DISARM

OTHER TITLES BY KARINA HALLE

Contemporary Romances

Romantic Suspense Novels

Horror Romances

DISARM

KARINA HALLE

Montlake
Romance

Text copyright © 2019 by Karina Halle
All rights reserved.

Published by Montlake Romance, Seattle

www.apub.com

Amazon, the Amazon logo, and Montlake Romance are trademarks of Amazon.com, Inc., or its affiliates.

ISBN-13: 9781542014915
ISBN-10: 1542014913

Cover design by Hang Le

Cover photography © 2019 by Daniel Jaems

Cover model: Matteo Capicchioni

Printed in the United States of America

DISARM

PROLOGUE

SERAPHINE

Seventeen years ago

I knew when I woke up this morning that today was going to be different.

Normally I wake up because Laura is shaking the bed below me, tossing and turning, like she's fighting for sleep even though we should be waking up soon. She never sleeps. It's the bed shaking that usually gets me up in time before Miss Davenport comes into the room and flicks on the lights. It's how I'm always the first one out of bed, ready to go, smiling up at her and hoping she'll notice.

She never seems to. It doesn't matter how hard I try to be good, to show her I want to please her, Miss Davenport ignores me. I've been back and forth out of this orphanage for a long time, and I think every time I come back, she hates me a little more.

But this morning, Laura never woke me up. I was sleeping all the way until the lights flicked on, and I scrambled like the crabs I used to see on the shores near Goa. I almost fell off the bunk bed.

Of course, Miss Davenport didn't like that. Her eyes narrowed as she looked at me, even though I wasn't the only one just waking up.

Still, once I got to the ground, I looked at Laura's bed beneath me, and she was still sleeping.

"Laura," I said, pushing on her arm. For a second I thought she could be dead, but she just mumbled and turned over. "Wake up," I hissed at her.

"Jamillah," Miss Davenport scolded me. "Leave Laura be. She's on new medication."

Almost everyone here is on some kind of pills. Everyone except me. I'm not sure why. I keep hearing the women here at the orphanage talking about us in terms of "bad" and "good" and "abuse" and "trauma." Sometimes it feels like every other girl gets special treatment. I just get shuffled around. Maybe it's because I don't seem to cry like the others do, even though horrible things are done to me every time I leave this place.

I'm only nine years old, but sometimes I think I might be within these walls for the rest of my life, never having a family, never having a place to belong.

"Okay, everyone, get ready for the day," Miss Davenport said. Then she looked at me. "Jamillah, do me a favor and watch over Laura this morning until she wakes up."

But breakfast! I wanted to say those words, my stomach growling as it was. But I knew that I was needed and it felt good, almost better than the dry toast with peanut butter we always have.

I nodded at Miss Davenport. "Okay. I will."

Everyone gave me a pitiful glance for having to keep an eye on Laura. I knew it wasn't fair that I wasn't getting breakfast, but I also knew that there aren't a lot of women working here lately, and if I didn't do it, no one would.

So while everyone got ready and went off to the mess hall to eat, I sat on the edge of Laura's bed and waited for her to wake up.

She finally did and looked at me through sleepy eyes. "What time is it?" Laura is thirteen and probably my closest friend here.

I shrugged. "I don't know. Miss Davenport told me to make sure you woke up."

She rubbed her forehead. "I haven't slept like that in, like, forever. What kind of pills did they give me?" She looked at me. "You missed breakfast."

"It's fine."

"Jamillah." Miss Davenport suddenly appeared in the doorway. "Thank you for doing that."

I exchanged a glance with Laura, surprised. She'd never thanked me before.

"It's okay," I told her.

Miss Davenport raised her chin and looked me over. I wished I were a mind reader, because I had no idea what she was thinking. "Laura, get dressed. Jamillah, you too. Something nicer."

I looked down at my clothes: leggings and a baggy T-shirt with Mickey Mouse on it that had once belonged to another girl. I loved this shirt. One of the few memories I have of my parents is that my mother loved Mickey Mouse too.

"I don't know if I have anything nicer," I told her. We don't have uniforms here; everyone just gets clothes that are donated.

"I'm sure you can find something. Put it on and then go and wait outside my office. Laura, go get dressed and wash up. You can see the nurse in a bit."

Oh no. Her office? What did I do?

As she left the room, I looked at Laura for answers, expecting to see pity on her face again. "Did I do something wrong?" I asked her.

But she looked impressed.

"What?" I asked.

"Put on something nicer? Go and wait outside her office?" she said, getting dressed. "I don't think you're in trouble. I think you might be getting adopted."

I stared at her for a long time.

We don't joke about that here.

It's sacred.

You can't even think about it or you'll jinx it.

So I didn't. I got dressed in the nicest thing I had, which was a striped dress over my leggings, then slipped on my ballerina flats that were a size too small, enough so that you could see the top of my toes making these bumps in them. I slept in braids because Miss Davenport said my hair was too messy for them to handle, so I spat in my hands and smoothed them over my head.

"Good luck," Laura said to me as I left.

And that's where I am now, sitting on the chair outside the door to Miss Davenport's office, swinging my legs in front of me, wondering what's going on behind that closed door.

Could Laura be right? Could this really be an adoption?

For me?

I don't dare think about it, so I start biting my nails, even though my last foster mom whacked me across the knuckles with a belt if I did it. At least I know I'm not going into another foster home; they never care about what you wear. One of the older girls told me that they don't even want you—they just do it because somehow you being in their house makes them more money.

It seems like hours before the door opens, and Miss Davenport looks at me, giving me a small smile. She doesn't smile often.

"Jamillah?" she says in a nice voice. "We have some people here who would love to meet you."

My eyes go big.

Could this be true?

I get up and go over to her. For some reason I hold my breath as I step into the room, like I'm afraid to breathe.

There are two people sitting in the chairs across from her desk. Both of them look so different from the usual foster parents. The man has glasses and gray hair at the sides of his head and has a kind smile.

The woman is wearing a lovely pink dress, with pearls at her neck and blonde hair pulled back. She's beautiful.

"Jamillah," Miss Davenport says, "this is Ludovic and Eloise Dumont. They're from France. They would like to adopt you."

My heart suddenly feels too big for my chest.

I'm so happy, so shocked, I immediately burst into tears.

Everything happens so fast, I barely have time to breathe. The whole week feels like I'm in a movie on fast-forward.

One minute I'm in Miss Davenport's office, meeting my adopted parents for the first time, the next thing I know I'm saying goodbye to Laura and the rest of the girls. I feel so sorry for them that they can't be adopted, too, that I almost give up my place and tell them to pick someone else instead.

But I don't. Because I've dreamed about this, more than anything. A home, a family. I want to take the girls with me, but I want this too much for myself.

Before I know it, I'm in the Dumonts' fancy car, in the back seat, and I'm watching London and the English countryside fly by. It's so beautiful and green, with so many rolling fields and cute houses. All the foster homes I've been in were in the city, in dirty areas.

I have a million questions, and I don't speak any French, but luckily Mr. and Mrs. Dumont both speak English as well as I do.

"What's your home like?" I ask them.

"I think you'll enjoy it," Mr. Dumont says. "It's just outside the city of Paris. Lots of space to run around and play. Lots of birds and trees and flowers. Very different from London."

"And you said you have two sons? Does that mean they'll be my brothers?"

Mr. and Mrs. Dumont exchange a look, smiling at each other. "Yes," Mr. Dumont says. "Olivier and Renaud. They'll be your brothers, as we will be your parents. I know it will take some getting used to."

"It won't," I say. Because that's the truth. I'm already used to it. It's like I've been waiting for this my whole life. The longer this car drives on, the more I feel like I'm actually escaping from that horrible place and the horrible people who would take me in and spit me out after a few months.

"I think you'll adjust to things very nicely," Mrs. Dumont says. "Now look, we're about to enter the tunnel. We're going to drive on the train, see, and then the train will take us under the water to France."

There's a train beside us and the doors on the side are open, and we actually drive onto it and down through the train. It's kind of scary, and reminds me of some space movies I've seen. I wish I had some sort of stuffed animal from the orphanage, but I'm always losing that kind of thing.

Mrs. Dumont turns around in her seat and hands me a teddy bear. It's fluffy and brown with big eyes. "I got this for you."

It's like she could read my mind! I stare at her in awe before I take the teddy bear in my arms, holding it close to me. "What's its name?" I ask her excitedly.

"Anything you want," she says.

I think about that for a moment. I think the bear should be called Ernest. Then I say, "Can I have a new name too?"

They look at each other again, in surprise. *"Bien sûr,"* Mr. Dumont says. "But of course. Any name you wish to have. You will be a Dumont now. You are free to become whoever you would like to be."

I think about that for a bit. I don't know what I want my new name to be, but I do want it to be French.

"Can I think about it?" I ask, scrunching up my face, hoping they'll give me time.

Mrs. Dumont laughs. "Take all the time in the world, darling. Until then, you'll be Jamillah. It's a pretty name too. When we saw your name and picture in the email the orphanage sent us, that's when we knew."

"Knew what?" I ask.

"That you were going to be our daughter," she says. "We had been wanting to adopt for years, but everything always fell through and nothing ever felt quite right. That is, until we saw your face. We said that's our girl. That's who we have been waiting for and who has been waiting for us."

"Did you used to wish for me? Because I wished for a family—a nice one—every single night."

Mrs. Dumont almost looks like she's crying, her eyes are all shiny. "We did."

Another few hours go by in the car as we drive through France, but it also feels like no time at all. My face is glued to the window as I hug Ernest tight, watching the landscape go past me. It reminds me of *Beauty and the Beast*, all the little towns that go past.

Finally we pull down a long driveway to a house right out of a fairy tale. It is large, the biggest house I've ever seen, made of stone and surrounded by sunlight and roses.

"We're here," Mrs. Dumont says cheerfully as the car comes to a stop right in front.

"This is where I'm going to live?" I ask.

"Bien sûr," Mr. Dumont says. "And that's Olivier and Renaud right now."

I look and see the large wooden door of the house open, and two boys step out. They look to be a few years older than me, and tall. At first I feel a bit sick at the sight of them, because the boys I've met in foster homes have always been so mean, and I don't want these boys to be mean to me too.

"Come on, let's meet them," Mrs. Dumont says as she gets out of the car with her husband.

She opens the door for me and holds out her hand. I unbuckle my seat belt, making sure not to let go of Ernest, and grab hold of her hand tight.

She leads me over to the two boys, who are staring at me curiously. They're dressed really nice—clean dark jeans and shirts tucked in. They're cute, and when they see me, they both smile shyly.

Maybe this won't be so bad.

Maybe they aren't bad boys like the rest of them.

"Jamillah," Mr. Dumont says, "meet your new brothers, Olivier and Renaud. They're your family now. We're all a family now."

I return the same shy smile to them. "Hello," I say.

"Bonjour," Olivier, the younger one, says. "*Est-ce que tu parles français?*"

I don't know what he's saying, so I shrug and say, "Nice to meet you. This is my bear, Ernest." I show my bear to them proudly.

Renaud steps forward and shakes the bear's hand. "It is nice to meet you, Ernest," he says in English. "As well as you, Jamillah."

"Welcome to the family," Olivier says. "As they say."

Welcome to my family.

CHAPTER ONE

SERAPHINE

What an officious fucking psychopath.

That's all I can think as I stare at my uncle Gautier's tired yet insidious face, like the old man has earned every wrinkle through the ravishing of someone else's soul. He stands at the head of the boardroom table and drones on and on about the new website and the online sales and everything he's done since he's taken over the company that once belonged to my father.

But of course, he's not just droning—he's gloating. He's bragging about the Dumont label and the boost in sales since he took the business online for the first time in the company's history, something my father and I had fought against from day one. The old world versus the new world. The good world versus the bad one.

Doesn't every conflict come down to that?

We always knew that taking the luxury brand online would increase our profits. But it would cheapen the brand, our legacy. It would take away the mystique of the label, the exclusiveness. My father believed that the impulsive, instant-gratification buying habits of today would work against us. "Isn't it always better to covet than to have?" he'd say.

Though I could always relate to that idea in some way, it was a terrible ideology when your whole career depends on people "having" rather than "coveting." But it kept the Dumont name up there—the best of the best, the purveyor of makeup and ready-to-wear clothing and iconic leather handbags meant to be worn with hard-earned pride. Subtlety was our specialty. Elegance was our mandate. Class was held above everything else.

But now, my father is dead.

And there's only me left to fight his battles.

Battles that I'm slowly but surely losing.

Nothing quite like waging war on behalf of someone who isn't alive to see it through.

It's been six months since my father died in the middle of our annual masquerade ball, and nothing in my life has been the same since. Gautier took over his position; my cousin Pascal took over what should have been my brother Olivier's role; and now my other cousin, Blaise, basically shares my job with me. Both Olivier and my other brother, Renaud, are in California; Gautier's family practically ran them out of the country. My cousins act like my father was nothing more than a hindrance, and despite being family, I've never seen even a hint of remorse or sadness in Gautier's eyes. You'd think he'd grieve the loss of his brother, but instead he's acted like he couldn't wait to step on his grave and take over.

And take over they have. Now I spend my days wondering how I'm going to survive this any further, because that's what my job has become. Surviving. My role in the company has been diminished, and my father's legacy has been snuffed.

The battle wages on and on, but I think I'm the only one fighting for the good name of the company.

Funny, because I'm the one with the most to lose.

Or I would be, if I hadn't already lost what meant the most to me.

"And you said to collaborate was a sin," Pascal says to me snidely, bringing me back to the discussion at hand.

I carefully take my eyes off Gautier and give Pascal a tepid look. The trick with Pascal is to act like nothing bothers you, because once my dear cousin finds your weak spot, he'll exploit it to no end.

"What?" I ask.

"You did say that, didn't you, Seraphine?" Gautier says, butting in with a smug smile on his face. The man is pushing sixty-five, and I know he's gotten fillers in his face recently, which makes him look like a cartoon monster, with his bloated cheeks and narrow eyes. Just needs a pair of goat horns on his head and he'll be complete.

I stare right back at him, that hatred filling me again. "I don't think I used those exact words." Gautier always wanted to bring on some famous collaborators the way that Louis Vuitton does every year for their bags and accessories, but my father and I thought it was tacky, a way of diluting the look of the brand.

His smirk deepens as he stares at me with his dark eyes. "Hmm. And yet our current sales are up sixty-five percent after our recent collaboration with Baptiste. Yet another thing you should be thanking me for, another smart move for the company."

I know I should be happy that the company is doing well. The papers love to shout about the Dumont label still being a success, just as much as they like to predict its demise. But I'm hanging by a thread here. We could make all the money in the world, and it wouldn't give me security, not when my uncle could let me go at any moment.

It makes me wonder why he hasn't yet. It's no secret that he hates me and has from the beginning. With my father gone, there's nothing stopping him from firing me. He owns it all now; I have no say. My shares are there, but they aren't enough to keep me here.

And yet I *am* here. He berates me day in and day out, ignores all my ideas and decisions that have made this company successful in the past, does what he can to make me feel as worthless and diminished as possible.

I glance at him as he goes back to talking about something else "amazing" that he's done since he's taken over the company, and all I want to do is get up and leave. I don't have to listen to this, I don't have to be here. Not with a man that I suspect may be more sinister than he lets on, a man I suspect of so many things I think about in the dead of night—things that make my heart cold.

But I know that's what they want. Even now, as I quickly glance down the table at Pascal, he's staring at me, rolling his tongue against his lower lip, looking like the smug bastard that he is. He's just waiting for me to quit.

When I look over at Blaise across from me, he's staring at me, too, though he averts his eyes the moment ours meet. I can't figure him out for the life of me lately. Ever since I was young, I've painted him with the same brush as his brother. After all, that side of the family is bor-derline psychotic, and I've had enough close encounters with Blaise to know that he's a crazy asshole like the rest of them.

Yet ever since my father died, it's like he's changed. When Blaise, Olivier, and I were involved in a car chase and subsequent crash not long after the funeral (yet another thing I think about in the dead of night), it came out that Blaise detests his brother and uncle, a fact that took Olivier and me by surprise. Though the Blaise I knew when I was younger had similar sentiments, I'd thought he secretly worshipped them.

And yet I don't see any sign of him changing. I've had to work closer with him lately, and he still seems to regard me with the same amount of animosity as I regard him, and when it comes to his father and brother, he acts no different.

But I know some truths about Blaise from back when we were young, back when we had something like a friendship forming. Things between us cousins were . . . complicated. I just don't think I can trust him, no matter what he says. I trusted him once before, and that didn't end well.

With that thought, the meeting is over, and I head straight out of the boardroom toward my office. The entire workforce has gotten an overhaul in the last six months, and I barely recognize any of the people who work here. After Gautier took complete control, he started to let everyone go, week by week, until nearly all signs of my father had been erased. The only one who has stayed is Nadia, the receptionist, because a good receptionist is worth her weight in gold.

I'm almost at my office when I feel a presence behind me.

I whirl around to see Pascal, grinning with a toothpick sticking out of the corner of his mouth. "What do you want now?" I snap at him, forgetting to play it cool.

His grin widens and he leans casually against the wall. Dressed head to toe in the Dumont label, all black, with sleek shoes, perfectly tailored pants, and a slightly unbuttoned shirt, he looks absolutely devilish. I know that most women would add "handsome" to the end of that sentence, since around the world they fawn over him like idiots, especially now that he's the face of our men's cologne. But I can't look at him objectively. All I feel is disgust.

"You seemed a bit distant at the meeting," he says. "Have a lot on your mind?"

"No more than usual," I tell him. "Now if you'll excuse me, I've got things to do." I turn and keep walking.

He calls out after me, "These 'things' you speak of seem too much for you. Perhaps you'd like some help."

I pause by my door and briefly close my eyes. I should just ignore him. He's dangling some kind of bait.

"What kind of help?" I ask despite myself, slowly turning around.

He's still leaning against the wall without a care in the world. He shrugs lazily. "Earlier you said that the beauty department needed some help."

"Yes, and they do. But not me. We need to bring in more people to work under me."

"That's what you think because you're too proud to admit that you're drowning. I think you need someone to help show you the ropes, make sure you do things properly, the way they need to be done."

My brows raise, along with my hackles. "What are you talking about?"

There's a glint in his eyes that I don't like. "I was talking with my father about this yesterday. I think perhaps it would be best if Blaise stepped in."

"Stepped in?" I cry out, aware that people in the office can hear me. This is worth raising hell over. "And do what? Are you firing me?"

That fucking smirk again. "Firing you? No, no. That would be up to my father, anyway. It's just that you and your father worked one way and we work another. If Blaise could teach you—"

"Teach me?" I repeat, my face growing hot. "What the fuck does he know about cosmetics and skin care? This has been my department for the last five years!"

"I know," he says quietly, his voice brimming with fake sympathy. "You started so young, when you didn't really know better. Picked up so many bad habits."

My eyes narrow and I stride toward him, sticking the sharp nail of my forefinger under his chin, wishing it were a knife. "You listen to me, okay? I know we don't see eye to eye on most things, but let's not forget we've been working together for the legacy of Dumont, and that's not going to change anytime soon. I've always done the best job, even if you're too proud to admit it, and I stand by our name."

He raises a brow, keeping his chin up. "But it's not really your family name, is it?"

I could fucking punch him for that. "Don't you dare," I whisper harshly, pushing my nail in deeper. "I took the Dumont name when my father and mother adopted me and brought me into the family. It's legal. It's official. It has been since I was nine. Sure, I don't look like you, I might have a different accent, but I'm a Dumont. As far as I'm concerned, I always have been."

"And as far as we're concerned," he says, removing my finger from under his chin, "you need help. Are you too proud to have your own cousin help you?"

"Eat shit," I tell him and whirl on my heel, heading to my office, where I slam the door.

I go straight for my desk and plop down in the chair, my head in my hands.

This is so fucking ridiculous. Since they let so many people go to cut costs, the entire Dumont beauty department needs help, not me—and especially not from Blaise. He's been trying to meddle in my business for the last few months, and I guess it makes sense why now. They want him to take over. I'll slowly be pushed out.

That, or they want me to quit. That's more likely.

I'm usually pretty good at keeping my head on straight. I have a short temper, but I try to keep my calm at work, especially since my father died and I know people have been watching me under a microscope.

But honestly, today is just another nail in the proverbial coffin.

Today is another reminder of how fucking alone I really am in this.

Both of my brothers are in California, working on their respective vineyards and hotels.

I'm divorced.

My father and mother are both gone.

I'm an orphan once more.

Surrounded by constantly circling sharks, wondering which one will try and pick me off first.

I let out a sigh that feels as heavy as my heart. I've been so good at keeping it together, but fuck it all. I need a drink.

"I hate to tell you this, but you look rough," Marie says to me as she reaches for the bottle of Dumont cabernet sauvignon and pours me yet another glass.

I give her a wry smile and take the glass from her. It's my fifth and yet it's not enough. "Is it because I have wine stains on my teeth? I always told my brother Renaud that he needs to grow grapes that don't stain your teeth."

"It's called white wine, Seraphine. And also, it's your eyes," she says, tilting her head sympathetically. Marie is a straight shooter and pretty low on sympathy for most people, so I should probably pay attention. "Plus, you're so skinny. Are you even eating?"

"No less than the typical Frenchwoman," I tell her.

Once upon a time I would have taken that remark as a compliment, but my appearance is the last thing I've been caring about these days. That, and apparently food.

"So do you want to tell me why you called me?" she says, taking a delicate sip as she folds her legs underneath her on the couch.

"I can't invite my friend over for wine at my apartment?"

She shakes her head. "No," she says emphatically. "You're impossible to get ahold of these days and you know that. I've been trying to get you out for coffee, for shopping, for cocktails, and you always push it off and off. Or you don't even text back or answer your phone. I feel like I'm dealing with a ghost."

I give her a sheepish smile, feeling ashamed at my neglect. "I've been a shitty friend."

She rolls her eyes and scoffs. "You aren't a shitty friend. You're just wrapped up in whatever you're wrapped up in, and I'm honored that you reach out to me when you need a little unraveling. And so, well, let's unravel you." She pauses. "Is it Cyril?"

I cringe at the mention of my ex-husband's name. "No. No, thankfully he's disappeared for now." I was embroiled in a long and bitter war with him over the divorce; despite the fact that he had cheated on me repeatedly, he still thought he had the right to all my money. He's dropped it for now, but that doesn't mean he's not coming back.

"It's your father," she says quietly.

I nod, willing away the lump in my throat I always get when I talk about him. For some reason, I can think about him all the time, and the sadness seems to stay at a manageable level, but when I talk about him with someone else, I can start crying at the drop of a hat.

"It is my father," I tell her. "I miss him. I wish more than anything that I could just ask him questions. You know, people always talk about how kind he was and a good man, but he was such a visionary, you know? So intelligent. So funny too. The two of us, we never lacked for words and stories when we were with each other, and I have so many things I want to ask him. I need his advice, badly. And there's none to give."

"It must be so hard, first losing your mother . . . ," she says, pushing her blonde bob behind her ear.

I know most people don't like to talk about the hard topics, but Marie only asks when she's genuinely interested, so I know I have free rein to say whatever I want, even the stuff that other people might judge me for.

"It's not just that," I tell her. "Well, I guess it's a lot of things. For one, work is getting harder. Now Pascal, my dipshit cousin, wants Blaise, my other dipshit cousin, to take over my job. They're basically trying to get me to quit."

"Wait, which dipshit cousin is the stupidly sexy one?" she asks.

I roll my eyes. "Neither."

Which isn't exactly true. When I was younger, my feelings for Blaise were a lot more streamlined and therefore a lot more complicated. But I'm not about to get into that right now with her.

"Okay," she says, not discouraged. "I'm sure they're both stupidly sexy. Your brothers are, too, you know. Runs in the family."

I wince internally. Little comments like that bother me. Marie doesn't mean anything by it, but it's a reminder that my family isn't through blood.

But it's also a reminder that blood means nothing. Just look at both sides of the Dumonts, one side always ready to stab the other in the back.

"Anyway," I say, glossing over it, "I'm not going to quit, but it's obvious that's what they're doing. So, suffice to say, work has gone from a place of joy to a place of stress and anxiety, and now they think I need to be babysat."

Marie gives me a tight smile before having a sip of wine. "I'm sorry. What a shame to have your own family turn on you like that, especially since you've been working together for so long. It wasn't always so bad, was it?"

"No. No, it wasn't. But my father was there. He was the buffer between us . . ."

"I see," she says with a nod. She sighs. "Well, I can certainly understand why you called me and needed to polish off a few bottles of wine." She looks around my apartment. "When was the last time you had anyone over?"

I shrug. I can't remember. My apartment has turned into a comfortable nest, the only place I feel safe. I did a rush job of cleaning before she came over, but it is in a bit of disarray. Once upon a time I had weekly dinner parties here and went out to shows and for drinks with models and designers and celebrities alike, but now I can't even imagine it.

As if she can hear my thoughts, Marie reaches over and, in a rare gesture of affection, puts her hand on mine, squeezes it, and says, "Grief takes a long time. It's not a linear process. There will be ups and downs. But if you're sliding backward, Seraphine, then you might need to talk to someone. You might need to get some help. Don't be too proud to ask."

I give her a sweet smile in return, though it falters with what I'm about to say. "You're right. I do need help. But not from a doctor or a psychologist, though you may think otherwise once you hear what I have to say."

She removes her hand and stares at me, urging me to go on. I take in a deep breath. "Promise me you'll keep this between you and me?"

She nods, her thin brows flitting together in concern. "Bien sûr. Of course."

"I think my father was murdered."

CHAPTER TWO

BLAISE

Sixteen years ago
Paris

It's an odd feeling to know that nobody loves you.

This isn't a sob story. I couldn't give a shit.

But what bothers me are the lies. If my family could admit the truth, that they're only legally obligated to have me around, then I could finally breathe. Maybe I'd know what it's like to be happy. You can't be happy when everyone around you is constantly pretending, when you know they're wearing masks, when you'd do anything to tear that mask off their face and tell them that you know the truth, you know how they really feel.

Today is my birthday. Other than Christmas, it's the worst day of the year. It's the middle of June, and it's hot as always, and yet it's the coldest, wickedest day.

Today they all pretend to love me even more. They turn up their game, they lay it on thick. They shower me with half-hearted attention and all the presents I could ever want. When I was younger, I used to wish on my birthdays for them to just actually love me. But as I got older, I realized how sad that was for a young boy. Love? Who needs that? Today I turn thirteen, and I'm over that shit. Over needing love. I'm afraid that what I really want—to expose the truth—will be the very thing that will hurt me more than anything.

My parents are tricky. My brother, Pascal? Even more so. To poke through their lies would really mess things up, and even though they've made it very clear that it's a unit of three, with me on the outskirts, I have no business rocking the boat.

And so I don't say anything. But I'm afraid one day I will.

I'm also afraid I won't.

That I'll live my whole life without ever telling them how I really feel and what I really know.

All this money, all this luxury, all this power that's built into the Dumont name and legacy is all fake. My family has done horrible, wicked things to get to where they are.

The sad thing is, I'm no better than them, and I don't even want to try. I'll cheat and lie and steal and blackmail my way to the top too. I'll just be a little more honest about it. I might be young, but I've seen enough to know age doesn't excuse anything.

There's a knock at the door. My room is large, and the sound echoes across the wood floors and cold stone walls. I live in a stupidly large *maison* on the outskirts of Paris. It's practically a castle, which isn't unusual for a family with a lot of wealth. It used to be my great-grandfather's and then his son's, passed down from generation to generation just like the Dumont business. It probably should have gone to my uncle since he's always been more of a family man, but I'm told my father snatched it out from under his nose.

Just as well. There's nothing you could do to make this place seem warmer.

The knock resounds again, and I turn away from the windows where I've been staring out at the backyard, watching the servants set up for the party. "What?" I ask.

21

The door opens, and my mother pokes her head in. It's early, but she already looks like she's been to the salon, every strand of her hair perfectly in place, every particle of makeup perfectly applied. Jewels and gold drip from her ears and around her neck. She's never been your typical Frenchwoman who is careful about showing off her wealth. Instead, she wears her money and stature with pride, a gaudiness that other people make fun of her for, but she clearly couldn't care. "If they think I'm tacky, fuck them! They're only jealous." I've heard her yell this at my father often, usually on a bender after too much gin and champagne.

"You're not dressed," she says to me. I'm still in my pajamas. I've been awake for hours but haven't actually gotten out of bed.

I shrug. "It's my birthday," I remind her. "Figured I could do what I want."

She cocks a penciled brow. "Blaise, it may be your birthday, but you do have company coming over soon."

I groan, running my hands over my face. "It's nine a.m. on a Saturday. My friends aren't coming over until later."

"Yes, but your uncle, aunt, and cousins are coming over for lunch, and you know you can't afford to look like a slob in front of them." There's a glint of cruelty in her eyes. It's not unusual for her to start my birthdays—or any day—drinking, and it's especially not unusual for her to start getting mean. But I already feel like today is different. Perhaps age thirteen is when they throw you to the wolves.

Might not be a bad thing, I think to myself. As long as the stupid charade is thrown away with me.

Besides, it's a known rule in this house that we must look better than my uncle's family at all costs. "Just give me a bit, okay?"

She narrows her eyes at my tone but pastes a smile on her face, which stretches tightly. "Take all the time you need. It's your birthday, after all."

She closes the door, and I roll my eyes, flopping back down on the bed. Mind games already. I'm not sure I'm ready for this.

Just before lunch, and after my mother has nagged me a second time, I head downstairs. The table outside is all set up with a white tablecloth and shining silverware under the olive trees. Nothing is out of place.

My father is absent and my mother is still running around like a headless chicken, but everyone else seems to have gathered around the table, taking their seats, and at the end of the table is a huge stack of presents.

I don't feel anything when I look at them, but knowing my family is looking at me expectantly, I pretend to be happy. Gee, presents. More stuff I don't need.

There's a flurry of activity at my approach. Uncle Luddie is the first one up from his chair, and he envelops me in a tight hug. I'm not used to being hugged, so I straighten up, going stiff.

"Happy birthday, Blaise," he says to me before pulling away and patting me on the back. He smells like the Dumont-label aftershave he always wears, a different one from my father's. "Thirteen is a big deal."

He smiles at me. It's kind of lopsided; my father says that he was hit in the head with a croquet mallet when he was young, but I wonder if that's true. It's a kind smile, though, and Uncle Luddie is always handing it out to everyone, even if they don't deserve it. I certainly don't.

I nod, say thank you, and proceed to get a light embrace from my aunt Eloise, who kisses both my cheeks. She smells like roses and radiates warmth. This is why I hate being around my uncle and aunt: it reminds me that I was born to the wrong family. I'm not used to this much affection.

Or maybe I'm rotten at heart, and my family is what I deserve.

Then there are my cousins. Thankfully all three of them are cool enough to not try any displays of affection with me. There's Renaud, who is stone faced and grumpy, like he's always hungry or something. He's nice to me, but I don't really know him that well. Maybe because he's a lot older—seventeen—and doesn't say much.

Then there's Olivier. Olivier is a year older than me. My mother always remarks on how handsome he will be, as if I'm going to grow up to look like a can of dog food. Olivier is easygoing and always smirking at something, and to be honest, it makes me want to punch him in the face. Why does he get to feel that way and coast through life when every day feels like a struggle to me?

Finally, there's Seraphine. She's not even a real cousin of mine. She's only ten years old and was adopted last year. I don't know her that well, either, other than the fact that my mother has said some shitty things about her. She's from India originally, I think, though she has a British accent. I actually think she could be quite pretty when she gets older, if she wasn't so tall and awkward with such messy dark hair. Plus she stares at you with these big bug eyes, like she's always thinking. I don't think she's judging you in a bad way, but either way, I don't like being the subject of her thoughts.

Right now her eyes are fixed on me, as usual, but at least she doesn't look put off by me.

I take the seat across from her, beside my brother, Pascal. I'm surprised he's even here; he's usually off somewhere else, pretending I don't exist.

"I didn't get you a present," Pascal says to me under his breath. "Sorry."

I glance at him, and he's smiling, not sorry at all.

I shrug. "I never want presents anyway."

"That's because you have everything."

"So do you," I point out, lowering my voice once I realize Seraphine has been staring at us in awe. Apparently she was adopted from an orphanage, and so maybe she's never even seen so many presents before.

Pascal looks over at Seraphine and frowns. "What are you looking at?" he snaps at her.

"Pascal," my aunt says quickly, giving him a tight smile. "Let's all be nice on your brother's birthday." My own parents would never try to talk back to him in public like this; they prefer to do that in private and in much harsher ways. But my aunt and uncle have been dealing with Pascal since he was born, and even though it's a tightrope to walk, it seems to work.

It's working right now, anyway. Pascal doesn't look remotely ashamed, but at least he leaves Seraphine alone. She has shrunk back in her chair, trying to avoid looking at us.

It feels like an eternity before my parents come out. They bring a tiered cake, which is made even more ridiculous by the fact that they have another cake for tonight's party. Always with the excess.

Everyone starts singing "Bonne Fête," and I should feel embarrassed, but honestly, I feel nothing at all. I just want this to end, to go to my room, and forget about everything and everyone.

But it's impossible. My aunt encourages Olivier to "play" with me, as if we're children, as if I didn't just become a teenager today. I show him some of the stuff I've gotten lately, like a remote control car, which is top of the line and does laps around the yard, and we occasionally chase Seraphine down with it until my real guests show up and the actual party begins.

I have a fair number of friends, but none that I'm particularly close to. Most of them are rich as fuck—birds of a feather, as my father often says. My only good friend is Jean, whose father fucked off when he was young and who has only his mother raising him and doesn't have a lot of money. My parents hate the fact that I'm friends with him—not just because he's poor, but because they say he's a bad influence.

Considering right now we're sneaking around the yard to the gazebo so we can drink the liquor he stole from his house, my parents probably have a point. It's evening now, and we have the cover of darkness on our side.

I've never gotten drunk before. I've had wine on some special occasions, but I didn't care for the taste. But now that we're sitting cross-legged on the floor of the shadowy gazebo, having escaped the party, I'm eagerly reaching for the bottle.

"You're thirteen now," Jean says as he hands it to me. "My mother says that's when you become a man. So you better drink up."

I pull the cork off and smell it. It causes my eyes to roll back in my head and reminds me a lot of my mother. I eye the bottle. It's some sort of almond liquor, so it's not even that strong. Not the big-league stuff, but it will have to do.

I take a deep breath before bringing the bottle to my mouth and swallowing some. It burns and I start to cough. By the time Jean takes the bottle back, the burning has turned into sweetness. It's actually not that bad.

I'm about to encourage him to try it, but he's already taking a giant swig. He coughs, too, and then laughs.

And then things get a little fuzzy. We drink a lot of the bottle, just hiding out in the darkness, hearing the music blaring—some kind of abrasive rock Pascal most likely put on that my mother will turn off soon. I should feel bad that I'm missing my own birthday party, but the more I drink, the less I care. Maybe this is why my mother does it all the time.

"Oh shit!" Jean swears harshly as he gets on his knees and peers through the fence of the gazebo. "I think your father is coming!"

I freeze, staring at the bottle in my hands and then back up at my father's silhouette, which is quickly approaching us. "Blaise!" he bellows, and the rage in his voice nearly makes me pee my pants.

"What do we do?" I ask Jean, but Jean is getting to his feet and jumping over the gazebo railing and running off across the yard and around to the front, leaving me and the bottle. Fucking coward just ditched me!

"I see you, Jean!" my father yells after him. "Running, just as your daddy ran from you."

Jesus, he's being so harsh. I hope Jean didn't hear that. I have a feeling that he'll never be allowed back to the house after this.

But none of that really matters right now because if my father catches me drunk . . .

I quickly toss the bottle behind me into the bushes along the other side and then hear a sharp but quiet "Ow!" as it lands on someone.

I whirl around and see only movement in the bushes. It was a girl's voice. Could it have been Seraphine? Did I hurt her?

But before I can even think about investigating, my father is entering the gazebo and looming above me.

"Get up," he says to me, his voice low and eerily calm. The kind of calm that makes shivers run down my spine and my heart turn into a loud drum in my head.

I stare up at him, so scared that I can't move.

"I said, get up," my father says again. I can't see his face, I can only see the shadows. For a moment he looks like a monster, the kind that shape-shifts in inky blackness. I expect to see a flash of red eyes.

Then, with lightning speed, he reaches down and grabs me by the arm and yanks me up to my feet until it feels like he's going to pull my arm right off.

I know I shouldn't show any weakness, but I'm screeching with pain.

He yanks me right up to his face, and I see a glimpse of his eyes, just a bit of light glinting off them. I've never been so terrified.

"Just as I thought," he snarls as he breathes in deep. "You've been drinking. You're drunk."

"I'm not," I try to say, but before I can further my feeble protest, he pulls back momentarily and slams his palm against my temple, rocking my world and sending me backward onto the floor. Everything inside my head explodes into jagged stars, and I scream in pain.

"Shut up," he says, almost hissing. "And get up. You want to be a man? You think that because you're thirteen, you're a man now? You can get drunk at your own party? Then stand up and take it like a man, Blaise. Come on. Get up."

I can barely hear, barely comprehend him. My father has hit me before on a few occasions, but they were usually a slap across the cheek or, when I was younger, the belt across my ass. But he's never hit me like this, with hatred and venom in his eyes.

What if he kills me?

"Get up, Blaise. If you don't, you'll regret it forever. You want me to be proud of you? You own up to your mistakes, and you get to your feet after you've been knocked down."

I have no doubt I'll regret it forever. My father doesn't give empty threats.

So I get up. I don't know how I do it. Maybe the hit rattled my brain cells. Maybe the booze already killed them off. But I get to my feet unsteadily.

He leans in. "Look me in the eye," he says in a low voice.

I do. His eyes are both calm and wild and completely unpredictable. I don't know what is about to happen, but I know that he's looking for something inside me, maybe to see who I really am and what I really deserve.

I hold his gaze and defiantly raise my chin, trying to pretend to be better than this, to be strong.

It is a mistake.

He hits me again, this time a backhand across my cheek, until tears squeeze out of my eyes and things turn swimmy and black.

Somehow I manage to stay upright, and I think that's why he stops.

"Don't lie to me, Blaise," he says after he composes himself, slicking back his black hair and straightening his tie. "Don't ever lie to me. If you think you aren't being watched, you are and always will be. You have to earn your father's trust, do you understand that now? And since you broke it, I fear it's going to remain broken for a long time."

You trust Pascal, you never had to put him through any of this, I think angrily, but I don't dare say it. I never will. I hate to imagine what that would earn me.

"Now if anyone asks you what happened, I dare you to tell them why. Explain why you deserved it. You won't find any pity from anyone, only disgust at what you have done. Now, I'm going back to your party, and I'm sending everyone home. If you're out here getting drunk with that half-wit, you don't deserve those kids as friends anyway."

He turns around and strolls out of the gazebo and across the grass and back to the party.

I just stand there, torn between wanting to pull my hair out and scream or collapse to the floor and cry. Neither seems like a good choice.

Then I hear a shuffle in the bushes behind me and turn to see Seraphine step out, her hand at the side of her head.

"What the fuck are you doing here, spying on me?" I sneer at her, trying not to sniffle, trying to hold it together. I'm further humiliated now, the fact that this little girl saw all that.

"I was here first," she says quietly in English. "And you threw a bottle at my head."

"That was an accident," I tell her, refusing to feel bad about it. Who cares if it hit her? I'm the one who was just smacked around by my own father.

But when she makes her way around the gazebo to the entrance, she's still holding her head and looking like she's in pain. I feel guilty.

Yet I still say, "Get out of here."

"What does being drunk feel like?" she asks, staring at me with those big eyes of hers.

I shake my head, not wanting to talk to her anymore. "It feels like none of your business," I say, waving her away as I turn my back to her.

There's a pause in the air.

"My mother was an alcoholic. It's why she died. My father was too. He didn't die, though, he just couldn't take care of me. That's why I was an orphan."

Against my better judgment, I say, "I thought you were born in India. Why do you have a British accent?"

She takes a step into the gazebo. "My father took me over to England. Outside London. I don't think he was supposed to, and that's when the social services took me away from him and put me in an orphanage."

"They still have those? I thought that was something from *Annie* or *Oliver Twist*."

She nods, still staring at me with those eyes. "I was in different foster families but would always end up there when it didn't work out."

"Why didn't they want you? Too ugly?" Though I'm smirking as I say it, the part inside me that wants to be mean to her shrivels a little.

She doesn't flinch. "Some were nice. Most weren't. Most hit me just like your dad did. Maybe even worse."

I raise my brows in surprise. "Really? Worse? Like what?"

She comes over to me and sits down on the floor, holding her knees up to her chest. She tilts her head down so that her bangs fall in front of her eyes and stares at the floor. "Sometimes," she says, her voice so quiet that I have to sit down next to her, "this one lady—her name was Jane, but I don't even think that was her real name. She wouldn't let me eat. Only if her husband was around would she act like everything was normal, but if he wasn't, she wouldn't give me breakfast or lunch or dinner or anything. Instead she made me watch as she ate. Said I was too fat and it would teach me."

I glance at her. Seraphine is as skinny as they come. "She was crazy. You aren't fat."

I'm not sure she hears me, because she continues. "Another time, there was this family, and there were three of us foster kids. If you misbehaved, they would lock you down in the basement for a day or two.

I was once down there for three days. It was gross. They only gave me water. And I never did anything wrong; one other kid was always trying to get me in trouble."

"And this happened in England? It sounds barbaric. And illegal." I sit down beside her on the gazebo floor.

"In London," she says, glancing at me briefly. "It probably was illegal, but I was too afraid to say anything. You don't want to be known as a problem child or they'll put you with families even worse. I've heard horror stories."

"So you were never knocked around?"

She nods. "I was. But they don't really stick out. I mean, it hurt. But it happened so frequently it was just . . ." She shrugs. "They were good at hiding it too. One lady would burn you with cigarettes on your arms and make you wear long sleeves." At that, she turns her arm over, and I can just faintly see a few marks, something I thought was just pigment earlier. "Some would do what your dad did and get you in the face or on the head. But if the social workers ever came to the door, your bruises were gone, and they pretended everything was fine."

"You never complained?"

"No one believes kids."

I know she's right about that. "I guess it's really lucky that my aunt and uncle found you."

She gives me the first smile I've seen on her in a while. "It's very lucky. I'm spoiled now and I know it. I guess . . . I still don't feel like I belong here, though. I used to pray every night for a family that loves me and cares about me, and now I have it and I guess I'm afraid it will be taken away."

"I think you're here to stay," I tell her. I open my mouth to tell her that my aunt and uncle are wonderful people, but it makes me feel bitter about it all, so I don't say anything except, "I've never heard you talk so much before."

She smiles again, and it's a pretty smile. "I suck at French, still. But if we're speaking English, it's okay."

"Well, if it makes you feel any better, I feel like I don't belong with my family either," I admit. Something makes me pause, something wants me to hold stuff back and not get personal. But for whatever reason, I feel I can actually relate to Seraphine now on some level. "It's hard to explain."

"You don't have to explain," she says. "I know." She picks up the bottle and shakes it. "Are you done with this?"

I nod and she tosses it over the railing, back into the bushes.

"Good throw," I tell her. "For a girl," I add.

She rolls her eyes, but she's still smiling.

CHAPTER THREE

SERAPHINE

I can't sleep.

It's been two days since I confessed to Marie my biggest fears, and I swear all that confession has done is make the fears even larger than life, invading my thoughts and my dreams.

The truth is, I've opened up to both Olivier and Blaise about my theories before, but Olivier stubbornly refused to even entertain the idea, and Blaise, well, he may hate his brother and father, but he's not about to accuse them of murder either. Besides, he has no dog in this race.

Opening up to Marie wasn't much better. She's as skeptical as sin to begin with, so I wasn't surprised she listened to me with one brow raised the entire time.

"Seraphine," she said when I was done, "don't take this the wrong way, but I think you're so overwhelmed with grief, you need to put the blame somewhere in order to process it. But there is no blame. Your father died of a heart attack. He may have been in great shape, but it happens. It just happens sometimes. That's life. It's not murder."

And with that I knew there was no point in trying to further convince her. We went back to drinking wine and talking about other things, all while the seed of truth inside me was growing and growing.

I know deep inside it's true.

That's why I've been trying so hard to ignore it these last six months. Working under the man I believe killed my father has been a special sort of hell, so most of the time I won't even let my brain entertain the idea. But lately, I can't seem to shake it.

I don't have any proof. None. It's just a gut feeling. It's that burning hatred I feel deep inside me mixed with the heart-heavy horror that this actually happened.

Gautier had everything to gain with my father out of the picture. He got control of the company, which normally wouldn't have happened had he not been blackmailing Olivier for his shares. It's been ten years since he set Olivier up for sleeping with Pascal's ex-wife, but the transfer of the shares and the death of my father created the perfect situation for Gautier and his sons.

I'm not giving up on the idea that it could be Pascal who did it either. He's just malicious and devious enough. But my instincts tell me that it was both Pascal and Gautier together.

As for Blaise, I know he didn't do it. He obviously thinks I'm insane for having entertained the idea, and I haven't brought it up around him since. But I know him, and I believe him.

I wish there had been an autopsy. The doctors were so quick to rule out anything other than a heart attack, even though my father was a very rich, very famous man who made a lot of enemies. He never did anything wrong and was always so gracious and giving and kind, but success creates jealousy—especially at this level, especially to an untrained eye who would say my father just inherited it all from *his* father.

Therefore, you would have thought the fact that he had just been given a clean bill of health by his doctor, and had no heart condition whatsoever, would have raised some alarm.

But that's the thing about my uncle. He has connections that run deep. You don't get to the top without stepping on a few throats, and Gautier goes for the jugular. He could have easily paid off the doctor. It might seem like a stretch, but I'm not ruling it out.

I'm not ruling anything out. That's why I'm lying here in bed, trying to sleep even though my brain wants to pick through every shred of evidence that there could be. I know I'd probably be better off if I believed what Marie said. Just chalk this up to grief and move on with my life. I just can't. I owe it to my father to at least see.

I stare up at the ceiling and sigh, wishing that I'd turned the light out in the hallway. I'm jumpy these days, and every shadow has me paranoid that there's someone lurking in the dark.

It's only your imagination, I tell myself, but a few seconds later I'm sighing and getting out of bed.

It's February and it's cold. My apartment is over two hundred years old and drafty as fuck. Even though I was only in India until I was four, I swear it's made me a weakling when it comes to winter.

I quickly hurry to the hall to switch off the light, the hardwood floors cold on my soles, only then noticing that the window is open and the freezing air is flowing inside, making the curtains billow.

I hurry over to it, my teeth chattering as I go. I can't remember opening the window at all, but I must have. Maybe all the wine I've been having every night is fucking with me.

I shut the window and quickly eye the bottle of wine on the coffee table that I had polished off with ease earlier. I need to get ahold of myself.

But as my eyes drift over the wine, they focus on the *Vogue* magazine next to it. I'd been flipping through it earlier since our new matte lipsticks were featured in a paid-for review, but I hadn't really paid attention to who's on the cover until now.

It's a famous French actress, one I've actually had the pleasure of meeting once at the Dumont runway show (or displeasure, since she was a bit of a cow). She's dressed up like she's going to a sexy version of the Venice carnival, wearing a gold dress, cape, and an elaborate gold mask.

The image of the mask makes my head spin. Suddenly I'm brought right back to that night at the masquerade ball. When he was murdered. I must have seen something. Someone must have seen something. I've been trying to think who was with my father right before he died, but I was off talking to guests. When I badgered Olivier about it, he didn't seem to know either.

If I could find out who he was with just before he had his alleged heart attack, maybe that will give me a clue. Poison seems so dramatic, but that would have to be it, something slipped to him in a drink or perhaps injected without him knowing. It all sounds so grandiose and farfetched, but if I don't explore this, I'm going to regret it.

And that's when it hits me. I know what I have to do.

And it can't wait until morning.

Even though a train to Bordeaux is fast and only takes two hours, there's none running in the middle of the night, and anyway, I'd rather drive. I get to the château when the sun is rising over the rolling vineyard.

The vineyard and castle belong to Renaud, but it's unusual for me to visit, especially by myself. I was hoping to arrive unannounced, before the morning workers show up. Because it's February, no one is tending to the vines on a daily basis, and there are only the occasional workers in the production rooms, keeping an eye on the vats.

When my car pulls into the gravel parking lot, I see I'm the only one here.

Perfect.

I walk between rows of giant cypress and oak trees, limbs like skeletons reaching into the misty morning sky, and head across one of the bridges that span the moat, swans honking noisily as I go, like an alarm.

But I'm not trespassing. I have a key still from the masquerade ball, part of my duty as the hostess. I head around the back of the castle to the glass doors that open up into the armory room.

The key slides in with ease, and I look around to see if I'm being filmed. I know that there are cameras everywhere—that's why I'm here, after all. I can just hope that no one other than me has current access to them.

The armory room is even more disturbing this morning. In this large, low-ceiling room with a musty red carpet, medieval armor is set up all around as if the knights are still alive and watching you under their tarnished metal masks. It's one of the highlights of the castle, but now it just seems ghostly and macabre, like the knights may have witnessed my father's murder.

I ignore them, trying not to get creeped out. I believe in ghosts and spirits, and there's definitely a heavy feeling in the air, like something is stuck and can't get out. Most people would blame dust and mildew—the castle operates as a hotel only in the summer months—but I know there's something else here.

Maybe it's the truth.

I know that the cameras would have been recording everything and that they would have caught something. It's up to me to try to figure out exactly what that is.

I head up the stairs to the main floor of the castle, past the old dining-room table that had been cleared out for the ball but is now back in place. With twenty empty chairs, it seems like I'm being watched by invisible diners.

The third floor of the castle is off-limits to the public. There are two grand bedrooms up there plus a mini-kitchen. Who knows what it was back in the day. There's also an office, and in that office is a computer with many screens where you can watch the CCTV. Though no one is here now, the caretaker lives here and watches to make sure nothing in the hotel is damaged. If there are any burglaries, this will record everything.

And, of course, in case this room is robbed, the footage is no doubt being sent to a hard drive and server somewhere, maybe in Renaud's house in California, maybe to a security company. I know I'll show up on today's footage, but I have doubts that anyone is monitoring it twenty-four seven. Besides, it's not like I can't come here. It does belong to my side of the family. In fact, once I'm done here I'll text my brother and let him know what I was doing.

He doesn't need to know the specifics.

Just like Olivier, he'd think I'm crazy.

I head straight to the office and sit down at the desk, flicking on the computer screen. It immediately splits into four screens, live footage of the castle. There's one of the dining room, one of the armor room, one of the kitchen, and one of the parlor. When I tap on the keyboard, it gives me the option to show more screens. Here I can see the study, the staircases, the back and front entrances, an overview of the property from several angles with cameras mounted on trees, plus one bedroom. I'm pretty sure it's illegal to have that last one, and I can only assume that it doesn't record anything when guests are staying over.

But, of course, this footage isn't what I want.

I need the footage from that horrible night in August when my world changed.

I select the calendar and go back into last year, up to August, then select the channel I want to watch. The problem is, I don't know which camera to view, which means I'm going to have to go through all the footage for that night from each recording.

This is going to take a while.

I take in a deep breath and start clicking.

Except, aside from a few outside shots, every time I click the interior channels, I see an error message that says "Footage Not Found."

What the fuck?

How can the footage not be found?

I click around until the day after the ball, and the footage pops up. I click around to the previous date, and that footage pops up as well. This happens on every single channel. It's only the day of the masquerade that's missing. In fact, when I watch the footage from the day after, I can see people straggling behind as the party came to its horrible end.

This makes no sense.

Or maybe it makes perfect sense.

The footage was deleted, which means that someone had something to hide. Someone who had access to this room.

Did it happen that night? If so, maybe anyone could have stolen away and come here when no one was looking, perhaps during the commotion of my father's death.

But if it happened later, then it had to be someone who had access to this castle.

Which narrows things down quite a bit.

Points in a direction I knew it could take.

And yet without the footage, I have nothing. There's something on it, something that someone (or several someones) doesn't want anyone to see. Someone who is covering their tracks, who knew there was a chance of getting caught, a chance that someone might be suspicious.

I'm not sure they planned for me.

I take out my phone and glance at the time. It's ten a.m. and I'm sure the workers for the winery have already arrived. I should probably get out of here, but I need to figure out how to get that footage back.

I google how to recover deleted or damaged footage from a security network DVR and discover to my surprise that all hope isn't lost yet. It's possible with software, or a professional can do it.

I look around the room, trying to figure out how to do this. If I take anything—and I'm not sure what to take—that might set off some alarm bells. The best bet I have is to find someone who can do this and bring them here.

Preferably someone who can keep their mouth shut until I know what's going on.

Someone who can help me, not just in this but in everything.

I need to hire a professional.

CHAPTER FOUR

Blaise

"What do you want?" I ask as I stand on the front steps of my parents' château, staring at my brother as he opens the door.

"That's the greeting I get?" Pascal asks, swirling amber liquid around in a snifter glass. He's still in a suit even though it's nine o'clock at night, and it's a different suit than he was wearing at the office earlier. Both Dumont, of course.

"What's going on?" I say with a sigh. I was comfortable back at my apartment, watching Netflix, drinking vodka, ignoring the outside world. Then Pascal texted me, saying he needed me to come over to discuss business. Said it had to be done in person, here, where he still lives with our parents—couldn't be done at work tomorrow.

So that, and the fact that I had to drive an hour outside of the city to get here, already put me on edge. I just want this, whatever the fuck this is, over with.

"You never were one for patience, Blaise," he says with a smirk. "You always wanted things now, immediate gratification. And when you didn't get it, you blew up, like a stick of dynamite. You could time it down to the second."

"Give me a fucking break," I snarl at him. "Either you tell me why the fuck I drove an hour here for something you couldn't tell me at work, or I'm leaving."

He rolls his eyes and lets out an exaggerated sigh. "Fine. I should have known you'd be like this. Come on in."

He opens the door wide as if I'm a guest, as if I didn't grow up in this house of horrors right alongside him. Lord knows why the hell he still lives here, but there are a lot of things about Pascal that have never made any sense, things I'd rather ignore and not get to the bottom of.

I step inside and look around. "Where are our parents?"

"Out for dinner in Paris. They won't be back for a while."

I raise my brow at him as he takes a calm sip of his cognac. "You're not planning to murder me, are you?" I ask, half joking. While it's a relief to be here when my father and mother aren't here, it's also a little odd to be alone with Pascal outside of the occasional discussion at work.

"Murder," he muses. "On so many people's minds lately."

I frown. "What?"

"Here, come into the study. I'll pour you a drink."

"Just one," I say, following him into the elaborate library, where my father keeps a large amount of alcohol along with rows of priceless literature. I remember being a kid and wanting to read all the books, but every time I tried, he'd bring out the cane he always kept behind his desk and rap it on top of my hand until I had bruises for days.

Instinctively my hands coil into fists and then relax. I still have some things to work out, some issues I'm sure a therapist would have a field day with. Coming to this house brings them back every time.

I think Pascal knows this and that's why we're in here. After he pours me a drink from the bottle, making sure to top off his as a show of trust that it's not full of poison—as if that's a real fucking thing normal brothers worry about—he goes around the mahogany desk at the end and brings out the cane.

"Remember this?" Pascal asks, stabbing the air with it. "Remember what he used to do with this?"

"Vaguely," I reply, sniffing the cognac. So far so good.

"You knew about this, right?" He puts his glass down on the desk, careful to use a coaster, then twists the brass horse head of the cane around and around until it comes loose and pulls it out. The head is attached to a long, skinny sword.

"All this time I wondered why our father had this cane since he never limped, never had any ailment," Pascal says, holding the sword up to the light. "Turns out he just liked having a weapon. I suppose we're lucky he didn't use this end on us."

This catches me off guard for a moment. *Us.* All this time I assumed whatever violence my father showed toward me wasn't directed at Pascal. Pascal was the golden boy.

"Is that why I'm here? To discuss Father and his weapons?"

"Not exactly," he says, sliding the sword back inside the cane with one fluid motion. "He doesn't know you're here, and I'd like to keep it between us."

Okay. This has my interest.

Still, my brother is as trustworthy as a snake. I have to be cautious.

"So then why am I here?"

He sits down behind the desk and leans back in the leather chair, looking both like he does it all the time and also like a child imitating his father. "I need a favor from you."

I raise my brows. This is a new one. "What favor?"

He licks his lips slowly before they twist up into a crooked smile. "I need you to keep an eye on Seraphine."

The sound of her name jars me, making me blink. "Seraphine? Why?"

I mean, what the fuck now? Just last week my father called me into his office and expressed concern over my cousin's role in the business.

He says he fears that the death of her father is too much for her and she's drowning in her responsibilities.

If I'm being honest here, I think Seraphine is handling everything exceptionally well. She's a hothead, so she's often fighting against my father and Pascal, especially since they want to change the company in so many ways. I don't blame her for the pushback—she's sticking up for her father's legacy that way.

But I also know that we're making more money now and with it, the perks. I know I've been given the opportunity to completely take over the health and beauty department if that's what I want. But it will mean Seraphine will have to quit or get fired in the process.

"We can't have an outlier on our team, and that's what she is," my father had said. "This company is ours now. We need to be a united front. We need to sweep away the past. My brother had a good heart but bad business sense. This is the dawning of a new age for us, for our legacy, for our name, for the brand."

The irony is that I think I'm more of an outlier than Seraphine is. My father and brother just don't know that yet.

"I have concerns," Pascal eventually says, taking a deliberate sip of his drink.

"Father already talked to me about her. He said she's slipping. I'm supposed to guide her. I'm guessing he wants me to replace her."

He nods slowly. "Yes. But this has nothing to do with that. And it's just between you and I. Nothing to do with Father, you understand?"

I stare at him, waiting for him to elaborate, my patience being tested. Despite disagreeing with my father about Seraphine, I don't like how tangled our lives are becoming lately. Once upon a time, I rarely saw her at the office. Now I see her all the time, and my feelings toward her are far too fucking complicated to try to make sense of. All I know is, the less I see her, the better off I am.

"Has Seraphine confided in you lately?" he asks.

I let out a sour laugh. "Confide? I don't know if you've noticed, but she hates me, just as much as she hates you."

Pascal hums, musing it over as he runs his finger over the rim of his glass. "I'm not too sure about that . . ."

And then my world spins as a memory slams into me. One night in Mallorca, where everything changed and then changed again. I can't be sure that Pascal even knows what happened, but I've always erred on the side of caution.

"Well, she hasn't," I tell him, my voice getting sharper as this conversation goes on. "So then what?"

"I was just wondering, that's all. You've been working together so closely."

"We barely exchange words. She doesn't even look at me."

"I suppose I can believe that. It will only work in our favor."

"Just what are you getting at?"

He stares at me for a moment. You'd think after growing up with Pascal, I would know how to read him, but half the time I don't. There's too much going on in his head at once, and I'm not sure if his thoughts make any sense to him.

He straightens up and fishes his phone out of his pocket, crooking his finger at me. "Come here. I need to show you something."

This can't be good.

Still, I get up and walk around the desk as he displays the phone to me. On the glass screen, a grainy video plays. It's of a car driving down a vineyard, dust rising from the wheels. The light isn't good, so I can't even make out the car, but it parks and someone steps out.

Then the screen switches to another shot, this time of a bridge over a stream and a woman walking over it, looking around nervously.

Seraphine.

"What is this?" I ask him.

"Renaud's winery, Château la Tour."

Where the masquerade ball was held last year. Where my uncle died in front of everyone.

The screen then switches to Seraphine using a key at the back door and walking inside.

"I don't understand," I tell him. "So what? She's not allowed to be there?"

"Keep watching," he says, seeming amused by all this.

And so I do. She definitely is looking cagey. Even though the footage is dark and grainy, her mannerisms are nervous, and she's looking around and over her shoulder as if she's going to be caught.

She goes up the stairs to the third floor and then enters a room that looks completely unfamiliar to me. Sits down at a desk and flicks on a computer. The rest of the footage is of her just sitting there and flicking through changing screens, though I can't make out what it is she's watching.

"I don't get it," I tell him. "Why are we watching this? More than that, why are you recording this?"

"You truly aren't that bright, are you?" he says as he stares up at me, contempt written all over his face. "Seraphine went all the way to the castle the other day. Arrived in the morning, so she must have left Paris in the middle of the night. She acts like she might be watched or followed, which means she's doing something she shouldn't, and goes straight up to the office on the third floor where the CCTV recordings are. If you zoom in, you can see she's checking the footage from the night of her father's death."

I shrug. "So?"

"So?" Pascal repeats, giving me a steady look. "We all know what she thinks. We all know she thinks we had something to do with his death."

He's right. I did know that. She told me so herself, months ago, before I told her she was fucking crazy.

Only I never really believed she was crazy.

I just didn't want to think about what she was saying.

Knew that if I let myself listen, she could easily lead me down that path.

Convince me that my father and brother are capable of murdering my uncle.

But that's something I refuse to entertain—for the sake of my life, for the sake of my own sanity.

"But you didn't have anything to do with his death," I point out. "Right?"

He narrows his eyes at me. "What do you think?"

"Then why do you care what she thinks?"

"Because she's sick in the head, that's why," he snaps. "You know it."

I flinch internally at his words. I don't know Seraphine like I once did, and maybe the way I once knew her was wrong too. But she's not sick, no matter how Pascal and my father try and spin it that way. She's just lost and she's angry and she's grieving. She should really be left alone.

"Blaise," Pascal says, calmly now. "She's angry and looking for someone to blame. She's going to blame us."

"Then let her. I have nothing to hide."

"It doesn't matter. She's very vocal and has a lot of influence. People like her. They want to listen to her, they want to help her. We can't even have the smallest amount of doubt thrown our way, do you understand?"

"I think you're overreacting," I tell him, straightening up and going back around the desk. I pick up my cognac from the side table and finish it in one go. This is ridiculous. I need to get out of here.

"She's snooping around because this is what she believes, Blaise. And once someone like that finds something—someone—to place the blame on, all hell will break loose."

"So let her find the footage from that night, then," I say as I whip around. "If we're all innocent, then the footage will show that."

He sighs, biting his lip so hard it starts to pale. "The footage is missing."

"Why? How do you know?"

"Because I wanted to see what she knew, if anything. But the footage from the party is gone. Just that night. Like someone came in and made it so it never existed."

Did you ask our father? The question is on the tip of my tongue, yet I don't let it spill out. Perhaps I'm too afraid of the answer.

"Shouldn't that make you relieved?"

"What if she can somehow recover it? What if she grows restless with not knowing and comes prodding and poking in different ways? You know I've never liked her, Blaise. She's never been one of us. She's never understood what it's like to grow up the way that we have, with the privileges and education we've had. She's going to use that against us."

"So tell me again how any of this involves me? What do you want me to do exactly? Tell her to knock it off?"

"No. I need you to follow her."

"Follow her?"

The very idea of it causes hot prickles in my chest.

"I can't watch her all the time."

My eyes widen as I stare at him dumbly. "You've been watching her?"

Those prickles in my chest are starting to flare, something fiery and wild. A feeling I don't entertain very often. One I try so hard to ignore.

He smirks at me. "I've had concerns for a long time. How on earth did you think I knew she went down to Bordeaux? I knew she left her apartment, I'll just leave it at that. But I don't trust people on the outside, and I can't be everywhere at once. So that's where you come in."

"Don't take offense to this, but I think you have a real problem when it comes to stalking people."

He just grins, his smile crooked and pleased. "That's what I do best. You have to play up your strengths, brother. So what do you say?

Can you watch her? Report back to me where she goes and what she's doing?"

"What if I say no?"

He seems to think that over, clasping his hands together and tapping his manicured fingernails against his chin. "Hmmm. I suppose you're allowed to say no. But I would have to ask . . . *why* are you saying no? Do you want harm to come to us? Do you want our legacies, our reputations, to be damaged by her wild lies and accusations? You know the moment it becomes public that Seraphine suspects her own family of killing her father that things will end for you. Your life as you know it will end. Do you understand that?"

I am sick and tired of Pascal asking me if I understand. I understand very well.

And I know he does, too, why I'm reluctant to do this. He could ask me to do many things that are creepy or immoral, and I'd do them because I honestly don't give a fuck about most things. His blood and mine are the same. I am no good.

"Fine," I say, and I am so very, very tired all of a sudden. "I'll keep an eye on her."

Pascal doesn't look convinced. "And you know I don't mean at work. Outside of work. She's bloodthirsty right now, and I'm depending on you to stop the bleeding before it gets worse. Can you do that?"

Can I stalk my cousin?

I've done worse things to her.

CHAPTER FIVE

SERAPHINE

Twelve years ago
Tuscany

"Why are you here?"

I glance over my shoulder as I pull the bag of flour out of the cupboard, careful not to let it spill.

Blaise is standing in the doorway looking at me expectantly. The villa here in Tuscany where we're staying actually belongs to his side of the family, so I automatically feel like I'm stepping on his turf somehow. His accusatory tone doesn't help.

"Why shouldn't I be?" I ask, my eyes going over him. With his jeans slung low, his black T-shirt looking like he might have put it on backward, and his messy dark hair, he looks like he just rolled out of bed even though it's three in the afternoon. He might have—I haven't seen him all morning.

"I thought you'd be at the river with everyone else," he says, ever so casual.

I go about my business with a shrug, setting down the flour beside the bowl of fresh eggs. "It's Olivier's birthday, so I'm baking him a cake. It's a surprise."

"You know how to bake?"

I give him a wry look before turning my back to him and getting out the measuring cups. "Of course I know how to bake. And cook. Don't you?"

"Why should I? We have cooks who will make anything for you."

I fight the urge to roll my eyes. Of course he has all that.

"Don't you?" he adds defiantly.

"My parents would rather we not become spoiled," I tell him, knowing just how spoiled Blaise and his brother, Pascal, are. On the surface, anyway.

"Oh, how high and mighty of them," he says with a yawn.

"Yeah, well, you're what, seventeen now? I think cooking is a skill you ought to pick up."

"Not if I get a wife."

I turn back to look at him and give him a grin. "I wouldn't count on that. Anyone who gets married to you needs to have her eyes checked. Or his. I don't judge."

"Shut the fuck up," he says, glowering at me. It's hard to get a reaction out of Blaise sometimes because nothing seems to bother him, but apparently this does.

I give him an overly sweet smile and then try to concentrate on the cake. Olivier is tough to shop for, so I figured baking a cake might be a nice alternative, and my brother eats like a horse. I practically shooed everyone out of the house to go to the river for a few hours so I could whip it up as a surprise, but I'm pretty sure Olivier will figure it out. I'm usually the first down there, swimming and sunbathing and trying to catch the eyes of the local Italian boys, especially on a sweltering day like today. August in Tuscany is no joke.

But as everyone—meaning my mother, my aunt, my brothers, my cousin Pascal—headed off to the river to cool down, I told them I was going to stay behind.

Of course, I expected some peace and quiet while they were gone. I didn't expect Blaise to be lurking around.

Which he is still currently doing. I can feel his presence behind me; he hasn't moved.

I do my best to ignore him, but the longer he stands there at my back, the more flustered I get. I don't know why he has that ability. Probably because I'm always on my guard when I'm around Blaise or Pascal—or even their parents. I just don't trust them.

I get so flustered that when I'm trying to crack the egg on the side of the mixing bowl, I hit it too hard and my hand slips and the contents of the bowl go flying in the air, getting me right on the face and in my bangs and down the front of my tank top.

"Fuck!" I cry out, even though I'm not supposed to swear. But I can't help it. My face immediately goes red from embarrassment as Blaise bursts out laughing behind me.

Ew. Ew. Ew! I'm covered in raw egg, and I want to cry.

I frantically look around for a towel, but I can't see anything with the eggs running in my face.

"Stop laughing and help me!" I cry out, reaching blindly, but then I nearly slip on the eggs on the kitchen floor. I grab the counter to hold me up, only that's slippery, too, with egg goo, and I'm starting to go backward.

And then Blaise is behind me, and I'm falling into his arms in the most mortifying way.

"Easy now," he says to me, his grip tight on my elbows. But his whole body is shaking from laughter.

I don't know what to say; my cheeks are burning, and I still can't see. Next thing I know, he's putting me upright and bringing a paper towel to my face.

At first he's trying to clean it off in a gentle manner, and the action is so confusing to me that I quickly yank it out of his hands and wipe it over my eyes while mumbling, "Thanks."

I turn away from him, away from the mess, and finish wiping off my face, my bangs goopy and sticking to my forehead. I sigh loudly, wishing I could just be swallowed up by the floor.

"Hey, it's not a big deal," he says to me, gently nudging me on the arm. "Why don't you get yourself cleaned off, and I'll clean up down here."

"Those were the only eggs," I cry out softly.

"The farm down the street is bound to have some. We'll go get more. Just . . . go take a shower or something, or else you're going to stink even more than you already do."

I try to glare at him, but it's impossible with the egg still lingering around my eyes. Besides, I'm kind of floored that he offered to clean up.

So I trudge upstairs to my room, where I share a washroom with my mother, and quickly jump in the shower. I hate having to wash my hair, especially when I'm so clueless on how to manage it. I've read so many magazines and online articles, but they're of no help. It's funny that I'm officially a Dumont now, but I have none of the class and fashion sense of the family (not to mention skin tone). I stick out like a sore thumb in so many ways.

When I'm done, I know I don't have the time to blow-dry my hair as usual, so I braid it back wet, slip on a clean and simple white summer dress, and head back downstairs.

To my surprise, Blaise has completely cleaned up all the eggs and is drinking orange juice the housekeeper squeezed this morning straight out of the pitcher.

He finishes, wipes his mouth, and puts it right back in the fridge. Boys, I swear.

But wait a minute. This boy is my cousin, and his eyes are taking longer than normal to coast over my body. It's not like the dress I'm wearing is revealing or anything; it's just something light and flirty, and yet there's a look in Blaise's eyes that I haven't seen before.

"Your hair," he says, nodding at me. "It looks different."

Check out the brains on this one. "It's back in a braid, dummy."

"I like it. And you don't have any makeup on."

"It came off in the shower."

"You shouldn't wear makeup. You don't need it," he says. He pauses, then adds, "You're only fourteen."

"I know how old I am," I retort. "And I can wear makeup if I want to."

He shrugs. "Suit yourself. Just thought you'd want to know why you're always single."

"Always single!" I cry out. "Need I remind you what you just reminded me of? I'm fourteen. I don't have time for boys."

"But soon they'll have time for you. You don't want to mess that up."

I roll my eyes. "Whatever. They can do what they want. I do what I want."

"You know," he says slowly, "you've changed a lot since I first met you."

"That was five years ago. I sure hope I've changed. You've changed too."

And that's true. Blaise used to be on the shorter side, but in the last year he's shot up so he's even taller than Pascal, who's older. He's got to be already over six feet. Plus, he's got muscles and abs galore out of nowhere. I try not to look, because that's icky, right? But when we're swimming down at the river, it's kind of hard not to.

"I mean, you used to be so quiet and shy. Now we can't seem to shut you up."

"Very funny," I tell him. I've never been particularly shy, it's just that the circumstances I was raised in made me that way, and then there is the fact that it took me forever to learn French. Now that I can speak it fluently, I guess I do have a habit of telling everyone what's on my mind, whether they like it or not.

His gaze lingers on me, on my lips, just enough to cause a strange butterfly feeling in my stomach, then he says, "Let's go get you your eggs for your stupid cake."

I let his comment slide as I follow him out of the villa. It's late afternoon, and the air is hot and sweet all at once. We've been coming to Uncle Gautier's place in Tuscany, which is not too far from Florence, every first week of August ever since I was adopted. Usually we're here for a week or two. Olivier told me that in the past, our father and uncle would both come, too, but I guess work has gotten more hectic over the years, so it's just my mother and aunt.

I close my eyes to the sunshine and sigh, and when I open them, Blaise is standing in the pebbled driveway and staring at me expectantly. "Are you coming or what?"

"I'm coming. Just taking time to enjoy the moment."

Now he's rolling his eyes. "Do you want your eggs or not?"

I hurry on after him, shaking a pebble out of my sandals. "So why are you hanging around the house and not with everyone else?"

He shrugs. "Didn't want to."

"Lazy."

He glares at me, the look intensified under the hot sun. "I'm not lazy. I just didn't want to. I don't have to hang out with anyone if I don't want to."

I guess I'm not floored by this. Blaise is always the black sheep and the odd one out. His brother is either tormenting him or ignoring him, and the same goes for his father. When it comes to the latter, the more his father ignores him, the better.

I sneak a glance up at him as we walk side by side down the narrow road lined with a crumbling stone wall, past sprawling vineyards and sunflowers. He looks and seems so different now. I remember going to his thirteenth birthday party at their house, hiding in the bushes at night because I didn't feel welcome. That's when Blaise and his friend came to the gazebo and started drinking alcohol. His father caught them, started hitting Blaise with a force that reminded me of so many of my foster homes gone wrong. It was the first time I saw Blaise even remotely vulnerable, and even though he was a lot nicer to me after that, we never spoke of it again. He kept his distance.

Until now.

I'm wondering if I should bring it up and say something when he glances at me sharply, squinting under the sun. "What are you staring at?"

Such a way with words. "Nothing really. I was just thinking."

"About me, naturally."

"Well, actually I was."

He gives me another odd glance. "Oh yeah? And what were you thinking?"

"About how you're doing. You know. In terms of your father."

His eyes narrow just as the road starts to, causing us to walk closer together. "What about him?"

The edge to his voice tells me he knows exactly what I'm talking about, but even if I've been intimidated by Blaise before, I refuse to be now. "Your thirteenth birthday."

He tenses up and wiggles his jaw, averting his eyes from me and back to the road. "That was a long time ago."

"I know. I was just wondering."

"If my father ever smacked me around like that after?" he asks and then shrugs. "Yeah. Sometimes. But not recently. I'm taller than him already, bigger than him. He wouldn't dare lay a finger on me. I'd fucking kill him."

But even as he says that, I can hear a tremor in his voice. Like he's still afraid of him. I don't blame him. His father terrifies me, too, and I go out of my way to avoid him.

Sometimes it makes me wonder how my own father can see the good in him. He never says a bad word against his brother, even though my mother has said plenty. We've all seen the way that he treats the boys, his wife—hell, anyone who crosses his path. He's creepy and manipulative and an outright asshole, but I guess that just means my father is that loyal.

"As soon as I turn eighteen, I'm out of here," Blaise adds.

"Where are you going?"

"School, maybe. University. Or not. Maybe I'll go to Greece and live off the land. Or Ibiza and party for months. Who knows. But I'll be gone."

I shouldn't feel that pang of disappointment because he's leaving. It's a strange feeling, and I'm not sure I like it.

"You're not going to follow in the family footsteps?" I ask him.

He sighs, kicking a stone before focusing his eyes on a truck coming toward us on the narrow road. "I'll probably leave that all to Pascal. He's the one who wants it, and he's the one that Father wants."

The truck slows as it approaches, but the lane is almost too narrow for all of us. Blaise puts his arm across me and pulls me to the side so we're back against the wall as the truck passes, the driver giving us a friendly wave. My shoulder is against his shoulder, and his arm is across my chest for just a second, but I swear it makes me dizzy, the fresh scent of his body wash or soap invading every cell in my body.

When the truck passes and Blaise keeps walking on—his arm dropping away, no big deal—I'm momentarily stunned. What was that? Why did it feel that way?

He glances back at me curiously and looks amused but doesn't say anything, just pushes back a dark lock of hair behind his ears. I've never noticed how nice and shiny and thick his hair is until now.

Damn it, Seraphine, what is wrong with you?

"It's just up here," he says, pointing to a dirt road that snakes off the main road through stunted cypress trees and rosemary.

I hurry to catch up, but here the driveway forks—one side leading to a stone farmhouse, the other side to a barn with a caved-in roof and a pen and chicken coop beside it. Out in the distance I can see a farmer going through the fields with a mower.

"What are you doing?" I ask. "Shouldn't we go knock on the door and ask?"

He just gives me a devilish grin. "I'm a Dumont. I don't ask for anything."

Then he strides over to the pen and opens the gate. "You can stay out here if you want."

Well, shit! He's going to go in there and steal chicken eggs and hang me out to dry.

"I don't think so," I tell him, hurrying along so that the farmer in the field doesn't see me. Blaise holds open the gate and I step inside, careful not to step in any chicken shit.

It's a huge space and chickens are everywhere. The chickens are cooing and squawking at us, making me nervous. "I really think we should leave a note or some money," I tell him.

"That's your side of the family for you, always so good," he remarks as he opens the door to the coop. We're met with darkness and the horrid smell of concentrated chicken shit.

"Why does it always have to be good and bad? Why can't we just be gray?"

"Speak for yourself," he says to me. "Would you consider stealing eggs from a poor farmer to be good or bad?"

I cough, trying not to breathe in the stench as he searches the nests for eggs. "Definitely bad."

"Then color me bad," he says.

I laugh and reach out, smacking him against his chest. "You're the worst, you know that?"

"I do. We're in the middle of discussing it." Even though it's dark and shadowy in the coop, I can see a flash of his smile.

"Okay, let's just hurry up and get out of here."

He continues searching, pulling out two eggs and handing them to me. "How many do you need?"

"Better make it four to be safe," I tell him just as we hear the mower in the distance getting closer. "And I think someone is done working in the field. We better get out of here."

But before we can get out of the coop, there's the sound of footsteps outside and a man yelling about the gate being open and the chickens being loose.

Shit!

He yells something at the chickens in Italian, shooing them.

I hold my breath and exchange a look with Blaise, a look of fear on both our faces, though I swear he has a mischievous glint along with it. He slowly puts his finger to his mouth, as if I didn't know to be quiet.

The farmer continues to berate and coax the chickens back inside the pen. For a moment I think maybe he's going to leave, but then I hear his heavy work-boot footsteps coming toward the coop's open door.

Even though it's a massive coop, there's barely any room in here for us, and Blaise has to slouch or he'll reach the ceiling. There's nowhere to hide.

Blaise stands beside me, right next to the door, and we're hidden in the shadows, unless the farmer happens to search inside the coop or just look in our direction.

I stare up at Blaise, trying to figure out how we're going to get out of this if we're caught, while Blaise is gazing down at me. His chest is rising as he tries to control his breath, and he has a wild look in his eyes, a change from the indifference that usually plagues him. His mouth is open slightly, lips full and glossy, and I'm wondering if it's the adrenaline that's causing me to look at him in such detail, as if I'm pushing aside the dark to see him clearly, or what's going on.

"Hey," a voice says as a shadow falls across the center of the door. "Qual é il problema?" Blaise and I both freeze. If the farmer looks to the right at all, he'll see us right there!

But the farmer seems to be satisfied with the silence of the coop since all the chickens vacated while we were looking for eggs, and he pulls back, chatting to the hens as he makes his way out, and we hear the click of the gate.

Once we hear the motor start, we both let out a large breath of relief. I start laughing nervously. "I can't believe you nearly got us caught."

"Me?" he says, the distance between us getting even smaller somehow. It makes my heart bump against my ribs, the hairs on my arms stand straight up. Just from Blaise moving closer to me, I'm full of anxiety and for different reasons.

Get a grip.

"You're saying I'm a bad influence?" Blaise says, his voice lower, almost husky sounding. It makes my stomach do backflips in a way it hasn't before, not even when my crush Pierre Tremaine told me I was cute during math class last year.

I stare back at him, feeling brave and bold, even when he moves closer, so that the toes of his shoes touch the toes of mine. "You definitely are."

"I could be worse," he says and then gives me a quick smile, a hint of something wicked flashing in his eyes.

Before I can even say anything he's leaning down and kissing me. Right on the lips. Right here in this bloody chicken coop.

I'm stunned. Everything inside me freezes. His lips press against mine, soft and warm and wrong. So damn wrong!

What are you doing? Make him stop!

And yet I don't.

Because . . . I think I like this.

And I kiss him back, even though my lips are unsure of what to do.

This is my first kiss.

And it's with my *cousin.*

The realization of that reality is enough to put my hand on Blaise's chest and push him back.

"What the hell was that?" I ask him, my face flushed with embarrassment, my heart and nerves dancing all over the place, butterflies in my tummy taking flight.

"Felt like kissing you," he says, and his voice sounds so calm and collected, I have to wonder if that even meant anything to him, if he's mocking me somehow.

"You're my cousin, Blaise," I tell him sternly, trying to take a step back, but I'm cornered in the coop.

"Most definitely not by blood," he says, reaching across and brushing my bangs away from my eyes. "But, hey, now I know."

"Now you know what?" I ask, keeping so still, my skin tingling from the contact of his fingers brushing against my forehead.

"What you taste like," he says.

The way he says it hits me deep in the gut, in a way I'd never felt before.

In a way that scares me to death.

I clear my throat. "Well, now you know. So you better not try that again."

"I won't," he says with a shrug, as if it doesn't bother him. He looks toward the door. "We should get going if you want to start on that cake."

With our eyes peeled for the farmer and the eggs cradled in our arms, we leave the coop and the farm. We leave it completely different people from the ones who first stepped in.

At least, it feels like *my* entire world has changed. I'm not too sure about Blaise. As we walk back down the narrow road, he seems so at ease and casual about what happened, about kissing me like that, out of the blue.

Me, I'm just a mess. Of feelings and emotions and hormones, I guess. A deadly cocktail.

I can't believe that just happened.

I just had my first kiss, with Blaise.

And I don't know how anything will ever be the same again.

But when we get back to the villa, and I'm a nervous, blubbering mess inside, he says he'll leave me to work on the cake, and then he's off, joining the others at the river.

I might not ever be the same again, but it's obvious in his eyes it's like the kiss never even happened.

Maybe it's for the best.

God, I hope I find a way to pretend that it never happened too.

CHAPTER SIX

SERAPHINE

"What are your plans for tonight?"

It takes me a few moments to register that those words are not only being spoken but being spoken to me by my cousin.

I glance up at Blaise. We're in the boardroom along with three interns Gautier hired yesterday, going over posters and images of past ad campaigns and comparing them with the sales data.

I look to the employees, but they aren't paying us much attention; they're totally engrossed in their work, as marketing and advertising students usually are when they have to fight for survival.

Still, I can't answer like I normally would—a.k.a. "None of your fucking business."

"I'm having an exciting evening at home with a glass of wine," I tell him with a fake smile pasted on my lips. "And you?"

He stares at me for a moment, his dark eyes flickering with unknown thoughts, and for that moment I'm brought back in time to when we were teenagers. In some ways, he's barely changed. He's still a smart-ass, still quietly observing one moment and cutting the next. Always so calm and composed, unless you really got under his skin. And how I wanted to get under his skin.

He never let me.

But so much time has passed since then, and we are different people now. He still has that height and the broad shoulders and cutting jawline and the dark hair that he often swoops off his forehead with fancy hair products. I swear his lips have gotten even fuller. But when I look into his eyes, I don't see the person that I knew, which tells me that perhaps I never knew him at all.

"Probably going to see a movie," he says. "Alone."

My brows come together. "Is this your way of inviting me to a movie?"

He grins at me but there's no warmth in it. "I wasn't inviting you anywhere. Just making small talk so that the interns here don't think we're all unsociable monsters at this company."

At that, the students all look our way, and I know they've been listening this entire time.

Blaise probably has a point, too, but I'm not about to tell him that. Besides, it's almost time to go home, and I actually do have plans, quite the opposite from what I told Blaise.

Ever since I got back from Bordeaux, I've been racking my brain trying to figure out how to proceed with what I've discovered. Google is your friend for only so long, and it's hard to know who to trust when it comes down to it. I need someone I can absolutely rely on, who will keep all this a secret, who's a professional and will do everything I ask of him without anyone else knowing. I need to feel like I have someone in my corner, even if it's someone who I'm paying the big bucks to.

It's just too big and scary for me to handle on my own.

So I reached out to the last person I wanted to, the only person I know who is so far removed from the Dumonts that there would be no issue of misplaced loyalty. Someone who owes me a lot. Someone with few morals who knows a lot of people with even fewer morals.

My ex-husband, Cyril.

Believe me, I have my pride, and all of that was ripped to shreds the moment I picked up my phone and gave him a call, telling him my problem and needing him to keep it all a secret.

I'm meeting him tonight at a divey bar in the Latin Quarter, along with someone he thinks is the right person for the job.

It's the last thing I want to do. I think I'd rather accompany Blaise to his movie, if he really is going to one. But I know it's the only shot I have.

And the one saving grace in all this is that Cyril didn't hang up. He didn't laugh, and he didn't call me crazy. He knows my family very well, and he's hated them as much as they've hated him. Yes, he was cheating on me; yes, he only married me for money. Both of those truths tore me up inside for a long time.

You'd think I would be used to rejection at this point. It's what an adopted child always goes back to: the rejection.

I managed to get over it, though. It still stings, it still makes me mad, but it no longer hurts like it once did. I'm guessing that's because I realized I never really loved Cyril, I just loved the idea of him. I loved the idea of being married, of maybe being a mother, of having someone who loved me.

It turned out to be a lie, but at least I didn't lose my heart in the matter.

I leave the office before Blaise can stare at me any longer. It's almost as if he doesn't believe me.

I don't bother going home. I park my car around the corner from my apartment and head to my favorite café on the street corner. I live in Saint-Germain-des-Prés, one of the more expensive parts of Paris. At one point in my life, the status and the power and the money of this neighborhood fueled me. It made me feel like I had to work harder and harder to be deserving of a place like this. It made me competitive, though more against myself than anyone else.

Of course, I know I don't have to work. I'm an heiress. With my father's death, I inherited a lot of money, and even before, that silver spoon was lodged firmly in my mouth from the moment I entered the family.

But the last thing I want is to not earn my place here. And so I've worked harder, smarter, better, to ensure I belong. It's probably why I didn't want to leave the neighborhood after Cyril and I got a divorce. I should have wanted a fresh start, but my apartment was mine before I left him.

I sit down outside under the heaters, wrapping my scarf around my neck tighter and slipping on a pair of leather gloves with a zipper running across them. They're by Acne Studios, a Swedish brand, and I was always so nervous to wear them around my father because he would immediately know they weren't the Dumont label. The craftmanship pales in comparison, but these gloves were €200 instead of €2,000, and, well, I find them cool.

I stare at the gloves as the waiter brings me an espresso, appreciating the modern and almost punk rock design. I find myself gravitating to these styles more and more lately. The Dumont label has always been about refinement and elegance—the classic chic look of the typical upper-class Frenchwoman. But I'm not French, and I'm feeling the need to expand my horizons. Try something new. When I put on a Dumont dress, I almost feel like I'm pretending to be my mother. There's nothing wrong with that at all—I love that it can make me feel that way, because I miss her so damn much.

But maybe it isn't me anymore. Maybe this job, no matter how hard I work at it, doesn't give me the joy and purpose it once did. Maybe this is a sign that I belong elsewhere, with a company I want to work for because I believe in the work, not because I'm bound to it out of loyalty and legacy. I'd never even given it a thought before, because I always did what my father wanted me to do, but now . . .

I sigh and sip my drink, bundled against the chilled breeze that sweeps through the darkness. Spring can't come fast enough. It doesn't help that I'm about to do something somewhat macabre.

When I'm done with the espresso, I move on to champagne. I'm not the only one out here on the terrace; there is a slew of Parisian smokers puffing away on their cigarettes, braving the cold to get their fix and partake in some conversation and people-watching.

I'm watching too. Seeing a couple of girlfriends laugh and lean on each other, smoking and drinking wine, and it makes me yearn for that. I should call Marie again, unless she thinks I'm too crazy to be her friend anymore. I should contact old friends, go out and have fun. I'm single. I need to get laid, or at least just a night of dancing.

But I can't. Not right now, not while this loss burns inside of me and the truth is all I can think about. I need to know what happened to my father; I need to know if the man I'm now working for is the very man who killed him.

And so then what? a voice inside me asks.

And so then I do everything I can to take him down.

Even though I know I might lose so much more than I bargained for in the process.

I end up spending a few hours outside, drinking champagne by myself, until my nerves have subsided a bit. I'm still nervous, but I'm a little drunk and that helps. Anything to help me get through seeing Cyril again.

I pay the bill and get up at the same time another patron gets up. I hear the scrape of their chair, see their figure in the background, but don't pay it too much attention.

Not until I'm crossing the street and heading to the *métro* to take the train to Cardinal Lemoine. I feel the presence at my back, like I'm being followed.

Once I'm on the other side of the street, I look around, expecting to see someone ominous-looking.

There's a crowd of pedestrians behind me. Bundled-up old ladies teetering together, businessmen in long coats with baguettes tucked under their arms, women puffing on cigarettes and pushing baby strollers. No one is paying me any attention, no one is following me.

I've been paranoid ever since the car chase last year, and I'm even more so since I got back from the castle. I know the odds of anyone having seen me are slim. Yes, it's possible that my car was spotted by a worker, but anything of concern with that estate would have been funneled up to Renaud, and I haven't heard from him.

That said, even on the short métro ride to my stop, I'm staring at everyone on the train. Some people stare back, maybe because they recognize me, maybe because I'm acting like a total weirdo. Still, I refuse to keep my eyes down.

The bar where Cyril wanted me to meet him is called the Terrible Cat, and it's in a part of the Latin Quarter that stops being charming and filled with broke students and now borders on dirty and unsafe. Figures this is the place we would meet.

I step inside the bar, surprised to see how busy it is, though not surprised that it smells like cigarettes, stale beer, and a pinch of urine.

Everyone's head swivels toward me, taking me in. Some men take me in longer than they should, and I try not to show any fear or shame, because this place is full of men who take pride in that. Using their leers to make women uncomfortable, particularly a woman like me, well dressed and polished and hinting at money.

I spot Cyril waving at me subtly from a booth in the back corner.

Here it goes.

I keep my head high and stride confidently through the bar, though I feel anything but. I hear a bald-headed white dude whisper, "Go back where you came from," in broken English, assuming that I don't know French, and it takes everything I have not to stop and pick up his beer and throw it in his face. I've done that before, and nothing good comes out of it, and the last thing I need is to draw even more attention to myself.

So I swallow my anger and keep going until I reach Cyril, who is trying to get out of the booth to get up and hug me.

"Stay where you are," I tell him sternly, gesturing with my palm out. "We don't need to play nice."

He pauses, half out of the booth, and then shrugs. "Okay. But you are the one that called me, remember that."

"And I wish I had another alternative," I tell him, sitting down across from him.

"Well, you look nice," he says. "Maybe too skinny. I liked you better when you had some meat on your bones."

I raise my brow and look him over the same way he looked at me. "And your hairline is waving a white flag. Didn't think it would recede so fast, but I guess that's what stress does to you."

He blinks beneath his black-rimmed glasses, and I know I've hit a sore spot. The truth is, Cyril looks more or less the same. He's tall, slim, has short-cropped blond hair and a long nose. Pale. He banks on his nerd charm, and I know that fooled me into thinking he was handsome in a quirky way. Now all I know is that I can barely stand to look at him, knowing what this gold-digging asshole did and how he took me for a ride. Cyril works for the United Nations and has a lot of connections and a certain amount of status here, as well as in the rest of Europe. Little did I know he'd also made many bad business investments, many of which were questionable, and that our marriage was supposed to be his ticket out of debt.

Didn't really work that way, though he fought me on it for some time.

"Still sharp tongued," he remarks bitterly.

I shrug. "You have to be when you deal with idiots all day long."

"You have an odd way of showing appreciation, you know that?"

I tilt my head and give him an impatient look. "And so, do I have something to thank you for? So far all I see is you, and if you think you're going to act as my private investigator, then you have another thing coming."

"He'll be here in a minute," he says.

"Who is he? And how do you know him? All you told me on the phone is that you knew someone who might be able to help. Is he a private investigator? Someone who likes money and has no morals? A lapsed police officer?"

"Let's just say he's all of those things and more."

"I'm surprised you know someone like that. Almost as surprised that you wanted to meet in a place like this."

Cyril is a notorious snob. He probably wiped down his seat with hand sanitizer before he sat down.

"You truly believe I don't care about you, don't you?" he asks, shaking his head. "Then why did you call me if you thought I wouldn't help?"

I lift up my shoulder and start to unravel my scarf. It's hot in this place. "You're the only one I know that hates my uncle's family as much as I do." Cyril didn't care for my family, either, but there's no point in bringing that up.

"I care about you. I always have and you know it."

"You sure showed it in a peculiar way, shoving your dick up a bunch of pussies," I tell him, then look around at the bar. "Do I even want to risk having a beer in here?"

"I'll get it for you," he says, his face going red at what I just said. Can't stand to keep sitting here while I let him have it. But even though I have plenty inside me left to hurl his way, I have to stay cool and remember why I'm here. He might be my only hope with all this, and if I push back enough, he's going to walk away. Reminding him of what a shitty husband he was isn't going to help.

When he comes back with a bottle of beer for me, I try to give him a genuine smile and tell myself to stay civil.

"So back to this guy and how you know him . . . ," I say before taking a tepid sip of my beer. It's warm but better than nothing.

"Let's just say in my line of business, security is of upmost importance. This guy will have your back."

"For a fee."

"For a high fee. But he knows what he's doing, and more than that, he owes me a favor."

"And you'd waste your favor on me?"

"Nothing is wasted on you, my dear," he says, and then his eyes flit over my shoulder to the door.

I turn my head to see a man walk in. He's not exactly what I expected, but I know without a doubt that this is him. He actually looks very blank, like if I tried to recall him later, I'm not sure how I'd describe him. He has no features or mannerisms that stand out, only that he moves in a way that can be described as animal grace.

Or perhaps predatorial.

I shudder at the thought as the man heads straight for our booth and stands at the end, staring down at Cyril with quiet expectation.

"Jones," Cyril says to him. "Thank you for coming. Jones, this is Seraphine, my ex-wife."

I cringe internally at that term. I hate being reminded that the marriage was a failure.

I nod at Jones and give him a tight smile since he doesn't seem like the shaking-hands or kissing-on-the-cheek kind of person.

"Here, sit down," Cyril says, moving over.

Jones sits beside him soundlessly.

I stare at him some more. He's average height, with an average build and average face. The only things that stand out to me are his dark eyes, pale skin, and the faint scars that run across his face, the kind of scars that look like they were earned in a few fights and then fixed with expensive laser treatment.

"So, 'Jones,'" I say. "Doesn't seem like a French name . . ."

"I'm from Romania," he says, and his voice is so even keeled and quiet I lean in a little.

"Doesn't sound Romanian, either," I say.

"Jones can be whoever you need him to be, Seraphine," Cyril says quickly, a hint to make me stop questioning his name. "So why don't you tell him who that is and what exactly you want."

I rub my lips together, my lipstick completely worn off at this point. I hope he doesn't think I'm crazy. I hope that by repeating myself again to Cyril, it doesn't start to make me feel crazy too.

I lean in and look around the bar to see if anyone is paying attention.

"No one is listening," Cyril says, tapping his fingers impatiently against the table. "Why do you think I picked this place? They've all got their own deals and problems going on."

I take in a deep breath and still I whisper. "Jones. I believe that my father, Ludovic Dumont of the Dumont empire, was murdered by his own brother or perhaps his nephew. Or maybe both. Or maybe even someone else. But I believe he didn't have a heart attack—he was poisoned and it was covered up. And before you ask for proof—because I know you'd dismiss the value of gut feelings—the security footage of the night of the party when he died in front of everyone, that footage is missing. And only that footage. I believe someone deleted the files and deleted evidence of the crime. I need your help to get those files back. If you can do more than that, I'll be even more in your debt."

Jones stares at me with his dark eyes, and for a frightening moment I'm reminded of the way that Gautier looks sometimes—it's like staring into a black hole you can't get out of. But then he nods sharply.

"I can do that."

"So you don't think I'm nuts," I ask.

"I have no idea about your mental state," he says in his quiet, calm voice. "But never dismiss your gut feelings. A lot of what I do is based on gut feelings and backed by evidence. It sounds like you're on the right track to the truth."

But even though what he's telling me should make me feel better, feel relieved that what I'm thinking isn't so nuts, he still continues to stare at me with those eyes. My gut right now is telling me to tread lightly with him. Those eyes hide a lot of lost souls, lives I'm sure he's taken. I know that right now in the heart of me.

I look to Cyril, who is nodding his approval, and then back to Jones. "I know you want to discuss money . . ."

"I do," he says. "But I also need you to give me some of your family history. Why your uncle? What did he have to gain?"

"There's so much history there that I'm pretty sure it will take the whole night," I tell him honestly.

"Don't worry," Jones says. "I charge by the hour. I have all night."

CHAPTER SEVEN

BLAISE

Ten years ago
Paris

The Dumont Masquerade Ball has to be one of the fucking stupidest, most self-indulgent events of the year. And every time August rolls around, I'm busy thinking of excuses of why I shouldn't go. Even if I'm traveling through Bali, like I was a few days ago, my family has some way of roping me into it.

The funny thing is, they don't guilt trip me. Instead they act like they don't care and that I ought to go for the sake of my reputation and career. Scratch that: they don't act at all, because they actually don't care. And I'm stubborn and stupid enough to let that spur me into going.

So that's where I am now. Being driven to my parents' estate outside Paris, where the party is being held. I'm wearing a $5,000 Dumont suit that I didn't have to pay for, and in my hands is a purple velvet mask that I'll put on before I go inside.

Of course, at these parties there is no masquerade. Most of the people there want to flaunt who they are, so the masks and disguises are minimal. It's just an excuse for people to act like high and drunken idiots, indulging in fantasies that never feel so good behind closed doors.

My uncle Ludovic has always insisted that the ball is about celebrating the mystique of fashion, that people can use clothes to either show the world who they are or to disguise it. That always sounded so trite. My father, on the other hand, says the ball is about getting people to behave badly and have the tabloids report on it the next day. It creates more publicity for the Dumont label and makes the guest list even more exclusive, the party more in demand.

But it bores me. The whole scene bores me. I'm nineteen years old, and being around the fashion crowd is the last thing I need. Bunch of vapid users is what they are.

"Blaise," Pascal says to me as I approach the front doors to my family home, tightening the mask around my head as I go. "Not so fashionably late," he remarks.

I haven't seen my brother for five months. For a moment I wonder if that warrants a hug or the shake of a hand, but then I remember what side of the Dumont family I'm on.

"I wasn't sure I was going to come," I tell Pascal, stopping in front of him. "Do I need an invitation?"

He smirks, and I know by that smirk that he wishes he could keep me out of the party. I've always been a third wheel, one reason why I've been rolling along on my own way. "I'll make an exception for you." He looks around my shoulder as if he's expecting someone else. "No date? Again?"

I shrug. "Can't help it if I'm picky."

"Picky with men or picky with women?" He's grinning again. He's always teased me for not having a girlfriend, and honestly, I like to play up the fact that he thinks I could be gay.

"Let's just say I don't waste my time with people who are beneath me," I say, brushing past him.

"Very noncommittal," he calls after me as I step into the house, but I don't acknowledge that I hear him. I barely do, anyway—the place is absolutely roaring with laughter and music and the sound of chatter and champagne glasses clinking.

The good thing about being fashionably late is that it's easier to blend into the crowd and everyone is well lubricated. My father will probably be too sauced to want to spend much time talking to me. I just need for him to see me, need to strike a few poses for the tabloids, and then be out of here.

But for the life of me, I can't seem to find my father, not right away. I do have a few giggling models coming up to me, asking how I am, teasing me for having no date, doing their best to get under my skin. Other than that, I don't see any of my family.

Until . . .

I have to do a double take. I'm walking past the dining room, which has been cleared out to make room for guests, and heading to the back doors where the party has spilled out into the yard, when I see a familiar face.

Seraphine.

But familiar is a vague term. I haven't seen her in nearly two years— she wasn't at last year's ball—and she's like an elevated version of the younger cousin that I knew.

Yeah, cousin, I remind myself. *Your sixteen-year-old cousin.*

This wouldn't be the first time I've had to remind myself of who Seraphine is to me. Memories of being in Tuscany come flooding back as I stand here and stare at her. I kissed her in that fucking chicken coop. I don't know what the hell I was thinking, but I can tell you I thought about it for a long time after.

Thoughts I never should have had.

Thoughts no one should probably have about their cousin.

I'm frozen in place. She hasn't spotted me yet because she's hanging off the arm of some guy in a yellow mask. He's tall, though not as tall as me, with a strong jaw. I immediately hate him. I'm no stranger to jealousy, and I don't try to bat it away. I already know she's too good for him.

I mean, she doesn't look sixteen, that's for sure. Maybe my age, maybe even older. Her height helps. Her hair is up, exposing her long neck. She's filled in a lot, and even though her limbs are still long, she has hips now and an ample amount of cleavage, both of which are accentuated by her yellow, curve-hugging dress.

I hate the fact that she matches the guy she's with, the yellow making him look sallow and jaundiced while making her darker skin glow. I also hate that she won't stop staring at him adoringly beneath her own mask and that his own eyes are roving all over the party.

Until they meet mine.

I stare right back, waiting.

Finally Seraphine tears her eyes off him and follows his gaze.

I can't tell if she's surprised or not, but she does mouth something to the guy, perhaps reassuring him that I'm not a threat, even though I feel like I am. She at least tells him that I'm her cousin, which immediately makes him stand up straighter.

He walks away from her, right across the crowd in the hall and over to me.

"Are you Blaise Dumont?" the guy asks, his accent German, or perhaps Austrian. He sounds refined or at least like he's trying to be.

"It depends who is asking," I tell him.

Seraphine comes up beside him. "Blaise, this is my . . . friend Emil."

I stare at her, brows raised. "No 'hello, dear cousin'? I haven't seen you in over a year. Just, this is your friend Emil."

Her eyes narrow beneath her mask, and I know I've struck a nerve. Ever since I kissed her, things have been kind of strained. I've acted like nothing happened, but I feel like that just pisses her off. But what does she want me to do? Act on it again? She made it more than clear that I was out of line. And perhaps I was. But what can I say, being out of line runs in my blood.

My eyes linger, just for a moment, on her chest and the low-cut lines of her dress, and I feel a painful thrill run through me. The kind of thrill that's rife with taboo and flirts with danger. The kind of thrill that I have never felt around any other woman before (or, for Pascal's sake, any other man).

"Yes, of course," Seraphine says with a sigh. She straightens up, raising her chin. "Hello, dear cousin. I haven't seen you for over a year, and this is my friend Emil."

Emil smiles at me. His teeth are way too straight. "I am such a big fan."

I frown. "A fan? Of what?"

"Of you. Of your label. I've wanted to work in fashion for years. I already design my own clothes. This suit, I made it. I grew up in Vienna, helping my father become a tailor, but I'm already far better than he is, and he's been doing it all his life."

I eye Seraphine, and I can tell she's trying not to look embarrassed. *What a charmer,* my look says.

"Oh, well, I have nothing to do with any of this bullshit," I say, waving at the crowd of idiots. *In other words, I'm guessing you're just using Seraphine to try to get ahead.*

Emil starts laughing, the kind of laugh I've heard my mother use. It's fake and it's loud and it's entirely for my benefit. "You're hilarious. I had no idea."

He looks at me with an odd glint in his eyes, something almost heated, and I realize that Seraphine was his stepping-stone to me, and then I'm his stepping-stone into the business.

Times like this, I really do wish I'd nipped those rumors in the bud.

I glance again at Seraphine, feeling sorry for her. She really seems to like this guy, as far as I can tell, and yet he's using her, just as everyone at this party is using everyone else.

"Now if you'll excuse me," I tell them, "I have alcohol to drink and people to ignore."

I hear him laugh as I continue toward the backyard, but I get as far as the shorn grass of the lawn before someone grabs my arm.

I turn, not surprised to see Seraphine. Emil is somewhere in the background, perhaps looking for another Dumont ass to kiss.

"I need to ask you a favor," she says, eyes darting around. She shouldn't lower her voice like that—it's almost sexy.

"What?" I ask her, feigning disinterest and leaning back a little, away from her grasp. It would do me no good to stand any closer to her.

"Emil means a lot to me," she says, and I roll my eyes under my mask. She doesn't seem to notice. "If you could do anything—"

"Me?" I ask. "You're not very observant, are you? Too busy putting out to pay any attention."

Her eyes widen beneath the mask, her mouth dropping. She gasps. "What?"

"I've been in Bali for the last few months, in Thailand and Sri Lanka before that. Do I look like someone who gives a fuck about this business?"

She's speechless and I expect her to go off on me about how I basically called her a whore, but she just shakes her head. "I haven't known where you've been, and it doesn't matter. Your father looks to you and Pascal as basically his employees."

I bristle. "That's Pascal. I'm nothing to my father."

"But you're here, aren't you?" she says smartly, crossing her arms.

I take in a deep breath through my nose. "You have more to do with this business than I do."

"I'm still in high school," she says. "My father doesn't tell me anything, and he doesn't listen."

"Ah, so there's trouble in paradise, is there? Your father isn't the saint he's made out to be."

"No one is who they're made out to be."

"Unless you show people they're right. And anyway, go ask your brother."

79

"Olivier wants nothing to do with the business. He did at one point, but now he just wants to open hotels. And Renaud just cares about wine. You're all I've got."

"You've got me as much as you've got Pascal, so you might as well go try him."

She closes her eyes and sighs, shoulders slumping for a moment. Pascal is always the last resort.

"Listen," I tell her, feeling just a bit bad. "This guy, Emil? He's not worth it. He's just using you."

She straightens up, like her spine was snapped back into place, and glares at me. "You're an asshole."

I raise my palms. "Whoa. Asshole? For telling you the truth?"

"You're just an asshole in general. I should have known you would have never helped me."

She turns around but before she can go, I reach out and grab her wrist tightly, holding her in place. "Believe it or not, I am trying to help. You should only do favors for people who deserve it."

"So then do this favor for me," she says, yanking her wrist away.

"No way. He's not worthy of it. Find someone worthy and then we'll talk."

She swallows hard, and I swear I see the shine of tears in her eyes. "He's worthy," she says quietly.

"Oh yeah? How long have you known him?"

"We've been dating for eight months. His father is good friends with my father. He's rich and accomplished and twenty years old. He's going places."

"Have you slept with him yet?"

I know it's in bad form to ask that, but fuck it. I'm curious.

She flinches. "None of your damn business." And maybe if she wasn't wearing a mask, I could read her a little better. Or maybe I could never read her at all.

I shrug. Whatever. "Just saying you seem to have it bad."

For a moment her chin trembles with vulnerability, but then she pulls it together. "I wouldn't trust your judgment on other people's relationships. I haven't seen you in one yet."

I cross my arms and study her. "You know, everyone seems so fascinated as to whether I'm dating or not; I'm surprised you're no different. I'm surprised you care."

"I don't care," she says haughtily. "I just notice, since Pascal and Olivier and Renaud—"

"Yes, they're all running around and fucking everything that walks. Don't you think it's possible to do the same and be discreet about it? Perhaps I don't have a girlfriend in the public eye, but I'm game for laying each and every one of my sexual conquests out for you in detail, if that's what you'd like."

"No thank you," she says.

"You sure? You seem awfully intrigued. And if you're fucking Emil, I wouldn't blame you one bit."

"You're disgusting," she says, nearly spitting on me. "Forget I ever talked to you."

And with that she turns on her heel and storms back inside.

Seraphine has always been a pistol, but now she's turned into a real firecracker. And it seems whatever I do or say nearly sets her off, though perhaps I deserve it a bit.

Okay, that's over now. Let's find Father and get out of here.

I try to shake Seraphine out of my head. We barely spoke and she's already thrown me for a loop.

I saunter off into the crowd that's outside, and after running into more models and celebrities and photographers and designers, I finally find my father talking to my uncle. As usual, Ludovic lights up when he sees me and pulls me into a hug, all while I'm watching my father closely, to see if the affection his own brother shows me bothers him.

I think it does. Just a bit. But not enough to become affectionate himself. Not enough to change.

"You decided to show up," my father says dryly, giving me nothing more than a nod and the slight upturn of his nose, as if the smell of me displeases him.

I shrug. "Figured the party might need a little excitement."

"We're glad you're here," Ludovic says, that familiar and friendly glint in his eye. "It's been too long, Blaise. It really has. Where have you been, anyway?"

"Galivanting around Southeast Asia," my father says. "Wasting his life away."

I stiffen at that but quickly brush it off. As if working for him is anything but a waste.

"Oh, come now, brother," my uncle says to him. "When we were his age, we wanted nothing more than to see the world."

"You saw the world," my father says, pointing his glass of champagne at him.

"Through the business. Through work. But to be young and free like Blaise . . ." My uncle trails off, and my father is glaring at him to shut up.

The funny thing is that it's true that my uncle was the one seeing the world for work when he was my age. He joined the company, working right beside my grandfather, and, as far as I understand it, never really took a break. Work is everything to him.

My father, on the other hand, was slow to join. I don't really know what he did when he was my age. He doesn't speak about it often, just says he tried university for a bit and then hung around Paris and New York. Eventually he was brought on board at the label, but he never had any kind of passion or enthusiasm for it the way that Ludovic did.

The only thing he really cared about was money and trying to outdo his brother in whatever way he could.

"Blaise isn't free," my father says simply. "He may think he is, but he's a Dumont and we all know that the word translates to *chains*." He stares at me as he says this, as if daring me to prove him wrong.

Which I take as my moment to leave this hellhole.

I give my uncle a polite nod to signal that I'm getting the fuck out of here, give nothing to my father, and then head back inside, ready to find my driver.

And that's when I see it: two things happening at once, a collision course in front of my eyes.

Just outside the back doors that are opened wide to the lawn and reveling partygoers, I see the yellow mask of Emil in a passionate, albeit sloppy, kiss with someone who isn't Seraphine. I can just see the back of her head and her long blonde hair and his hands running under her dress. So fucking brazen and bold—this kind of public shit is something Pascal would do.

Then I watch as Seraphine steps out and sees Emil kissing this girl. The mask can't hide her expression as it turns from shock to humiliation to anger.

"What the fuck, Emil!" Seraphine yells, and it's like the music almost stops as she says that. Everyone turns to look.

The blonde breaks away from him and looks around sheepishly as Seraphine continues to yell. "Who is this? How could you do this to me, in front of everyone!"

My cousin is awfully good at making a scene.

Part of me wants to chuckle and watch in amusement as all the drama explodes in front of my eyes.

But the other part of me actually feels for Seraphine, a feeling that is so peculiar because I don't normally feel anything. And yet there it is, stabbing me in the chest. The hurt in her eyes, the humiliation flushing on her face, her trembling hands as she rips off her mask and then lunges forward to rip the mask off the blonde.

"Who are you?" she screeches, trying to pull it off.

The blonde pushes her back. "Get the fuck away from me!"

The mask snaps and reveals her face, but it's no one that I know.

The look on Seraphine's face tells me it's someone she knows.

It spurs her on to push the girl, who stumbles back into Emil.

I know I have to intervene before Seraphine does something stupid. Emil is already trying to distance himself from it, as if he can just slink away.

I stride over and grab Seraphine's arm, pulling her away from a fight that's about to get ugly.

"Let go of me!" she hisses, but I don't. I just tighten my grip and put my arm around her waist, pulling her back until we're enough at a distance; then I take her by the wrist and lead her around the corner of the house, away from prying eyes.

I expect her to yell at me some more, but once she sees that no one is around, she immediately bursts into tears, putting her face in her hands.

I don't know what to do. I want to console her, but I feel like that will make it worse. So I keep my distance and watch her cry.

After a few minutes she looks up at me, her makeup running over her full cheeks, her eyes shimmering with sadness and regret, and says, "You were right. Are you happy now?"

I swallow thickly. "I'm not happy," I tell her, my voice low. "I don't think I ever am."

"About Emil!" she cries out. "You knew he would do this to me."

I nod. "At some point, yes. But not here in front of you. I didn't think he would do that."

"He broke my heart!"

And if I had a heart at all, I think mine would break a little for her too.

"I stand by what I said," I tell her, taking a step closer. "You're too good for him."

She shakes her head, tears continuing to spill. "No, no. He did this because I'm not good enough. Because I'm ugly. I'm dark skinned. I'm foreign. I don't belong. He thought all those things to begin with, and then he used me. He used me to get what he wanted." She pauses, letting out a shaking sob. "God, I feel so stupid. I feel like Jamillah."

I frown. "Who is Jamillah?"

"Jamillah was me. It was my name until your uncle took me in."

I feel stupid now. "I had no idea."

She wipes under her eyes with the heel of her palm and sniffs. "Yes. I didn't want to be Jamillah anymore, and he said I could change it to whatever I wanted. I wanted to fit in here, so I chose the French name that I thought was the prettiest."

"It is the prettiest."

She glances up at me. "Really?"

I nod. "I've always thought so."

She studies me for a moment as if trying to gauge my sincerity. "Well, most of the time I feel like I picked wrong. I should have stayed Jamillah. Or just someone with no name. I mean, fuck, half my foster parents just called me 'girl' or even 'brown girl.' And yet I thought I was deserving of being Seraphine. Seraphine is the name of a girl who doesn't have a boyfriend who cheats on her in front of everyone she knows."

"Seraphine is a beautiful name for a beautiful girl."

The moment those words leave my mouth, I know it's a mistake.

"You . . . ," she says softly, obviously taken aback. "You think I'm beautiful?"

Fuck.

Yeah, I think you're beautiful. I think your lips should be outlawed. I think your eyes are as big and dark as the night sky, but a million times more mysterious, a million times more mystical.

"Yeah, I guess," I say, trying to sound bored. "Look, I'm just trying to make you feel better."

She gives a few small nods and averts her eyes. I see what little hope there was in them vanish and feel like now I'm the one to blame.

Shit. Why the hell is this so complicated? Is it only complicated to me?

"Well," she says with a heavy sigh, one I feel in my bones. "You succeeded for a moment. And I guess a moment is all I can hope for. Now, if you'll excuse me, I need to be alone."

She gives me one sad little smile and walks off down to the front of the house, her shoulders slumped and head hanging low.

Jesus. I could have handled that better. She doesn't deserve any of this.

There's only one way to make things right.

Or, at least, there's only one way that will make *me* feel right.

I march around the corner, right back into the drama, where Emil has his arm around the blonde bitch, trying to console her.

"Hey, asshole," I cry out, not slowing my approach toward them.

Emil looks up in time to see me swing back and punch him squarely on the nose. Blood spurts out as he screams and goes stumbling back.

"That was for Seraphine Dumont," I tell him, ready to hit him again. My knuckles have burst and they're throbbing wildly, but I don't actually feel any pain. I'll do it again and again until I feel something. "Are you still a fan of mine or what?"

"Fuck you!" Emil yells, covering his nose, spitting out blood. If he makes one move to come at me, I'll hit him again, making sure his nose shatters into pieces.

"A fair-weather fan, then," I comment as I lean in and grab him by his bloody collar, the mask crooked and half-up his face. "Do me a favor and never set a foot here again. Take this blonde bitch with you. If you try and get a job anywhere in Paris as a designer, I can guarantee I'll go out of my way to make your pitiful little life a living hell."

A crowd has gathered around, all probably wondering what's come over me. I couldn't give a shit. I'm done with them, done with all this. If I grow a spine in the next year, I won't be back here again.

I walk back toward the party, hoping to get out of here once and for all, when my father steps in front of me and pulls me aside.

"What the fuck was that?" he says in my ear, his voice low but simmering and barely contained. I know that voice. That's the voice that comes before a strike. Well, I fucking dare him.

My eyes must say that exact thing, because when I pull away from him, my gaze fixes on his and I'm not backing down. He manages to, just an inch.

"That fucker isn't welcome here," I tell him.

"You couldn't have made that more apparent," he says, jaw tense. "And now it's going to be reported that Blaise Dumont is not only the most useless member of the family but the most violent as well."

"That will always be Pascal. You've trained him so damn well."

"Pascal always knows his place, and he knows not to make a scene."

"But that's what you've always wanted, isn't it? For them to write about us in some way. Your brother makes headlines one way, you make headlines another."

He flinches like he's been slapped. "What did you say?"

"I said I'm doing exactly what you want, and I fucking hate it," I say, my voice tight, anger building up inside me. All around us are fairy lights in the trees and beautiful people decked out in elaborate jewels and gowns and masks, yet all I can see is a hell burning around us, a fire that started inside me.

"Then why did you do it?" he asks me, brow arched. "Whose honor were you defending there? It sounded like Seraphine's, but that couldn't be right. That girl is nothing. She has no honor. Why on earth would you waste time on her?"

My eyes narrow as I take in the sharp, stiff face of my father, a person I hate more than anything in the world. "Because she has more honor in her little finger than you do anywhere."

He doesn't say anything at first, just takes me in, breathing in long and deep through his nose. I don't care what he's thinking, but he's thinking something.

"You're mistaken, Blaise, and I hope this is the last time you ever make this mistake. You hear me? I hope this is the last time. I hope you realize that there are few things in this world that you stick your neck out for, and your cousin isn't one of them."

"And neither are you," I tell him and then turn to leave.

"She's not even one of us," he says as I walk away. "She's not a Dumont."

"Yeah," I reply under my breath. "Maybe that's why I did it."

CHAPTER EIGHT

BLAISE

I have no fucking idea what Seraphine is doing.

What I do know is that Pascal was right.

There is something going on with her, something that's making her hole up inside that dirty bar called the Terrible Cat in the forgotten seedy section of the Latin Quarter, the last place I expected to see Seraphine disappear into, let alone have some sort of meeting with her ex-husband and some nondescript guy who moves like a hit man.

The sight of Cyril is most confusing. I'm outside the bar, just out of sight, pretending to be on my phone and sneaking a look inside the joint every few minutes. It's not like she's happy to see her ex. In fact, she's sitting on the opposite side of the booth and watching him with disdain. She hasn't cracked a smile once, though he's done plenty to try to charm her.

My stomach knots up with jealousy. Over the years I've had to watch Seraphine date others and fall in love, and all this time I've dealt with it. I didn't see her often anyway; it was easy to pretend she didn't exist. And then, when I decided to join forces with my father and brother and start working for the company, I had to see her every day.

I was there when she first started dating Cyril.

I was there when she'd bring him to the office, all proud and in love and showing him off, and it was like my heart got a jump-start for the first time. It moved in my chest, poking and prodding sharply, reminding me that I used to have feelings at one time. I used to want and yearn and lust. I haven't felt any of those things since the day I left Mallorca and wiped her clean from my mind.

Then they got married. It happened quickly. I knew it was a mistake for her, but that didn't mean it didn't hurt in a very acute, very unreasonable way. They had a wedding. I didn't go. I was invited out of formality, but I knew she couldn't care less if I was there. In fact, if she'd remembered at all what happened between us once, she wouldn't have wanted me there.

They were married for two years, and during those two years I had to look at that wedding ring on her finger, and I had to pretend that it didn't bother me. I'm her cousin; I'll always be her cousin. It's fucked up that she could even affect me that way.

But I'm used to being fucked up. I don't fear it. I don't feel shame in it.

It made me bitter, though. It made me angry. It made it so that my interactions with Seraphine were sharp and harsh and full of spite. She hated me, too, adding fuel to the fire, making it easier to be around her when she looked at me with disgust, and so I looked at her the same way.

Then she and Cyril broke up. Marriage over. He cheated on her repeatedly, caught by tabloids, and I know it destroyed her. It reminded me of the masquerade ball, when she was just sixteen and I'd caught her douchebag boyfriend making out with someone else. She was publicly humiliated, though part of that was my fault too.

During the divorce, she did her best to hold her head up high and let it roll off her. She put up a strong front. But I knew she was hurting inside. Beneath her beautiful and polished veneer, she has a big heart, and she comes from a lost and damaged place. She's sensitive and delicate, and sometimes I think I'm the only person in her world who knows that.

Of course, that didn't stop me from secretly delighting that her marriage failed. I know you're supposed to want what's best for someone and you shouldn't take pleasure in someone's pain, but that's not how it works with me.

"What are you doing, Seraphine?" I say out loud, my words swallowed up by the noise and traffic on the nearby street. In this narrow cobblestone alley there is thick silence tempered by the occasional drunken shout from inside the bar.

I end up watching her for two hours.

She talks the entire time, looking emotional with a lot of hand gesturing. Cyril tries to butt in every now and then, but she's dismissive with him. Meanwhile, the hit man only asks her questions.

I wish I had known they would be here so I could have gotten a spot somewhere inside, though the chances of me hearing their conversation would be low. The minute she abruptly left work, I had to do the same, following her to her apartment and then to the café around the corner, where she stayed for a few hours, drinking champagne by herself. Then she hopped on the métro, and a few stops later, got off here. I nearly lost her in this unfamiliar area and just happened to be looking in the window of the bar when I saw her and Cyril together.

I'm not sure what to say to Pascal about this.

Part of me thinks that she's getting in over her head with something dangerous. I mean, she drove all the way down to Bordeaux in the middle of the night and snuck into her brother's castle, and now she's meeting with her ex-husband and a stranger who looks like he strangles people for fun. Part of me wants to protect her from whatever this is.

The other part of me agrees with my brother. That she's fishing for information on her father's death, and that information could lead back to me. Now, I know I'm innocent, but I'm not certain about Pascal or my father. I couldn't imagine either of them killing anyone, and yet . . .

And yet you know your father is capable of that. Capable of worse. There are so many events that have happened around you that have exposed his true nature, yet you choose to put your head in the sand and ignore it.

I close my eyes and take in a deep breath, wishing I could ignore that voice that grows louder every day. Growing up, I had no loyalty to my family, and now I'm being asked to show it. What happened to me over the years that made me tuck away all my anger and distrust of my family? What made me want to give up my carefree life roaming around the planet and decide to work for the Dumont label? When did I stop looking out for myself and become a sheep and a coward instead?

When did I fall in line with exactly what they want me to be?

I open my eyes and notice that they're getting up from their seats.

Shit.

I spin around and look for somewhere to hide. I'm useless at this whole stalking thing, whereas Pascal turns it into an art form.

I tuck myself away between a garbage can and a storefront, watching as the three of them exit the bar.

"So you'll call me the moment you know of anything?" Seraphine asks, her voice clear as day and full of hope.

The man just nods, his face grim, while Cyril says to her, "Let me walk you home."

She shakes her head. "I've ordered an Uber. He'll be picking me up in two minutes."

Good. The last thing she needs is Cyril following her. If he did, I might have to intervene.

"Okay, well, keep your chin up and stay vigilant," Cyril says to her, trying to sound tough. "You need to keep a low profile with this sort of thing, so let Jones take care of everything."

Jones. Funny name.

The Jones guy just nods while Seraphine gives a polite smile. "I'll talk to you later. Thank you again."

"Anytime," Cyril says, watching her walk away toward the main street. I keep my eyes on him, hoping to see his angle. He watches her the entire time, but what disturbs me is the lack of lust or affection in his eyes. If anything, he looks completely disdainful, as if she took a piss in the middle of the alley.

He then looks at Jones. "So what do you think?"

Jones gives him a quick glance. "We learned nothing new. So I think nothing except the lip service I'm going to provide and the paycheck she's going to give me."

"But, just for the sake of argument," Cyril says, crossing his arms across his chest, "if she is onto something—"

"You know she's onto something. But she didn't hire me first. She hired me second. My loyalty lies with the highest bidder. And it's not her."

"You're sure about that?" Cyril asks, narrowing his eyes.

Jones doesn't look too impressed at being questioned. "Maybe you should ask yourself why you're doing this?"

Cyril shrugs. "Let's chalk it up to revenge and leave it at that."

Revenge?

I didn't expect this.

"Fine," Jones says. "Then let's go report to the boss. Where is he right now?"

Cyril takes out his phone and glances at it. "Still at this fundraiser in the Trocadéro." Jones makes a face. "Hey, you're the one who insists on doing everything in person and not by phone."

"Then let's go," Jones says.

They walk off in the opposite direction of Seraphine.

I glance down the alley in both directions. Seraphine is gone, and I probably should get in a cab and follow her to her place, but there's no way I'm going to let this go. I know what Pascal asked me to do, but this is about more than that now.

I wait until I see Jones and Cyril disappear around the corner, then I follow.

Crouching down and keeping a low profile, I watch them get into a black car.

I immediately wave for a taxi, lucky to flag one down in this spot.

I get in and do something I never thought I'd do.

I tell the driver to follow that car.

The driver eyes me in the rearview mirror. "Are you serious?"

"I have two hundred euros for you," I tell him, opening my wallet and showing him. "Now go. Now!"

The driver shrugs and then we're off, heading down rue Linné. The taxi catches up to the black car with ease, and we stay two to three cars behind them all the way through the twists and turns of the Left Bank until we end up on the Right Bank at a fancy hotel gleaming with lights.

I tell the driver to park and wait, and I watch from my seat as Jones and Cyril step out of the car.

They linger at the steps of the hotel, and through the large, well-lit windows, I can see a party going on. Jones texts something on his phone, and they both stare at the entrance to the hotel expectantly.

Then someone comes out, and because of the people walking past the taxi, I can't quite see who it is at first.

But when the crowd clears, my heart stops.

It's my father, dressed in a tuxedo and shaking Cyril's hand as if they're long-lost friends.

CHAPTER NINE

BLAISE

Nine years ago
Mallorca

What a fucking mess.

I should have known better than to step foot on this island. I should have known better than to answer that phone call. I should have known that my mother would cry over the phone, begging me to come, just as she's crying now.

Only she doesn't know I can see her.

She also doesn't know that I can see my uncle Ludovic in the dark corner with her, trying to console her.

She's drunk. I knew she would be. She always is. But I especially knew that since this was my parents' thirtieth wedding anniversary, a whole bunch of pent-up and raw feelings would come out, as they always do in these situations. Too many complications all in one spot.

Earlier we had all been having dessert and drinking wine around the table on the white-sand beach, immaculately set up just beneath the villa here on Mallorca. A lot of wine was had, far more than normal. I guess that's what happens when both sides of the family are in one place—an event as rare as an eclipse.

I had a lot to drink, too, so I wasn't really paying attention to what happened. I was more focused on the dessert in front of me, a type of flan created by the famous chef my parents had hired for the event.

The next thing I knew, my father was saying something to my mother, whispering in her ear—something malicious judging by the smug look on his face, a look I know all too well. She looked across the table to Uncle Ludovic, yelled something that made no sense, and burst into tears. When she got up to run away, the tablecloth caught on her tacky jeweled bracelet, and she ended up pulling everything off the table in one messy swoop.

The dessert, all the wine, everything went falling into either our laps or on the ground. My mother fell onto the sand, screaming and crying, and the only person that would help her was Ludovic, who got her to her feet and brought her up the stone steps and inside the villa.

Suffice to say, after that everyone went off on their own. Dessert was over, but more booze was brought out to compensate. Big, expensive, rare bottles of single-malt Scotch that my father usually hoarded like a miser but decided were the only way to save this night.

We each got a bottle. My aunt, Olivier, and Seraphine wandered off down the beach with one, Pascal and my father sat on the sand just a few feet from the mess that the servants were busily trying to clean up. Renaud went off for a walk by himself.

Which left me to my own devices. I decided to head up to the house and get a new shirt since mine was covered in red wine and gooey flan.

That's when I came across my mother being consoled by my uncle.

There's nothing out of the ordinary about any of this. It's always my uncle who is the first to console anybody. But still, I stay silent as I pass by them, pausing when I'm out of sight. I don't think they even know I'm around the corner, hidden by a marble statue near the sitting area.

"He knows," my mother says between sobs. "Luddie, he knows."

"Everything is fine, Eloise," he says to her reassuringly, but I swear there's a hint of tremor in his voice—very unlike him.

I peek around the corner of the statue and see him put his hand on my mother's shoulder, but she swats him away. "No," she says sharply, racked by another sob. "He knows and he'll kill me. You know what he's capable of." She looks up at him with the wildest eyes I've ever seen. This might be one of the few times I've really seen fear on my mother's face, and I don't think I like it.

"You need to calm down, please. This is your anniversary—"

"It means nothing!" she yells.

My uncle shushes her, and my mother looks around, expecting to be seen. I quickly duck back before she has a chance to spot me. Not that I understand what I'm eavesdropping on, but it sounds important. A little too important. Probably something I need to walk away from.

So I do. I walk away just in time to hear my mother say softly, "We all know what he can do and will do. No one is safe. He holds grudges until he dies."

She's slurring her words, though. She's drunk and she's crazy, becoming more and more unhinged as I get older. I have no doubt she's talking about my father, but when it comes to my family, the less I know and the less I'm involved, the better off I am. I didn't just spend the last few months in Brussels trying to get an education so I couldn't step away from this family and this god-awful business.

My mother obviously did something wrong. Maybe my uncle did, too, but that doesn't seem likely. He's too good for that. Perhaps it was a business deal gone south. Whatever it is, it's not my concern. It can't ever be.

I head upstairs through the sprawling interior to the third floor, where my bedroom is, and take off my shirt. Then, as I'm pulling out a clean one from my carry-on suitcase, I realize that I don't owe anyone anything. I don't have to get dressed, I don't have to go back down. I have the bottle of Scotch with me, and that's all that I need. I can finish the bottle, drift off to sleep, and see if I can get a flight out tomorrow, a day earlier than the one I have scheduled.

So I sit at the foot of the bed and proceed to drink straight from the bottle, wishing once again that I'd just stayed away. But the more I stay away, the more I have to ask myself, where am I staying? I'm twenty years old, and I have no fucking idea what I'm doing with my life. I just know what I'm trying to avoid.

I drink and I think about this, and I'm not sure how much time has gone past, but then I look up and see a figure passing in front of my door, the door I'd left halfway open.

It's Seraphine.

I've barely said two words to her since I arrived yesterday.

There's not much to say.

Everything I want to say can't be put into words, and if it could, it would be inappropriate.

Just the sight of her makes something inside me unravel.

I can't let that happen.

I have to stay intact. I have to avoid her.

And yet I get to my feet and walk unsteadily over to the door, leaning out of it in time to see her silhouette disappear into her room.

I quickly follow her, putting my arm out against her door just as she starts to close it.

"Jesus," she swears as she jumps. "You startled me."

"What are you doing?" I ask her.

"I was about to go to bed," she says, looking me up and down. I'm shirtless, and her eyes trace over my bare skin with more care than she'd like to show. "And it seems so were you."

"Have a drink with me," I tell her, showing her the Scotch and pushing the door open even further. "Talk to me."

Her eyes go wide. "Talk to you?" She sweeps her long hair over her shoulder and puts her hands on her hips. "Since when do we ever talk,

Blaise? The last time we even spoke, you punched my ex-boyfriend in the face."

"He deserved it. You know it."

"It doesn't matter. It was uncalled for. It made it all a bigger deal than it was. Had you not done that, no one outside the party would have known how humiliated I was. After you did that, all the tabloids reported on the story. Made you out to be a violent and crazy drunk, made me out to be some loser whose boyfriend cheated on her in front of everyone."

"Jamillah," I say.

"*What?*" Her brows knit together, eyes hard.

"Your alter ego."

"She was my old self," she clarifies. "And I regret ever telling you about her."

"What else do you regret? I mean, now that we're laying everything out."

She takes a step toward me, her fingers curled around the edge of the door. "We're not laying anything out. Don't get it twisted. I think it's time you go to your room."

But I don't move away. I lean in and whisper, "Do you regret kissing me back?"

"Get out." Her voice trembles slightly.

"I'm not going anywhere," I tell her, moving forward until I'm pressed up against her. She tries to push back, but I keep going until I'm inside and clear of the doorway.

I'm not sure what I'm doing, I just know we need to talk. Maybe not about everything, maybe there's nothing to talk about on her end. But I hate this whole back-and-forth thing we have, the ignoring each other for months and months and then the forced conversation, the formalities we put up in front of everyone else when there is something so much more raging underneath. Perhaps all unbeknownst to her.

This is what I need to find out.

"What do you want?" she asks quietly. She doesn't look scared, really, just wary.

I reach over and brush her bangs out of her eyes so I can see them more clearly. Perhaps *now* she looks scared. The fact that I touched her.

I then hold up the bottle, keeping it between us. "Just have a drink with me."

She eyes it. "That's probably a bad idea."

"Not true. I only have good ideas." I lift the bottle to my lips and take a swig. "Don't tell me you don't need it after tonight."

"I think I've had enough wine," she says in a feeble protest. Then she takes the bottle from me and turns, walking over to the window. I watch as she takes a long swig, doesn't flinch even once. For a seventeen-year-old, she can handle her liquor phenomenally well. Can't say the same for my mother.

"What a mess," she whispers to herself.

I come up beside her and look out the window with the clear view of the beach below. The table is set up again, everything in place from the dessert plates to the empty wineglasses. Renaud is back, and my father and brother are sitting around it, drinking from their bottles of Scotch, just as we are.

"I bet you never thought you'd be adopted into such a dysfunctional family," I tell her.

She snorts lightly. "Speak for yourself. My family functions just fine. Your side is fucked up."

Then she stiffens and gives me an apologetic look. "I'm sorry. That was rude of me to say."

"I like it when you're rude," I say.

I don't add that it fucking turns me on. I think she's barely tolerating me enough as it is.

What a mess, indeed.

"I figured that," she says, and for the first time tonight, there's just a hint of a smile.

That hint means far more to me than she can possibly know.

"So, if your family functions just fine, why aren't you down there with them? Why are you up here alone?" I ask, reaching back for the bottle.

She doesn't let go. "Why are you here alone?"

"I think you know why."

"Because you still hate everyone?"

"Do you ever wonder why I'm never around?"

"To wonder would mean I think about you. And I don't."

Though she must mean her words to hurt, she looks away as she says it. I loosen my grip on the bottle and let her have another long sip. I probably shouldn't let my younger cousin drink like this, but there are a lot of *shouldn'ts* tonight that I want to keep doing.

"I think you're lying."

She presses her lips together, swallowing the booze. "What do you want from me?"

"I told you, I just want to talk."

She glances at me furtively. "About what?"

I'm drunk and have only liquid courage and a smidgen of hope.

"I want to know if you liked it when I kissed you. I want to know if you thought of it again."

Her cheeks flush, and she looks back out the window as if to escape the question, but there's no relief for her out there on that black ocean and that dark night sky.

"That was years ago," she finally says.

"Doesn't mean it didn't happen."

"No, but you acted like it didn't happen," she says sharply, eyes flying to mine. "You kissed me, and then we went back to the way we were before, like it was nothing."

Something rises in my chest, hot and burning. "And that bothered you. You cared."

Her nose scrunches up. "No. Yes. I don't know." She brings the bottle back to her lips, but I take it from her.

"I think you should slow down."

"You're the one who brought me that!"

"And I want to hear things from you while you mean them."

"Oh, like you ever mean a single thing you say."

"I do," I tell her, feeling defensive. "I always mean what I say."

"I can't trust you," she says. "I can't trust any of you. You're all . . ."

"Terrible?" I fill in. "My side of the family is terrible. I know that. And I'm not standing here in your room pretending to be a good guy. I am not a good guy. I'm just a guy who knows what he wants."

A long, heavy pause fills the room, laden with tension. "And what is that?" she asks quietly.

But she knows.

I reach up and put my hand on her cheek. She flinches slightly as I press my fingertips into her skin, holding her, a war raging inside my chest. Torn between doing what I want and doing what is right, and I have never done what's right.

So I do what's wrong.

I lean in and kiss her.

Hard.

My hand slides back into her hair and makes a fist, and the bottle drops to the floor between our feet and rolls across the rug. Everything else slips away because all I care about, all I want, is her. I want her. I want to be inside of her. I want to kiss her until she's hopeless, helpless, then I want to throw her on that bed and show her the way.

But she's fighting it. She's trying to do things right, as she's always done. She's stiff in my hands, not pliable, not succumbing to the kiss. She's trying to hold her ground.

And yet she's not pushing me away. She's not telling me to stop.

She has a war inside herself too.

And I know who the victor is the moment her mouth opens to mine and I slide in my tongue, grazing the tip of hers, and she lets out a soft and breathy moan, which I feel reverberate in every cell in my body.

Fuck.

This is all I've wanted.

Seraphine is kissing me back, and more than that, she's enjoying it.

Our kiss deepens, my hands sliding farther up into her hair and then down her back as her hands tentatively rest on my biceps, as if she's not sure she can touch me. I'm sure the fact that my shirt is off is making things more complicated.

My heart is a jackhammer in my chest. I'm not sure if I can have a heart attack on my feet, but there wouldn't be a better way to go. Our lips are fire, the flames building between us, and with each long, hard pull, each tangle of our tongues, I feel like I might just explode.

I'm harder than I've ever been in my life.

I've slept with enough women at this point to know that I like sex, but kissing Seraphine has just erased every single fuck I've had. It's created a new beginning, a clean slate, the basis to which everything will be measured against.

I press against her, needing her to know how I feel.

She gasps as my erection digs into her hip.

"This is what you do to me, Seraphine," I murmur as I pull my mouth away from hers, just an inch. "Does it scare you?"

She swallows. "Yes," she whispers, her eyes falling closed as my hand slips under her shirt and skims across the soft curves of her stomach.

"Do I scare you?"

She shakes her head slightly. "No."

But there was hesitation in her voice. "What are you afraid of?"

She takes in a wavering breath and glances up at me through her long lashes, her eyes a mix of fear and yearning. She's turned on too. When my hand travels up to her breast and over her thin bra, her nipple is as hard as a rock.

She sucks in another breath and bites her lip.

Dear God. I might come right now, just like this.

"You know why I'm afraid," she says.

"You're a virgin."

"You're my cousin," she says. "This is wrong."

"Is it?" I ask.

"Are you kidding me? Yes. It's wrong."

"We aren't related."

"It doesn't matter."

"It does matter." I slip my fingers underneath the underwire of her bra, finding her soft bare skin. "And yet nothing matters."

"Blaise," she warns, but as I stroke her sensitive nipple, she lets out a fluttering sigh, her eyes closing, mouth opening.

"Seraphine," I say, my voice coming out rough with the lust that's threatening to tear me apart. "I've wanted you from the moment I saw you."

"We were just kids," she manages to say.

I lean in and kiss the side of her mouth. "It didn't matter. I saw you and I knew we were alike. I knew you were like me. Alone in this world. Unmoored. Looking for something. Family."

"You have family."

"But I don't. I don't have anything. You're the closest thing to family that I have and yet you're so much more than that." My voice is starting to shake, a whirlwind of complicated emotions swirling inside me, competing with the hard sexual drive that's wanting to take over. "I'm obsessed with you. And I'll never stop wanting you. For the rest of my life, you're the only thing I want."

I kiss her softly this time, our lips barely touching and somehow feeling more erotic than anything else.

"You just want me out of your system," she whispers against my mouth, breathing hard.

"No," I tell her hoarsely. "I want you in my system. You'll never be out, not if I can help it."

"Where can this go? What happens next?"

"What happens next is that I'm not going to let you go. I'm going to take you right here, possess you, keep you. You're mine, you always have been, even if you didn't know it. But I think you did know it. Didn't you?"

"We can't . . ."

"We can. And I'll show you exactly how we can."

I grab her by the hair, by the waist, pulling her against me, kissing her so hard that our teeth knock against each other, and I feel my breath being stolen from me. I spin her around and throw her on the bed, climbing onto her, my hands roaming over her body, trying to pull her shirt over her head.

She's grabbing me with the same hunger and force, her fingers digging into the hard planes of my back, bucking herself up into me, gasping for air.

I manage to get her bra unhooked before bringing her full breast out of the cup, my mouth sucking her nipple, drowning in the taste of her.

"I need to come inside you," I murmur against her hot skin. God, I had no fucking idea it would be like this. I dreamed about it, jacked off to it, but I had no idea.

This is going to ruin me for the rest of my life.

Because it's at this moment that I realize I'm not sure I'll ever be able to truly have her.

As if she knows what I'm thinking, or perhaps because she's put off by my crude words, she stops, pulling her head back and pushing her hands up against my chest.

"No," she says, her words so breathy and weightless they almost dissolve in the air. "We can't. I can't. I'm not . . . I don't think . . ."

Whether she's a virgin or not is none of my business, but if she is, I'm not about to pressure her into anything, no matter how badly I want and need it. And if she's not a virgin . . . I guess the same stands.

"It's fine," I say, brushing her hair off her sweaty forehead. We'd barely gotten started and yet the heat between us is palpable. "We can slow down."

She stares up at me, her eyes searching my face. "I don't think it's a good idea."

"Tonight or any night?"

"Tonight."

"Are you sure?"

"I just need to think."

"I'm not going to hurt you," I tell her, kissing the tip of her nose. "I promise you that. I won't hurt you unless you want me to."

Her cheeks go a deeper red, and she gives me a shy smile. "I just . . . I don't know if I can trust you still. I don't know if you're just using me. I don't know that if I give you myself, you'll toss me away because that's what boys like you do."

"Because it's in my blood?" I arch a brow.

"Because you're you, and I've never gotten a handle on you, though Lord knows I've tried."

"You just need to spend more time with me. So spend more time with me."

"Tomorrow, maybe . . ."

"Tomorrow night, meet me at the beach at nine o'clock. By the rocks to the left, way down the beach."

"I'll see."

"You'll do it," I tell her. "You'll do it because you want me as much as I want you. And you want to know what's going to happen next. You want to know what it feels like to have me inside you, making you moan, making you come. You want me to become your world, and that's exactly what I'm going to fucking do."

She's speechless.

Good.

I hope that knocked some sense into her.

I get up, my hard-on still straining against my jeans, begging for mercy. I'll have to deal with it later.

I reach down and pull Seraphine off the bed until she's standing in front of me. She gives me a sheepish look before she redoes her bra and pulls her shirt down, but I'm looking over her shoulder.

I'm looking at the door that I thought I'd closed, but I guess I didn't.

I'm looking at someone in the doorway.

Just a glimpse of a face in motion.

Pascal.

Fuck *no*.

"Well, I didn't expect this tonight," she says, looking up at me, and I avert my eyes to hers before she sees where I was looking, hoping that my face isn't registering my shock and the very realization at how fucking screwed we suddenly are. If Pascal saw anything . . .

"To add more to the dysfunction of the Dumonts," she continues, a tiny smile on her lips.

I can barely smile back. I can't even think. I have got to get out of here.

"You're right," I say dumbly. "I should go."

"Okay," she says uneasily. "Are you okay?"

"Yeah. Yeah, I'm fine." I move past her toward the door.

"Tomorrow on the beach at nine?" she calls after me, and I nearly jump at how loud she sounds. Pascal is sure to hear her if he's anywhere out in the hallway.

I nod, afraid to speak, and quickly exit her room.

I see Pascal down the hall just as he goes into his room, closing the door.

Fuck.

Fuck me.

If Pascal heard us, if he saw us, the first thing he'll do is tell my father. He'll tell him and then my father will make our lives a living hell.

If not that, he might just kill me.

It's no secret what he thinks of Seraphine. Both he and my mother look down on her, pity Ludovic for taking her in. The fact that she was an orphan, that she was poor, that she came from what they consider "scum" would have been enough, but that she's brown really disgusts them. She's not white, not French, not rich by blood—she's not *them*.

And while I have no doubt her saintly mother and father would go above and beyond to protect her, I also know that this dalliance would touch on my father's pride. The very idea that his failure of a son and his brother's unworthy adopted yet much-loved daughter got together would embarrass him more than anything else.

I can't let that happen.

And yet I don't know what to do.

I don't want to talk to Pascal about it, just in case he didn't see or hear anything damaging. And I'm not about to bring it up with my father either.

There's only one thing that I can do. One thing that will probably break me.

I can't be with Seraphine ever again. I probably shouldn't even talk to her, because Pascal might be watching for any sort of sign—something to fuel his suspicion, if that's all there is to go on.

I'm going to have to pretend she doesn't exist.

Or face the consequences.

CHAPTER TEN

SERAPHINE

Nine years ago
Mallorca

I'm in big, big trouble.

I mean, major shit.

One minute I was lost in my thoughts as I headed to my bedroom, the next minute Blaise was blocking the doorway, badgering his way inside.

I should have shut that door on him. Tried harder. Been quicker.

I shouldn't have let him in my room.

I knew the moment I let him in my room, I'd let him in my heart. For once and for real. And that's exactly what happened.

He came in with the look in his eyes of a man who has been lost at sea, finally seeing land. I've never been looked at that way before. I've dreamed about it. I've seen that look in movies, I've read about it in books, but I never thought it existed in real life. That hunger, that yearning. It was written on Blaise's face, clear as day.

And his body too. If the thought of feeling his erection scared me at one time, it didn't then. In that moment, the fear melded into something else. It was a fear of myself. A fear that I might become someone else if I give myself to him, and if I give myself to him, I might never get myself back.

It's scary to want something so badly.

It's even scarier when you're not sure if the other person feels the same.

I mean, I know what Blaise wants from me. It's always been there, an elephant in the room. Sexual tension that morphed into bickering and insults because that's the only place for it to go. For God's sake, we could never act on it.

Or so I thought. It was the one thing that held me in check, even in the days and nights that my thoughts turned to him. When I thought about kissing him again. What it would be like to feel his body. What it would be like to have sex with him, to be naked, to be the object of his primal and lustful affection. My teenage hormones were always kept in line because I knew that we could never be anything more than just cousins.

But Blaise is braver than I am. Or perhaps he's just stupider. I always thought he was the one so carefully composed and in control, and I expected nothing but that strength around me. That facade that we both weren't feeling anything for each other. To see him weakened . . .

I'd be lying if I said it hadn't turned me on. How fucked up is that? Not just to want your own damn cousin but to want his walls down so that he's vulnerable around you and only you.

Now it's eight o'clock the night after, and I'm sitting with my mother on the large terrace overlooking the beach. Thankfully the spot where Blaise wants to meet me is far out of reach, and I have another hour.

"Are you all right?" my mother asks.

I notice I'm tapping my fingers against the arms of the rattan chair. It's hard to act normal when all I can think about is him. I don't even know what to expect tonight. Are we going to talk? Make out? Will I end up sleeping with him? I'm pretty sure he knows I'm a virgin, even if he's tried to hint otherwise.

"I'm fine," I tell her, reaching for my glass of wine and having a large sip.

"Careful," she says, eyeing the glass. "You're only seventeen."

"Mother, it's France," I say, giving her a dry look. "You can't pretend that this isn't part of the culture."

"Be that as it may, you've been drinking like a fish while you've been here. I know we're here to celebrate and everything, but I think it's worth having a sharp and clear head." She pauses and lowers her voice. "Tensions are a little high, if you haven't noticed."

No fucking kidding they are. Oh, but she's talking about everyone else. The drama last night over my drunken aunt, which has made everyone cagey and hungover today.

I should care about that. I should be more in tune to the fact that something is going on, something I know nothing about. But family drama is prevalent every time we get together. Over Christmas, Pascal and Renaud got in a fistfight, and Uncle Gautier had the nerve to call the cops, trying to get Renaud put away even though Pascal started it. Other times my aunt will get my mother drunk and then pick a fight with her over something in the past. It's always something.

"I'll be careful," I tell her. I need the wine for my nerves. I didn't even eat dinner; I just picked at my food and did my best to ignore Blaise, who was sitting across from me.

He did the same. In fact, he did it a little too well. The times that I did look up at him, lost in the beauty of his handsome face, an attraction that I've denied myself for too long, he didn't even give me a glance. It's like I didn't exist at all.

That's another reason why I'm nervous. Because I'm trusting him, someone I've always told myself I couldn't trust. One of *them*.

God, I hope I'm making the right decision. My heart right now feels so precarious, like it's balancing on the edge, and if I lean just an inch, one way or the other, I will fall. One side and I'll fall forever. The other side and I'll hurt forever.

You should have slept with Emil. Or Armand. Or anyone else. You shouldn't be a virgin for Blaise. If this goes wrong, if he screws you over . . .

It's like it's on autoplay in my head.

And my mother, well, I suppose she's trying her best to ignore everyone and whatever sort of drama there is floating around this vacation house, and she's talking my ear off about this and that. I keep checking my phone for the time, wondering how I'm going to excuse myself. Thankfully, at about ten to nine, she gets up and says she's heading to bed.

I hug her good night, catching a glimpse of frailty in her face, suddenly struck by the realization that my mother is on the older side (especially compared to my aunt Camille, who is considerably younger than my uncle), and that I love her so much and I've only known her for eight years. It reminds me of what I lost as a child. I know it's better late than never, but I should have had my mother from the very moment I was born.

"I love you," I tell her. I feel like I need to tell her more often.

From the surprised look on her face, I know I need to. She's not used to it. I used to say it all the time as a child, when I was first adopted and learning what love is. Then the last few years, I don't know. Maybe I've been the stereotypical bitchy teenager, subconsciously pushing her away.

"I love you, too, sweetheart," she says to me with soft eyes, patting me on the cheek. "But try not to drink so much, okay?"

I roll my eyes. "I'm not drunk. I mean it."

She gives me a gentle smile. "Good."

I watch as she walks into the house. The lights are on in the lounge, and I see my father and Olivier sitting around talking, my mother stopping by them briefly before continuing on her way upstairs.

I exhale loudly and shake out my arms, turning my attention back to the beach. I need to get down there before anyone sees me out here and notices me leaving in the opposite direction.

I hurry down the long stone stairway that leads down to the beach, taking off my sandals as soon as I hit the sand. I look both ways but it's dark, with only a half-moon to light the way. I don't see anyone in either direction, but I hurry to the left, walking quickly through the soft sand until I'm around trees and bushes and the rocky outcrop that cuts into the sea.

This has to be where he meant. To go any farther would be to climb on the rocks, and with the waves crashing against them, it would be completely dangerous, especially in the dark.

So I sit down and I wait, running grains of sand through my fingers, over and over again.

I'm so nervous about what's going to happen that time seems to pass even slower. Each second stretches on with each crash of the waves. And yet time is also skipping. I keep thinking that I'm going to see him, and then that's going to be it and everything is going to happen so fast, and I don't even know what I truly want.

I just want to trust him.

I want to let him in.

I want to lose myself to him, go up in the heat and flames, and somehow manage to not get burned in the process.

But he doesn't show up.

I don't see him.

I keep looking at my phone and watching the time tick on while the grains of sand run through my hands. Nine fifteen turns to nine thirty. Nine thirty turns to nine forty-five, then ten o'clock. I don't even have Blaise's damn phone number, so I can't text him and see where he is.

I end up staying until eleven, thinking that maybe he got held up and couldn't escape. That has to be it. He was so into me last night; I saw it, I *felt* it. That wasn't a show. He would have come, right?

Even though it's May and the days are hot on Mallorca, the nights can get cold, and by the time I get back to the villa, I'm shivering from head to toe.

And that's when I see him.

Blaise, sitting on the veranda where I was earlier, drinking by himself.

I walk right up to him, rubbing my hands down my arms in an attempt to get warm even though the anger that's starting to flare through me is doing a good job of it.

"Blaise," I whisper harshly to him. "Where have you been?"

He doesn't even look at me, just takes a drink from a glass of amber liquid. Probably Scotch.

"Blaise," I say again. "What's your problem? What happened? Just fucking look at me, will you?"

But he doesn't. His Adam's apple bobs as he swallows thickly and continues to stare out into the open. His jaw is held tensely, warring with his relaxed pose.

Something inside me starts to break.

I know I shouldn't jump to conclusions, but I'm a mess inside; my heart, my gut, my pride, it's all getting so twisted and tangled, threatening to choke me.

He's going to fuck me over, isn't he?

I put my trust in the wrong guy.

I need to be wrong.

I go and stand right in front of him, and he finally looks at me, his eyes looking me up and down. Maybe he sees the goose bumps on my skin and my shivering. Maybe he sees the confusion in my eyes. For a second he looks at me like something inside him is breaking too.

And then it's gone.

Just like that.

The wonderful world of promises that his eyes held last night in my room, it's all gone. Replaced by a void.

I thought he wasn't like the rest of them, I think. Then I correct myself.

No, you hoped he wasn't like the rest of them.

And I was wrong.

"Where did you go?" I say, trying to keep my voice calm but failing. "I was waiting out there for you for two hours," I add in a harsh whisper.

He stares at me blankly. "Hi, Seraphine. Bit late to be out, don't you think?"

What the actual fuck?

"What are you talking about?"

"You should probably head to bed."

Wait, is that innuendo, like a hint, or . . .

"Just tell me what happened," I tell him. "Why didn't you show?"

His gaze gives me nothing, and his voice is bored. "I have no idea what you're talking about."

No.

I try to form words but can't. My lips flap soundlessly as I try to understand why he'd do this.

I look around, wondering if maybe we're being watched, but I don't see anyone.

I lean in closer to him, my eyes searching his. "Blaise. Just . . . tell me that things are going to be okay."

He tilts his chin up and gives me a chilling look. "They'll be okay when you stop fucking annoying me like some little fangirl."

It's a fucking shotgun blast to my chest.

Little fangirl?

Is that what he really thinks?

Is that how I've been acting?

"But last night," I say, my words shaking, falling from my lips as my heart continues to shatter in my chest. "Last night you . . . you . . ."

"Sounds like last night was a product of your imagination," he says, motioning for me to get out of his way. "Now if you'll excuse me, I'm going out."

"What? Out? Where?"

What the hell is going on? What is he talking about?

"A bar in town," he says. "Have a good night."

"Blaise!" I cry out, reaching for his arm.

He looks down at my hand and then pulls it off him, as if my touch suddenly disgusts him.

"I said have a good night. Maybe I'll see you again in a year or two. Don't go falling for the wrong boys, okay?"

And then he's gone, walking down the stairs and around the side of the house.

And I'm left behind with a hole in my heart.

I can't believe it.

I can't believe him.

How could he do this to me?

But then I know why.

Because he's a liar.

He's an asshole, a selfish prick.

He's like his father, his brother.

And I'm me.

I'm not a model. I'm an orphan, I'm from India. I can change my name and learn French, but I can never lose that past, that person I was—the person nobody wanted. The person people abused and spit on and humiliated.

And here I am, humiliated again.

By someone I dared to put trust in. Even when I thought I was keeping a cage around my heart, even when I thought I was protecting myself from the worst-case scenario, he still managed to find a way in through the bars.

I've been so stupid to think anything could be different for me.

I'm just a young, stupid girl who was fooled into thinking she was someone more.

Well . . . fuck that.

Never again.

Never again.

He's as dead to me as I'm dead to him.

And that's the way it's always going to stay.

CHAPTER ELEVEN

SERAPHINE

It's been five days since I had the meeting with Cyril and Jones.

Five days in which I've tried to keep myself as busy as possible while waiting for news from Jones.

Five days of staring at my uncle at work and trying to imagine what I'll say and do if Jones uncovers the truth and the truth points to him.

Time has never passed more slowly.

I feel like I'm living *Groundhog Day*.

I get up, I go to work, I ignore the curious stares from Blaise that seem more inquisitive and intrusive as time goes on, I put my head down more than normal and focus on doing the best job I can while helping to train the interns. I then go home after work and drink myself silly and pass out on the couch at nine, the phone always in reach, the phone that never beeps.

All this waiting for a text or a call reminds me of how little of those I get these days. It makes me fall asleep with the thoughts that tormented me my entire youth in my head.

You're alone.

Nobody likes you.

You have no one.

My dreams aren't great either. Nightmares in which I'm trapped in the castle, and I have to witness my father dying over and over again. Sometimes Gautier slips him a drink, and my father chokes to death, turns blue, his mouth frothing after the first sip. Sometimes it's Pascal, stabbing my father in the back with a silver butter knife as my father sinks to the floor, staring at Pascal in horror.

And in one dream . . . there was Blaise.

Blaise, who was across the room, yelling at me soundlessly, trying to get my attention. He looked like he did when he was almost twenty and in my bedroom. All young, with mussed-up hair and wild, passionate eyes. But there was something he was trying to tell me, something important that I just wasn't getting.

I didn't get it until I felt hands around my neck, tightening into a noose. Tighter and tighter, until I couldn't breathe and couldn't scream, and the last thing I saw before I woke up, sweating and gasping for air, was Blaise running toward me with his hands out, reaching but never arriving.

I'm sitting on my couch tonight—waiting, always waiting—and I stare down at the glass of wine in my hands, lost in the darkness of the cabernet. I think about Renaud and how I should contact him about all this, but Renaud wants to be left out of everything. That's why he left for California all those years ago.

I think about phoning Olivier. We had been so close once, but somehow our father's death made a gap form between us. Now he's out with his fiancée, Sadie, and Renaud, and even though he does call every week to have a chat and he checks in via text every couple of days, there's so much unsaid on my part. He fills me in on everything that's going on—his new hotel, the wedding, Sadie, his future mother-in-law, a damn cat. He's so excited about life that he talks a mile a minute. When the conversation comes back to me and how I'm doing, I don't have the heart to tell him the truth.

No, this is something I started and something I'll have to shoulder on my own. I'm not involving my brothers. They'd only worry about me in the end, and they both have enough on their plates.

The phone buzzes, making me spill wine on my blouse.

Shit.

It doesn't matter, though. It's black and it'll come out. Plus, it's Dumont.

I quickly pick up the phone and see a text from an unknown number.

Meet me at the same bar in thirty minutes.

I'm going to have to assume it's from Jones.

Jones? Okay see you soon.

There is no response to that, so I quickly dab off some of the wine in the bathroom, throw on my coat and a scarf, and head out.

I take an Uber this time, remembering his words to be more discreet and eschewing the métro system.

But now I'm early. I step inside the bar, and I don't see Cyril or Jones, though I don't even know if Cyril would be coming anyway. Even though I hate seeing him, I don't feel as comfortable meeting Jones alone.

I go straight to the bar and order a shot of tequila and quickly down it in front of the bemused bartender. Then I get a double Scotch on the rocks and try to find a place to hunker down.

The booth is occupied with some biker dude and his girlfriend, so I find a high-top table that's free and take a seat.

As before, I'm getting a lot of stares, and I hate the fact that I'm alone. I wish I had brought a book with me. All I have is my phone, so I scroll through the social media accounts of the major fashion houses, trying to see what Chanel and Hermès are up to, forcing myself to look interested.

But it doesn't work. The same ugly guy from last time, the one who told me to go back to where I came from, stumbles on over to me, leaning against the table. His eyes are bloodshot, and his breath reeks of onions. I try hard not to recoil.

"Hey," he says to me in broken English. "You again. You speak French or Muslim speak?"

I raise my brow at him, and in fluent French, I say, "I speak French, English, and Hindi, but I don't speak idiot, so I'm afraid I can't understand what you're saying."

The guy stares at me for a moment like he can't believe what he just heard.

Then his nostrils flare, his face goes red. His fat fingers grip the edge of the table like he's about to throw it. I feel like he's two seconds from spitting in my face.

"Pardon me," comes Jones's calm voice from behind him, breaking the scene.

The guy whips around, and I'm pretty sure he's about to punch Jones in the face. But there's something that makes the guy stop, and I'm not sure what. Could be that Jones is staring at him in such a way that would make holy water boil. Subtle but intense enough to make you squirm.

That's some skill.

The man mutters something under his breath and then waddles back to his table, Jones holding eye contact as long as he can.

Then he looks at me, and I get just a hint of that stare that he was giving the man. It makes my skin crawl.

It quickly dissolves and a blankness comes over his face, and he sits down on the stool across from me, hands folded in front of him.

I'm so nervous.

"Do you want a drink?" I ask him, swirling the ice around in my glass. I realize that when I get to the bottom of this, I am going to be tanked, so I put it back down and push it away from me.

"I'm fine," Jones says.

"So . . ." I raise my brow.

"So I was able to recover the data," he says simply.

"What? How?"

"I went to the castle, went into the office you told me about, and I managed to recover it."

I'm totally taken aback. "You were supposed to call me if you needed me to take you there."

"I didn't need you."

"How did you get in?"

"How do you think?"

"You broke in?"

"Listen, Seraphine. I told you that you might not like my methods, but they are my methods. Take it or leave it."

"But if Renaud finds out . . ."

I can see I'm testing his patience. A vein on the side of his temple starts to vibrate even though the rest of him remains calm. "I'm not sure you really understand who I am and what I do. And what I've done to get here."

I swallow thickly and reach for the Scotch. With shaking hands, I take a burning gulp. I think I need another after this. "So what did you recover?" I ask, afraid to hear the answer.

"Nothing," he says, showing his empty palms as a gesture.

My heart sinks. "What do you mean, nothing?"

"I reviewed the lost footage, and there's nothing on it. I watched the entire party from all the angles for hours, keeping an eye on your father the whole time. There's nothing there."

"Well, I'd like to view it myself."

"Sure. Take the next train."

I shake my head. "I'm serious." I hold out my hand. "You must have put it on an SD card for me to review?"

"That was never what you asked. You asked me to recover the footage and review it, and I did, and I'm telling you there is nothing out of the ordinary there."

"But the footage was missing. Someone deleted it." I nearly slam my fist onto the table.

"It could have been corrupted. Or deleted by accident. This is your brother's winery. Why not ask him?"

"Because he wasn't there during the ball, he's never there."

"Then ask security or whoever is in charge of the place. A caretaker. I can ask if you'd like."

"No," I tell him, shaking my head, trying to understand this. Without the footage, I have nothing again.

"I'm sorry," he says to me, not sounding sorry in the least. "But at least this makes things less complicated."

"How?"

"The trail ends there. You have nothing to go on. It's time to ignore your gut."

"But you said that gut instinct counts for everything."

"It does. Which is why you follow up on it. But not everything turns out to be true. Sometimes your gut is telling you something because you *want* it to be true, and I believe that to be the case here."

"You think I *want* my very own uncle, who is now my very own boss, to have murdered my father?" I hiss, leaning in across the table.

Jones watches me for a moment, making some sort of calculation in his head. "I do."

I narrow my eyes at him. "I should have known you weren't on my side. I should have known not to trust Cyril."

"I'm not on anyone's side. I just follow the money. And that's something we need to speak about right now."

I finish my drink and slam the glass down, my bangs falling in front of my eyes. "Why the hell should I pay you when you've produced nothing? I only have your word, and I'm starting to think that's worthless."

In a flash Jones leans across the table and grabs me by the back of the neck, squeezing so hard that my arm falls limp to my side and my head is frozen in place. I can barely breathe; my mouth is open and gasping, and I think he could kill me if he wants to.

I've never been so scared.

"I'm not worthless," Jones says calmly. He reaches across with his other hand and brushes the bangs out of my eyes and stares at me. I know he can see the pain and shock and horror in my face, and he smiles. It's the kind of smile I've seen on Gautier and Pascal. Evil. Soulless. Merciless. "I know my exact worth, and it's fifty-five thousand euros. You knew my price when you hired me, and I did my job. And if I don't get the money within twenty-four hours, I'm going to do this to you again, only this time I'm going to move my thumb an inch to the left, and I'm going to cut off your oxygen supply until I'm the last thing you see. Are we clear?"

I can only gasp quietly, aware that he could kill me right here and I don't think anyone in this bar would care.

Finally he releases his grip and I slump back, falling off the stool and onto the floor. It happens so quickly I don't even have time to yell. The back of my head hits the dirty carpet, and everything fades in and out until I'm being brought to my feet.

Only it's not Jones.

It's the racist guy from earlier, his hands sliding around my waist as I struggle to keep the room from spinning and find my balance. Without his hands I'll fall over again, my head feels too heavy, but then his hands are roaming everywhere.

"Get off me," I tell him, trying to push him away. "Let me go."

"Like hell I'll let you go, you brown bitch."

I stare into the guy's eyes and try to figure out what to do. One minute Jones was here, the next minute I was on the ground. Now I'm with this guy, and I don't have anyone in my corner. I was afraid for my life before, and I'm afraid for my life now. Out of the frying pan and into the fire.

I look around the bar, hoping to see someone, anyone, that will help me.

I only see blurry faces of people who don't give a shit.

But then I see someone coming toward us, a familiar form.

He barely comes into focus as he grabs the guy roughly and spins him around.

The guy lets go of me and I stumble, my hands grabbing the edge of the table and managing to hold on and stay on my feet. I try to focus my hazy eyesight enough to see what's going on.

It's Blaise, of all fucking people.

And he's winding up, punching the racist fuck right in the jaw, a swift uppercut that sends the guy flying to the floor beside me.

Then Blaise is jumping on top of him, straddling the guy's thick stomach and laying punch after punch into his face, blood spraying.

I yell at Blaise to stop, because I know everyone else in this bar is ready to fight him.

But Blaise keeps on hitting, like a wild animal on the loose.

Finally, when I see the big biker dude get up from the booth looking like he's about to intervene in a bad way, I find the strength to grab my purse and whack Blaise over the shoulder with it to get his attention.

Dumont handbags are heavy.

He looks up at me in shock, hair across his forehead, damp with exertion. His crazed eyes focus on me, and he stills.

"We have to get out of here. Now." I point at the door.

Blaise blinks at me, looks down at the bloody face of the man he's just beaten, takes a quick sweep of the room, and gets to his feet.

He grabs my hand, and we start walking quickly toward the exit.

The bartender, though not as tall and built as Blaise, steps out in front of us, blocking the doorway.

"I don't think so," the man says.

For a second I fear Blaise is going to get into another fight. His grip on my hand tightens in a squeeze. Then he takes his wallet out and hands the bartender a stack of bills.

"For all the trouble," he says firmly.

The bartender stares him down for a moment, then glances at the money.

He gives us both a grim nod. "That guy had it coming," he says and steps aside an inch.

We both squeeze past him into the night and the darkness and the putrid smells of the alley.

Blaise is jogging lightly and pulling me along, and it isn't until we're around the corner and onto the main street that I stop, breathless and dizzy, and lean back against the cold stones of a building.

"Are you okay?" he asks me, and he's standing close to me, too close. I can feel the heat from his body. "Are you cold?"

That's when he starts taking off his coat, and I realize that I'm shivering through mine. He gently pulls me off the wall and slips the coat around my shoulders, pulling it together over my chest.

I stare at him, breathing hard, trying to put everything together as his gaze focuses on the coat collar, making sure my scarf is tucked in beneath it.

"Wh-what happened?" I'm finally able to say.

He glances at me, swallowing hard. "I saw what that guy was doing to you."

"What guy?"

His jaw tenses for a moment. "The one who was trying to take advantage of you."

"You didn't see what happened before?"

He pauses, then shakes his head. "No."

I'm having trouble making sense of anything, and I'm not sure if it's because I'm drunk, because I hit my head, or because a private eye turned thug just threatened to kill me if I didn't pay him.

"Why were you there?"

"I was in the area. Passing through. I heard a commotion and went into the bar and saw you."

I shake my head and then wince at the pain. "Bullshit," I spit out. "That's bullshit, Blaise. Why were you there?"

A drop of rain falls on my nose, cold as ice.

"We need to get you back home."

"No, you need to tell me what's going on!"

He looks up and down the street. "I'll tell you later. First we get you home."

As the rain starts to fall, the kind of rain that feels like a prelude to snow, I have no choice but to let him. I'm too tired and out of it to argue, too scared over what happened and too suspicious to appreciate the fact that Blaise is here.

Things start to pass by in a blur.

With his coat around my shoulders, I'm now wearing two coats, and Blaise leads me over to a taxi, and then the next thing I know we're going up the stairs of my apartment.

He takes me right to my door, and I'm wondering how the hell he knows where I live. When did I ever have him over? But then there were so many parties that I've had over the years, especially with Cyril in the picture. It's possible he had been an uninvited guest.

I fumble for my keys and open the door.

He closes it behind us, locks it, takes me by the arm, and leads me over to my bed.

I immediately collapse on it, facedown, and the world starts to whirl around, black.

"What were you doing there, Blaise?" I manage to ask, my words slurring together into one. "Were you following me?"

There's a pause as the lights in the bedroom flick off.

"Yes," he says.

CHAPTER TWELVE

BLAISE

Four years ago

"She's dead," my mother says over the line, the hardness in her voice fading at the end. Before I have a chance to ask who, before my mind and heart run away on me, she goes on, "Eloise. She was in a car accident early this morning."

My heart lurches to a stop in my chest. "Was she with Seraphine?"

"No, she was alone," she says, and I can hear the clink of ice cubes. I can't blame her for drinking now. "It was a bad accident on the highway between Paris and their house. Many cars smashed up. Eloise, she . . ." She trails off. "I need you to come home, Blaise. The funeral is next weekend, and I need you there."

I'm surprised at the route she's taking. My mother rarely needs me for anything, nor did I think she was that close to Eloise. I know that the relationship between them was always strained, particularly in the later years; even so, my mother acts like she doesn't need anyone.

"Blaise," she says abruptly. "You will come."

The thing is, I probably would go anyway, without my mother demanding I do so. I liked Eloise deep down, even if my parents did a lot of talking behind her back, even if I was raised to view that side of the family as being inferior in some way. But I've been in Thailand for a long time, and I have a feeling that if I set foot back in France, I'm not going to be coming back here.

"Okay," I say with a sigh. I stare out the window of my villa into the hills of Mae Hong Son. There's a jungle fowl strutting along the edge of my infinity pool, and the sun is making the water sparkle. I don't want to leave this place, leave the person I've become here. I especially don't want to put a stop to my Muay Thai classes.

"I can leave next Friday," I tell her. That gives me the week to get my head on straight.

"Next Friday?" she practically barks. "Blaise, you will come immediately. Get the first flight out. You know money is no expense."

"I can't just up and leave," I tell her.

"You can. What are you doing there, anyway? You know I haven't talked to you since it was your birthday, and that was only because I called you."

Well, how incredibly gracious of you.

She goes on, "It's for family, Blaise."

I snort. "Don't take this the wrong way, Mother, but since when have you ever given a shit about family, particularly that side?"

Silence fills the air. "I care," she says after a moment. "Blaise . . . you have no idea what it's like to be me, what I've gone through. What I've done." She sniffs. "I can't deal with this alone. Your father and your brother, they don't understand. I need . . . I have to talk to you. Before the funeral. I need your support, you're the only one who might even care a little about me."

She sounds so small and broken that my stupid hardened heart softens just a bit. Fuck me, this is going to be a horrible week. I almost envy Aunt Eloise. She doesn't have to deal with any of this shit, any of us, anymore.

"Okay," I tell her. "I'll get the first flight out."

Questions hang on my lips: *How is Seraphine doing? Is she okay? Is she alone?*

But I press my lips firmly together.

I'll find out soon enough.

◆ ◆ ◆

Nothing had ever felt so wrong as landing at the Charles de Gaulle airport and seeing the gray, gloomy, and smog-filled landscape. Such a drastic change from the clarity and peace and quiet of the hills of Northern Thailand that my brain actually felt rattled. The long flight didn't help either.

But if I thought that was bad, the moment the car pulls up the driveway of my parents' house, that's when I feel like I'm caught in a terrible dream.

"This is it?" the driver asks me when I make no indication I'm going to get out of the car.

"This is it," I tell him and finally step out. He brings my suitcase out from the trunk—the same suitcase I've been living out of for years, the metallic exterior beaten and burnished by my many travels—and I take it, bringing it up to the house.

At first glance I notice that my mother's car is here but no one else's. I don't want to get ahead of myself, though.

I knock on the door, and after a moment my mother answers.

I didn't expect this. Usually she has a maid answer the door. And more than that, I don't expect my mother to look so horrible. That's a cruel thing for a son to think, but it's true. Normally she's on top of everything in regard to plastic surgery and other vanity treatments, but she just looks haggard and old.

Vulnerable, even.

"Blaise," she says to me, holding out her arms. I should be glad she doesn't have a drink in her hands for once, though when I give her an embrace and kiss her on the cheek, I can smell the booze on her like it's perfume.

"Mother," I tell her, stiffening as she holds me for longer than she normally does.

"I'm so glad you're here," she says, and when she pulls back, I notice the mascara smudges under her watery eyes. "You must have had such a long travel day. Here, here, come to the sitting room, and I'll get you something to drink."

"Water would be good," I tell her as I pull the suitcase into the hall and shut the door. She walks off, a bit unsteadily, toward the kitchen. "Don't you have someone to get that shit for you?" I call after her.

"I sent them into Paris to get some provisions," she says.

I look around. Nothing in this place has changed, and it's unsettling. Even more unsettling is the feeling that I never left. "And so I'm guessing Pascal and Father are out too?"

"Yes, but who knows where," she says. "And frankly, who cares?"

I slowly walk across the marble floors of the hall to the parquet floors of the sitting room. Normally this room gets a lot of sun through the big glass doors, but a drizzle is starting to fall outside, making everything look dark. I can tell my mother must have been in here a lot today, because there are a few empty glasses out that are smeared with her lipstick.

When my mother comes back from the kitchen, she has a glass of water for me and another empty glass. She sets both down beside me and then sits on the adjacent love seat, leaning back and picking up a bottle of rare Scotch from behind the couch, one of my father's prized possessions. She quickly pours herself a glass to the brim, her bracelets clanking against the glass, and then does the same for me.

I down half the water and then pick up the glass of Scotch, raising it toward her. "Are we celebrating something?"

She shakes her head quickly, and then, before I know what's happening, she's bursting into tears.

I can't remember the last time I saw my mother cry.

Wait. Actually, I can.

Mallorca.

And some instinct deep in my gut is telling me that the past is here in this room.

"Mother," I say gently, sitting up straighter. I've never had to comfort her before, so I don't know what to do. When I was really young, I'd often find her drunk and crying in the corner of a room late at night, but if I ever approached, she'd scream at me to go away, like she was a wild animal nursing her wounds.

"I didn't realize you and Eloise were so close," I say, and this somehow makes her cry harder.

She shakes her head and then puts her face into her hands. "We weren't. We weren't close," she mumbles and sobs. "Oh, Blaise, I need to get something off my chest. I need to tell you what I've done. It will eat me alive if I don't."

She's not joking. That's the look that she has. Not just haggard but like something dark, guilt or shame, has been eating her from the inside out, starting with her heart.

"You can tell me," I say. Against my better judgment, I slam back my glass of Scotch, feeling the burn, then slowly get up and sit next to her on the love seat, putting my hand on her shoulder and giving it a squeeze.

She flinches at the contact and looks up at me with tears running down her face. "You are the good son, Blaise. You know that. If I tell you, you'll have leverage against me forever. I have to know that you won't use it against me. I have to know that I can trust you. You can't tell your brother or your father. This is just between us." She swallows. "Please promise me that."

Jesus. Now she's freaking me out.

I nod. "Okay. I promise. I won't tell a soul."

She presses her lips together and nods softly, trying to suppress another sob. "Good. Thank you," she says in a quiet voice. With shaking hands, she finishes her drink and then pours herself another. I wait patiently for her confession.

"Blaise," she says after a moment, staring down at the amber liquid. "Years ago, I made a mistake. A big mistake. And at the time I was never ashamed of it, because your father deserved it. He deserved it and so much more, and he still does." A resolute look comes across her brow. "No, he still does deserve it. But Eloise . . . she never did. And I never got to tell her that I was sorry."

My stomach starts to churn. I have a feeling I don't want her to continue. I don't want to be in charge of keeping my mother's secrets, something that she's done. It's a burden more than anything.

"I had an affair with Ludovic." She says it so softly and with such finality that it takes me a moment to really hear her.

"You . . . what?"

Ludovic? My mother slept with Uncle Ludovic?

She nods, her chin trembling. "It's true. Long ago."

"When?"

"When you were a teenager," she says. "That long ago."

"For how long?"

"Years."

"Years!" I yell, getting to my feet. "Years . . . Mother, you . . . how could you do that? How could you do that to Eloise, to Father . . . my God."

I can't even begin to deal with this. I sit back down, feeling faint, my head in my hands. "Uncle Luddie. He would never do that to her. How could he? He was the good one."

She lets out a caustic snort. "There is no good side, Blaise. Don't you see? Your father and your brother are just worse than most." I notice she's left herself out of the running.

"I can't believe it."

She looks at me sharply. "I assume that's meant for your uncle and not for me?"

"I can't believe either of you." I sigh and reach across for the Scotch, pouring myself another glass. I need this. "So does Father know?"

"Oh, come on, we would know if he knew."

"I don't know. He does like to store things away for future black-mailing." I pause. "In Mallorca. You got drunk and fell down and ran off with Luddie. I heard you. You said to him that he knows."

"You heard that?" She looks startled.

I shrug, swirling the Scotch around in the glass. "I didn't know what I heard. I assumed you did something wrong, but not this."

"Well, I thought he knew. He had said something to me that night that made me think he knew. Basically called me a whore. I could have sworn he knew right there and then. But nothing ever came of it. I thought that he would have divorced me or done something awful to his brother, but nothing happened."

"That still doesn't mean that he doesn't know," I tell her. "But for your sake, let's forget about that. Let's just forget about everything. It's done."

"Don't you see? I can't forget. And Eloise knew."

"How did she know?"

"Because your uncle is an idiot and he confessed. Said he couldn't keep it to himself. He thought he was being the bigger man, but he shouldn't have burdened her with that."

"When did he tell her?"

"A year ago."

"And had you seen Eloise after that?"

She shakes her head, and a tear spills out. "I did everything I could to avoid her. And now . . . I wish I had reached out. I wish I had told her how sorry I was. Now she's dead, Blaise. She's dead and she died knowing what I did, and I never got the chance to make amends."

Now I completely understand why my mother seems to have aged before my eyes. This secret would have weighed a lot on her heart.

And now, I suppose, it has to weigh on mine.

"You think less of me," she says.

"To be honest, Mother, I never thought very much of you."

She flinches, her eyes turning from soft to hard. A look—a *mother*—I know too well. "I suppose I deserve that."

"I hate to say it, but you probably deserve all the guilt and shame too," I point out.

"Blaise, you have a wicked tongue," she scolds me, looking aghast. "Though what should I expect? I raised you. You have my wicked blood, as well as your father's, running through your veins. And yet I can tell that you think you're better than us. Better than me."

Oh, how quickly this has changed, as it always does with alcohol.

I stand up and stare down at her. "I came here because you asked me to. I let you unload your burdens on me. But I don't have to listen to this. I am free to leave and never look back."

Her face crumples in an instant, and I'm having a hard time believing it's real. That is, until the tears start to flow again and she collapses across the love seat, sobbing into the pillows.

I run a hand through my hair, trying to figure out what to do. The best course of action would be to leave, forget the funeral. I'm sure that side of the family wouldn't care if I were there or not; I haven't talked to them in years.

And Seraphine?

I swallow at the sound of her name in my head.

"Blaise, you can't leave me," Mother says through her muffled cries. "Don't you understand? I have no one. I can't trust your father, I can't trust Pascal." She sobs and sobs and then finally pushes herself up onto her elbows. "It's you and only you. I don't know what will happen to me if you leave. I need someone good around me. Someone better. I need you to help me. There's no way out of this."

I stare at her for a moment. She looks absolutely pitiful, reaching for the Scotch, the Scotch she will surely drown in. She's never shown any love or need for me for my whole life, and suddenly she's acting as if I'm the golden boy, the good son, the one who will absolve her of her sins.

I can't do that.

And yet I also know, in the darkest, deepest part of me, that I can't leave her like this. I *hate* that. I hate that I'm better than them. If I weren't, I would go. I would shun her and turn away from her as she has always done with me, and I would leave her to a life of alcoholism and an early death.

But I don't want that on my shoulders either.

And that small, sad part of me, the one that yearned for recognition and love and respect when growing up, that part is happy that she needs me. She *finally* needs me.

"What do you want from me?" I ask wearily, sitting back down in the armchair. I swear I feel it tighten around me, like a mouth that wants to swallow me whole.

She wipes her tears on her sleeve and slams back the Scotch. After she seems to regain her breath and some control, she says, "I just need you to stay with me for a while. Just a few months. I know you have a life in Thailand or wherever, but you also have a name and a duty here. A family legacy. Stay in Paris. You can work for the company."

I let out a sour laugh. "I am not working for the company."

"Fine," she says. "Don't work for them. Do whatever. But it would be good for you. To become who you are supposed to be. This could be your opportunity to start over. Don't you want to make us proud?"

I give her a steady look. "Does it look like I do?"

She nods. "I know you. Deep down inside, all you wanted was your father's affection. You wanted to be Pascal. You wanted him to respect you. This would do all of that. That's why you left, isn't it? Because you didn't feel worthy or wanted? But you can change that, Blaise."

I wave my hand at her dismissively, my throat choked up with anger that she's saying that. I don't even want to think about what she's saying. "You can think what you want," I tell her sharply. "I'll stay because you asked, and because, for some reason, I still believe in honoring my mother. But I won't stay long, and I won't be your shoulder to cry on when you find it convenient. I'll help you through this, and then I'm gone. And I don't plan on coming back."

She gives me a gracious smile over her Scotch.

God, I hope I have the spine to leave this place in the end.

◆　◆　◆

Saturday rolls around. It's been raining all week, and today is no exception.

The funeral is at a cemetery just outside the city lines of Paris, where my grandparents are buried. Everyone is huddled under black umbrellas, the rain pouring off the edges; everyone's shoes are wet.

I stand beside Pascal, my mother, and my father. There is no chatter today, no murmurs, even though the place is packed with people, some I'm sure are even tourists, braving the weather to see who might be attracting such a crowd. Eloise wasn't a true Dumont, but she was well known and well loved in both Paris and in the fashion community for all her charity work and for being a lovely human being in general.

"Oh dear," my mother whispers in my ear, grabbing my hand.

I turn to see Ludovic, Olivier, and Renaud approaching, looking absolutely devastated. Suddenly I feel the deepest shame on my mother's behalf, and I don't know what to do if Ludovic looks my way.

. But he doesn't. He is inconsolable, and I know that this must weigh so heavily on his heart too. I can only pray that he and his wife were able to get things right before she died, that there was still love between them.

137

However, as much as I feel for my uncle—even for my cousins, who are staggering with their loss—Seraphine steals my attention.

She's coming up behind them, her arm linked with that of a man I don't recognize.

I feel jealousy swirl through me, but more than that, I feel my own sense of guilt. I haven't seen or talked to Seraphine in years. Even though she's overcome with grief, she still looks as beautiful as I remember, and I wish that things between us had ended differently. We were both so much younger and naive, and I really ruined the fragile thread that connected us. Even if fear hadn't driven me from her, I could have stayed friends somehow. I could have handled it better.

I could have been someone to her.

Now she has someone.

Let her be, I think to myself. *She doesn't belong to you.*

And yet as she takes her seat beside her brothers, she looks over at me, and her eyes meet mine.

In that one glance I see our entire relationship. I see shock and then fear and then love and then hate.

But she leaves me with hate.

"Who is that with Seraphine?" I whisper to my mother, even though I can see Pascal give me a curious glance out of my periphery.

"That's her boyfriend, Cyril," she says with a lowered voice, her eyes darting over to them. "He's with the United Nations. Bit of an odd duck, if you ask me. But they seem very serious. Wouldn't be surprised if they get married."

The word *married* burns into me like a lit cigarette.

I look back at Cyril, taking in his ill-fitting suit and glasses. He seems older than her, and boring. Stuffy. Safe. The complete opposite of Seraphine. What could she even see in him?

"Not the kind of person you'd expect her to end up with, is it?" Pascal asks. I bring my eyes to his, and there's that damn smug smile on his face, like he's been able to see into my thoughts.

I shrug, slipping on a mask. "I don't know her enough to make that assumption."

"But you will," Pascal says. "Once you start working for us. You'll be working alongside her every single day."

"I'm not working for *you*," I remind him, looking forward at the casket, trying to pay my respects. "I'm not working for anyone. I'm here for a little bit, and then I'm out of here."

But even though I'm staring at the casket as the rain falls down and the priest comes up in front of the crowd, out of the corner of my eye, I can see Pascal smirking at me. Like he knows something I don't.

Like he knows there's no way I can leave now.

Not after seeing her again, after being reminded of what I've really been looking for all this time away.

Her.

CHAPTER THIRTEEN

SERAPHINE

I'm dreaming.

One of those dreams that teeters between sleep and consciousness, where you wake up and fall asleep again for a few minutes, and in those minutes a world unravels. The twilight of dreams.

In this dream I'm being choked again at the masquerade ball. Blaise is across the room, reaching out and running in slow motion. He freezes on the spot, hands stretched out, never getting to me. But where I was paralyzed before, this time I can move my hands. I put them over the hands of my attacker and pry them off.

I turn around and see a man in a black mask lined with silver zippers.

I reach up and take his mask off.

It's Gautier, grinning at me with eyes as black as his soul. Inky tar, sticky and fathomless.

Then he morphs into Pascal.

Then into Jones.

And finally . . .

Into my father.

I gasp, unable to hold back my shock.

"Father?" I cry out.

He leans in and winks, and in that moment I realize it's not my father at all, but someone else pretending to be him. "It all started with me," he says in a raspy voice.

Then I'm awake again.

In my darkened bedroom.

The light in the hallway is on, and the hair on my arms is standing at attention, just as it's happened on many nights lately.

Except this isn't a matter of me leaving the hall light on and passing out.

There's a man in the doorway.

A familiar silhouette.

"It's okay." Blaise's voice cuts through the dark. "I think you were having a nightmare."

Everything comes flooding back to me. Drinking here, getting the text from Jones, meeting him at the bar, hearing that he had no evidence against my father and the whole thing was in my head, the Vulcan maneuver he pulled on me when he threatened to kill me if I didn't pay up. Then falling off the stool, hitting my head on the floor, the racist guy helping me to my feet and groping me, followed by Blaise.

Blaise, who seemed to come out of nowhere.

Blaise, who is now in my bedroom.

"I *am* having a nightmare," I manage to say, my throat thick and dry as dust, my head throbbing. I run my hands down my body, feeling relief that my clothes are still on, everything except my shoes. "The nightmare is that you're in my bedroom."

"Not quite," he says. "I'm standing just outside."

I prop myself up on my elbows and let my eyes adjust to the dark. I still can't see his face. "Why were you there, Blaise? That wasn't a coincidence."

Karina Halle

I wish I could see his face. He's hard to read in the light, but even so, I want to make some guesses. He remains in the doorway, a shadow from my past even though I see him nearly every day.

He doesn't say anything, but the room is thick with tension.

"You should get some more sleep. It's only two in the morning," he finally says. His voice sounds strange. Like he's in pain.

"I'm awake now," I tell him. "And everything is coming back to me. So why don't you tell me why you suddenly became my knight in shining armor tonight? And please tell me the truth. I'm so very tired of being lied to."

He laughs dryly. "You would never trust the truth from me."

He has a point. "You're right. But I'd still like to hear whatever lie you have so I can figure out the truth from there. Usually it's the opposite." I pause. "You were following me."

I don't know what made me come to that conclusion before I passed out, but the moment it left my mouth, I knew it was right.

"I told you I was," he says.

This surprises me. His admittance. I sit up straighter, ignoring the swirling of the room and the ache in my head, and lean over to flick on the light on my bedside table.

Now I can see him, blinking at the light, leaning against the doorway. Now he's real, and I'm less afraid.

"Why were you following me?"

He stares at me for a moment, gathering his thoughts, maybe picking apart the lies or weaving together the truth. "I was told to."

I feel my chest seize up with something cold. My whole body is stiff. I didn't expect the truth so easily, and because of that, I'm not prepared.

"By who?" I whisper.

"By Pascal," he says. He sounds torn, like he knows he shouldn't have said anything but wants it off his chest.

"Why?"

142

"He knows about you."

Oh fuck. My hand goes to my chest, my fingers gripping the neckline of my blouse. "What do you mean he knows about me?"

Blaise doesn't say anything and averts his eyes to the floor, taking in a deep breath. It's only now that I realize he's in the same suit that he was in at work earlier. Dark gray, his white shirt splattered with dots of blood from the man he beat.

If Blaise hadn't been there, I would have been in a world of trouble. I should be thanking my lucky stars that he was following me.

Protecting me.

And yet I don't dare let myself dwell on that feeling. I've had the rug pulled out from under me too many times, especially by him, and the man just told me he was there because his brother told him to be.

I switch gears. "Were you supposed to protect me?"

He looks up at me, dead in the eye, and shakes his head. "No."

"But you did."

"I know." He licks his lips.

"Why did you? Why did you protect me?"

He frowns at me, his posture straightening. "Why do you think?"

"At this point, I'm going to say it's because you were paid to do so."

His lips twist into a smile, and even though it's a bitter one, it transforms his face. For a moment, I'm thrilled to have his protection.

"I wasn't paid to do so. I wasn't paid to do anything. Pascal told me to follow you because he thinks you're dangerous."

"Me, dangerous?" I burst out laughing. "What the fuck is that about?"

"You should know," he says simply.

My brows knit together in confusion. "Come here."

He looks at me in surprise. "What?"

"Stop hanging out in the doorway like a creeper and come over here."

Now he looks as wary as I feel. He slowly makes his way across the bedroom floor and stands at the foot of the bed.

I smack the space beside me. "Sit here."

He studies me as if he thinks I'm setting some trap, but all I really want is to see him up close. I need to see what he says to me from here. I need to find out the difference between the lies and the truth.

He takes a seat beside me, and now, fuck, now everything is a million times more complicated. I could ask him questions when he was across the room, and I could take in his responses, but it felt like I was talking to a hologram.

Now that he's beside me, sitting on the edge of my bed, I'm struck with too many competing feelings and emotions.

He smells fucking terrific, for one thing. Like cinnamon and sugar and coffee and a comforting cold day. Even though his shirt is splattered with blood, and some blood remains in a smudge above the dark arches of his groomed brows, it's like I'm seeing him as a teenager again. Back in those hot summer nights when I saw him as something else. Not a cousin, not family, but something else. Some intangible mysterious thing that belonged in my life. More than a friend, not quite a lover. Unrequited love, perhaps.

You've hit your head, I remind myself. *You need to be careful right now.*

And I'm right.

I close my eyes for a moment, gathering my thoughts. I hear the pounding of my heart in my head and the unsteady rasps of Blaise's breath.

He's the first man I've had in this room in a long time.

He's supposed to be family.

I'm not sure what he ever was to me.

Maybe just the man who is trying to steal my job.

Maybe a man who just beat the shit out of someone for harassing me.

"I don't know who you are," I burst out, unable to hold my confusion back. "Who are you right now?"

He's looking not at me but at a blank spot on the floor. His shoulders are slumped forward, his hands clasped, wringing them together. "I'm trying to do right by you." His voice is low and rough and rich with something that sounds like emotion. Something I haven't heard from him in so long. "That's who I am."

"Do you think I'm dangerous?"

His gaze goes to me and he holds my eyes in his, and I see so many things in them that I'm overwhelmed. This isn't the man I work with. This is someone in pain, someone who is showing his cards even if he doesn't know it.

"You're only dangerous to me," he says hoarsely.

"Why?" I whisper, sitting up even more, leaning forward so that I can stare at him in greater detail. "Why to you?"

"Do you really want to discuss that right now? Or do you want to know why Pascal had me following you?"

I want both.

But Blaise is fickle and subject to change with every passing second, so I have to run with what's most important. "Why were you following me?"

"Pascal called me over to the house the other day," he says, staring down at his hands. "No one was home. He showed me footage on his phone. Security footage. Of you, going into the castle and up to the security room."

My mouth is open. My body is prickling, like a million fire ants are running through my insides, making me hunch over. "He saw that?" I whisper, horrified.

He nods. "Yeah. He did."

"I had no idea. I thought . . . why, how would he find out I was there?"

"He was following you himself."

145

Fucking hell. "Why? What did I do?"

"He knows what you think."

Anger flares through me like a bullet, and I suddenly grab Blaise's shirt collar, pulling him right into me. "You told him," I grind out. "You told him what I told you and Olivier last year, right when we got into the car accident. You told him what I thought."

He rubs his lips together, his head shaking ever so slightly. "No," he says, his eyes pausing at my mouth in such a way that my stomach does a backflip. "I didn't."

I don't let go; I just stare at his eyes inches away from mine, searching for the truth, searching for some simplicity in this messy matter.

"I didn't," he says again, his voice a whisper. "You don't have to think I'm a good guy, Seraphine. I'm not. We both know it. But I didn't tell him. I don't . . . I haven't told anyone anything when it's come to you."

For some reason I believe him.

Maybe it's because of the look in his eyes.

An old familiar look that I've dreamed I'd see again.

One of sincerity. Of wanting.

I breathe in deeply and let go of his collar. "Okay. I believe you. But then why did Pascal follow me?"

He stares at me for a moment, a wash of sadness coming over him. "Maybe he knew you'd figure it out."

"Figure what out?" I say sharply.

"That you'd want someone to blame, and it would be him or our father. Either way, he was following you. He knew what you did and what you're looking for. So he asked me to follow you and find out more. And so I did."

I grimace, feeling so violated. "What did you see?"

"Whatever you've been doing this last week, that's what I've seen. Most days you just go into your apartment. But some nights, like tonight, you go to that bar, and you have a meeting with some pretty untrustworthy people. People who will put you in danger more than I ever could."

For some reason, knowing that Blaise was there watching on both those nights makes me feel relieved. Like if something had gone down when Cyril was there, he would have had my back.

"So then you must have seen what happened earlier tonight. With Jones. The other guy, who wasn't Cyril."

He shakes his head. "I didn't. I was late. Traffic. I saw him storm out of the bar, and that was it. I went inside, thinking that it couldn't have been good, and I saw you and I . . . I don't know, I just reacted. I shouldn't have but—"

"I'm grateful you did," I tell him softly and instinctively reach out and touch the blood on his shirt. "You're usually so cool and collected, I didn't think you had it in you."

"So what happened with Jones?" he asks, his eyes focused on my fingers, the fact that I'm still touching his chest.

I take my hand away, and it takes more energy to do that than to keep my hand there. "He . . . he didn't find anything."

Blaise frowns. "What do you mean? What did you have him do?"

"I had him try and bring back the files from the security camera, the footage from that night. It'd been deleted, and I figured that it had evidence on them. But Jones said he went down there and checked out the files and that there was nothing unusual about that night."

"And you trust his word?"

I think back to the way he held me—how powerless I was in his grip—ready to kill me. I shake my head, surprised at the tears springing to my eyes. "No."

Blaise continues to frown, his brows knitting together. "What happened before I got there?" he asks.

I bite my lip, closing my eyes. The shock of the earlier trauma is wearing off, and now it's all coming back to me. The fear. The utter fear in knowing I made the wrong choice, that Cyril betrayed me even if he didn't know it, that I hired the wrong guy.

A tear rolls down my cheek.

Blaise puts his hand at the back of my neck and I flinch. "No," I say through a wet, messy sob, trying to move away.

Blaise puts his hands on my biceps instead and holds me steady, trying to meet my eyes. "Seraphine, what happened before I got there? What did this man do to you, say to you? Tell me. Tell me because I'm the only one who can help you now."

"He . . . I told him that he didn't deliver. I was so dumb. I felt brave, I felt entitled, I don't know. I thought this man would be my savior, that he would expose the truth, and I was so mad that he said he went to the castle and produced nothing. He didn't even have any proof to give me. I wanted to see it all with my own eyes, not through his, not through a stranger. And then he reached back like you just did now, to my neck, and he did something that paralyzed me and . . . my God, I've never been so scared. I almost pissed my pants. I couldn't move and he had me, and I looked into his eyes, and he told me that if I didn't pay him in twenty-four hours, he'd do the same thing to me and cut off my oxygen supply."

Even though my vision is blurry as I struggle to control my tears, I can see Blaise is about to explode. His face is red, there's a muscle ticking at his jaw. His eyes are wild again, like when he was slamming his fist into that guy's face, over and over again.

He doesn't say anything either, he's just trying to compose himself. His breath is short, his nostrils flaring. I'm almost scared to set him off.

"I'm going to pay him," I add. "I don't want any problems. Not from him. I just . . . I don't know. Cyril wasn't there tonight, and I thought he would be. He's who set me up with him."

"Fuck Cyril," Blaise says through gritted teeth. "I swear to God I'll kill that fucker the next time I see him."

"It's my fault. I shouldn't have reached out to him. I just . . . I had no one to turn to."

"But he sold you out," Blaise says.

"I don't know," I say but my words are shaky with doubt. "Maybe he didn't quite know how Jones would operate. He wasn't there to keep an eye on me."

"No," Blaise says sharply, his hands sliding down to my hands and holding on to them, and I hate the feeling that washes over me, the comfort and the warmth and the calm amid all this fucking chaos. "He sold you out."

I don't get it. Blaise sounds adamant. "What do you mean?"

He swallows. "I told you what Pascal asked me to do. It was to follow you and see what you were up to. He was afraid you'd try and blame him or my father for your father's death."

"Because they did it!"

He gives me a hard, dismissive look and holds my hands even tighter, thumbs pressing into my palms, as if he thinks I'll fly away.

"That's all Pascal asked me to do," he continues. "And I did watch you. And I didn't see anything interesting until you were at the bar that first night, and I saw you with Cyril and Jones, and I had no idea what was going on. Then you all parted ways. Pascal told me to follow you and I didn't. I lingered in that alley long enough to catch the conversation between them. The conversation about you."

"What did they say?" I whisper, and the walls are already caving in around me, because I know in the heart of me where this is going. I know.

I am so fuckin' stupid.

Cyril hired someone who would never help me so he could split the money with him. Simple as that. "It was a scam, wasn't it?" I add.

But Blaise shakes his head. "No. It wasn't a scam. You just weren't the highest bidder. Jones was already hired by someone else. You were a conflict of interest."

"Who? Who hired him?"

Blaise stares at me for a long beat, and the room seems to get darker. "They were meeting with the highest bidder, the person who would cancel you out. And I followed them to their meeting."

I can barely breathe as I wait for him to go on.

When he doesn't, I squeeze his hands back. "Blaise, please. Who was it? Who is he really working for if it isn't me?"

He presses his lips together grimly. "He's working for my father."

The words don't sink in. Not at first.

But then they do.

And then I know how fucked I really and truly am.

CHAPTER FOURTEEN

BLAISE

The look on Seraphine's face is enough to bring me to my knees, if I weren't already sitting on her bed beside her, her hands in mine.

I knew it was going to hurt when I told her the truth.

I also knew the moment I saw my father I had no choice but to tell her the truth.

I'm a traitor to my family in this moment.

And yet I don't see I have a choice.

"Your father?" she whispers. "Jones is reporting to him?"

I nod. "I don't know how it happened. But it looked like he and Cyril were long-lost pals. Maybe your ex-husband sold you out right away. Maybe he didn't know and Jones was already on my father's payroll."

"No," she says bitterly, looking at me with war in her eyes. "No, it wasn't a coincidence. I called Cyril asking for help, and he went immediately to your father. He ratted on me."

Revenge.

Cyril's admission rings inside my brain. But there's no point in sharing that with Seraphine. She knows. Only a pathetic excuse for a human being like Cyril would take revenge against his ex because he was the one who got caught cheating.

"I'm sorry," I tell her, and I'm not sure she knows I mean it. "I know this is hard. You trusted someone and he betrayed you."

Her gaze sharpens. "This is on me. Cyril betrayed me before, I was stupid to think he wouldn't do it again. I should be used to it by now. He's not the only one to break my trust."

From the way she says that, I know she's taking a shot at me. Maybe it's a shot I deserve. Maybe this is the time to finally discuss what happened between us.

"Why are you telling me all of this, anyway?" she goes on, squinting at me.

"Because you have to know the danger that you're in."

It sounds dramatic but it's true. It's one thing to go snooping around, trying to uncover evidence against my father based on a hunch. It's another thing to get tangled up with a dangerous thug on my father's payroll.

She rubs her lips together uneasily. "What's going to happen to me?"

"I don't know. Probably nothing, if you pay Jones and if you drop this whole thing."

"But I'm so close to the truth, Blaise," she says, leaning forward with pleading eyes. "I have to be. There wouldn't be this pushback if I wasn't. I'm on the right track."

I've put off thinking about this seriously for too long. I look away, not sure yet what to say or believe, though I know what my gut would say if I dug a little deeper.

"You know I'm right," she adds. "I can tell. You know in your heart what your father and brother are capable of."

"I don't think Pascal killed your father," I tell her. "I just don't see it."

"Brotherly love, huh?"

"No," I say with a shake of my head. "There is no love lost between Pascal and me, because there never was love between us. You know that, Seraphine. You've been there. You've seen how I grew up. You know how I was treated."

"I don't know what I know," she says, looking away and giving me a tired sigh. "The boy that I knew . . . that all turned out to be a lie."

"I never lied to you," I say adamantly. "All those times I confided in you, I never lied. You were the only one I thought who understood me."

"Oh, so that's why you came on to me, told me you wanted me, wanted to be with me, then acted like I didn't even exist!" she snaps, fire in her eyes. "You broke my heart, Blaise!"

And there it is. Her words about what happened so long ago have the ability to break mine.

It's a blessing and curse to be reminded how much one can feel.

"I was young and I was stupid, but none of what I said to you was a lie," I tell her sternly, hoping she can read the sincerity in my voice, see it etched on my face.

"You're full of shit. It's fine, Blaise, it is. I've gotten over it. I've learned my lesson."

I let go of her hands and put my palm against her cheek. "I fucked up because I panicked. I did the only thing I thought I could do. I had to pretend that nothing was going on, I had to act like a dick to you, because if I didn't, then they'd know."

I can tell she wants to move her face away from my hand, but so far she's letting me touch her. Her skin is so soft, so warm, I'm losing all sense of self.

But let's be honest. I'm not sure who I am most days to begin with.

"Who would know?" she asks.

"Pascal. My father. They'd know." I pause. "The night that we . . . the night that we were on the bed, when we got up, I saw Pascal standing at the door, looking at us."

Her eyes go wide and shining. "What? He saw us! And you didn't say anything?"

My cheeks burn hot with shame. I was an idiot back then for keeping it to myself. "I thought it would make things worse. And I couldn't be sure if he saw us or not."

"But you just said——"

"I know what I said. I saw him, okay? He might have seen everything, might have heard everything. Or maybe he didn't. I wasn't going to risk it by having an affair with you, my cousin, from the side of the family my father hates. And yeah, we were young and we could chalk it up to being stupid, but if my father had ever found out . . ." I brush her hair behind her ears, and she seems to stiffen at the gesture.

"I don't understand," she says, eyes closing. "You could have told me. You could have talked to me."

"I know what I should have done. But I did what I thought was best."

She opens her eyes, and there's a world of hurt swimming in them. Disappointment. Regret. I've wrestled with those feelings for the last nine years. Just knowing what could have been if I hadn't acted the way I did.

"You could have reached out to me." She reaches for my hand and gently places her palm on top. Then she wraps her fingers around my hand and removes it from her face. I bring my hand to my side, feeling the distance grow. "There was so much time."

"And said what? You didn't want to see me again."

"Because you acted like a monster to me."

"Do you really think if I contacted you and tried to explain, you would have listened to any of it? You're not exactly a calm, levelheaded person, Seraphine. You're a fucking firecracker. You would have hung up, you wouldn't have given me the time of day."

"You should have tried."

"Maybe I should have, but I didn't. Maybe I was afraid that you'd just reject me anyway."

"You were afraid of me rejecting you?"

"You were just seventeen. I was the one pushing you."

"You weren't pushing me," she says quietly.

"I was. Because I knew that's the only way I could have you. Wear you down. If I stepped back, you would have stepped back too. I know you. You have too much pride to be the one who puts herself on the line. You want to feel wanted. You need it. You wanted me to chase you until you surrendered."

Her eyes roam around her bedroom as if I'm boring her, but I know she knows I'm right. I've got her pegged.

"Well, you stopped chasing," she eventually says, her voice so low and light it's barely more than a whisper.

I lean in close, my face inches from hers. "Did you want me to keep chasing you? All this time?"

She presses her lips together and doesn't say anything.

"Did you want me to still think about you at night, to wish I could touch you, to get off to thoughts of your lips on my body?"

I'm pushing now and pushing hard, needing a reaction, needing this conversation to go somewhere, anywhere, even if I don't like it.

"I forgot how crude you can be," she says, her tone sharp, her eyes even more so.

I grin at her. "I don't think you forgot at all. I think it's what your mind fixated on all this time. What I had promised to do to you. I think whenever you were having sex with Cyril, it was the only thing that got you wet."

"You're a pig," she says with a sneer.

"You bring it out of me."

"And I should be flattered, is that it?"

"Yeah. You should be. You're the only one for me, Seraphine. There has never been anyone else."

She frowns, scoffing. "That's a lie."

I'm staring at her lips now, wondering how long I can hold off, wondering how badly I'll fuck things up if I kiss her. "It's not a lie. After you I kept my distance and I bided my time."

She's beautiful when she's confused. "What are you saying? That you . . . no, that's impossible. You were with plenty of women."

I give a slight shake of my head. I'm not ashamed of any of this. "I wasn't. I dated some, discreetly, but . . . I wasn't physical with them."

Her eyes nearly fall out of her head. "Oh my God. Blaise, why? I mean . . . have you seen you?"

I'm unable to suppress the smile. I know I'm good looking, and it's not a matter of modesty. It's just fact when the media reports on this worthless shit your whole life. But to hear her say it . . .

"I never felt anything for them," I admit. "No one measured up in that way. No one else was you."

"Blaise," she says softly, looking demure. "We didn't even sleep together."

"I know. But it doesn't matter. What I felt for you, what you did to me, body and soul, I was never able to find in anyone else. Not even close." She swallows, licks her lips, her eyes wavering with something I should expose. "You raised the bar. All the women I had before you were erased, and after you . . . there was just no point."

"So you just . . . were celibate? All this time?"

I nod. "It was easier that way. Fewer complications. Sure, people thought I was gay, but let them think that. It's nothing to be ashamed of anyway."

"And so . . . I mean, I dated. I got married. You knew I did. I invited you to the wedding. You should have known that . . . that . . ."

"That I wouldn't have a chance again?" I fill in. "No. I didn't believe it. I decided to be patient. I decided to wait for you."

"Wait for me? But that's ridiculous. You've given me no sign. Instead, you've acted like you hate me, especially at work."

"Patience is a virtue, as they say. Even though virtues aren't always my strong suit."

She looks down at her hands in her lap. "I don't know what to say."

"You can just believe me. You can take my word for it. And if my word won't do . . ."

Impulsively, I lean in to kiss her, something I knew I was going to do tonight, no matter what happened.

But she's fast.

Her hands are up against my chest, pushing me back, my lips so close to hers.

"This isn't a good idea," she says, her voice loud and firm, even if it trembles a little.

"That's what you always said." I search her eyes, trying to get a feel for her. I know she's scared, of many things and not just me. But if she could only see . . .

"And then maybe it was never a good idea. You kiss me and then what? I sleep with you?"

"Yes."

"And after that?"

"I keep fucking you."

"Until the end of time?"

"Something like that."

"We can never be together, Blaise," she says, like frustration is rolling through her. "I know you understand that."

"But it doesn't mean we can't try."

"No," she says and suddenly gets up to her feet, walking out of the room. "No. I can't do this. I can't handle this," I hear her cry out as she heads down the hall.

I get up and run after her, grabbing her by the arm and pulling her right up against me, and she opens her mouth to protest and then my mouth is on hers, swallowing her words.

I kiss her with everything I have, every bit of anger and frustration and the years of lust and pining and wanting. I should be more gentle after the night she's had, but I can't help myself; in fact, I think I'm seconds from turning into an animal as I hold the back of her head and press my hand at the small of her waist, keeping her pressed as close to me as possible.

She gasps. "Blaise," she says, trying to pull away, but I won't relent. Not until she sees that I'm done waiting for her, that she needs to be with me, now more than ever.

I kiss her until she kisses me back.

Her tongue slides across mine, hot and fevered and—

She pulls back, gasping for breath, and slaps me across the face.

Whack.

Fuck me, that hurt.

"What the hell is wrong with you?" she says. "What are you doing? What am I doing?"

Her face is red with anger, perhaps even shame. I mean, my cheek is stinging from her powerful wallop, but even so, I expected it. She's always been the type of woman to put you in your place. But I didn't expect her to slide so easily back into hating me.

"Don't pretend you haven't been dreaming about that," I tell her, trying to control myself. "Don't pretend that you haven't wanted that, wanted me, all these years."

"The only thing I've been dreaming about, Blaise, is getting justice for my father. That's it. That's all that matters. And as far as I'm concerned, you're no better than the rest of them."

Anger pokes at me, building up inside. "Hey," I say, my inflection razor sharp. "I risked my neck tonight for you. I saved you from a bad situation. And more than that, I let you know the truth. I chose you over my family."

"And I'm choosing not to trust you," she says. "You've given me no sign over the years that I mean anything to you at all. Why should

I believe you now? Why do that when it might derail everything I'm working on?" Something comes over her, a flash in her eyes, as she's realizing something. "This is all a setup, isn't it? This is just something that Pascal is having you do, just like you followed me. You're supposed to tell me all this shit, all this nonsense about wanting me and staying celibate like some joke and waiting for me, and it's all a lie to get my guard down. If you're telling me I'm in danger, it's because you're putting me there."

I knew she'd go this route at some point, but even so, it stings. "That's not it at all. Seraphine, please, I'm serious."

"You just want me to back off because I'm close to the truth," she says, shaking her head wildly as the idea takes over. "For all I know, every single thing this evening that's come out of your mouth has been a complete lie, all to throw me off."

I run my hands down my face, trying to squash my frustration. I knew this was coming, and yet that tiny coal of hope was always burning inside. "That's not true," I mutter into my hands, but I know when she gets like this that there's no changing her mind.

"Get out," she says.

I look up to see her opening the door and gesturing for me to hurry up.

"You're making a big mistake by not trusting me," I tell her.

"And I don't take threats very well. Get out, and if I see you around me again . . ."

I almost laugh. "You will see me again. At work tomorrow."

"Right. I almost forgot that you're taking over my job." She runs her fingers under her eyes and sighs so defeatedly that leaving her feels like a crime.

"It's not like that," I tell her.

"Just go," she says quietly, holding open the door and looking away, like she can't be bothered to face me.

"You know where to reach me, if anything happens," I tell her as I walk past and out into the hall.

"If anything happens, you'll be the first one I'll blame," she says to me.

Before I can say anything in response, she closes the door in my face.

◆ ◆ ◆

Later that day I wake up feeling like shit. I have a headache from the lack of sleep I got from staying half the night at Seraphine's, my knuckles are all cut and bruised, and it's snowing.

It's not the nice kind of snow, either, not the kind that blankets Paris in white flakes and looks like a postcard. It's dirty, wet snow that the traffic on the Champs-Élysées churns up and splashes everywhere, the snow that gets your shoes wet and chills you to the bone.

I'm running late to work because of the snow and my headache, and I park around the corner from the office. I'm only a few strides from my car when I run into Pascal, clothed in a thick wool overcoat.

Smoking a cigar.

At nine thirty in the morning.

"What are you doing?" I ask, expecting him to walk alongside me to the office. "Acting like a mob boss already?"

But he doesn't follow. He calls after me, "You can stop following Seraphine now."

I stop in my tracks, almost slipping, then turn to face him. My heart has started to pick up the pace in my chest. "What do you mean?"

"I mean just that. Stop following her."

"But why?" I walk back over to him, keeping my coat closed tight against the blowing wet snow. "You haven't even asked me how it's been going. What I've seen."

"Okay. Then what have you seen?"

Now this is where it gets tricky. Pascal is uncannily good at picking through lies, so I have no choice but to tell him the truth.

"A lot. She's been meeting with her ex-husband and someone else."

"Oh really?" he asks before taking a puff. He blows dark smoke into the air. "Do tell."

"I don't know. It looked pretty suspicious."

So far, not a lie.

"Uh-huh," he muses. "Well, thank you for that. But we've found out some things on our own, and we'll be handling it from now on."

I blink at him, my veins running cold. "What things? Who is 'we'?"

"Father and I," Pascal says casually.

"You said you wanted him out of it."

"I did say that. But you have to understand, he has experience in this sort of thing. I told him what I was having you do, and he told me to tell you to knock it off."

"Why didn't he tell me himself?"

He smirks. "Because. He's busy. But hey, thank you for that. You were a great help."

I stare at Pascal, feeling more hopeless with each snowflake that melts in my hair. "What's going on?"

"Nothing for you to worry about."

"But you see, you brought me into this, and so I have the right to know."

Pascal sighs, tapping his cigar so that the ash falls into the slush at his feet. "How much do you care about Seraphine? I mean, really? Honestly, truthfully?"

I'm careful. "She's family."

"But not really," he says. "She wasn't born into our family. She doesn't have our blood."

"But family is more than blood, isn't it?"

Pascal narrows his eyes thoughtfully. "That's almost poetic coming from you."

161

"She's been with us since she was nine, Pascal."

"And we were a lot older when she came around. Frankly, I thought of her the same way I thought about the children of our help. Beneath us. Not one of us."

He sounds just like our mother. I recall her once talking about Seraphine to my father, saying, "I just don't know why they had to adopt a child from India. Everyone is going to think they couldn't afford a white one. It's just like charity."

"Well, I told you how I feel," I say with a shrug. "I feel the same way about her as I do about Olivier or Renaud. They might annoy me, but they're family and they've always been there, whether I like it or not."

"Mm-hmm. But how much do you *care*?"

A drop of melting snow falls on the tip of my nose and I shiver. "I don't know what you're getting at. I care enough that I don't want her to fuck anything up, and so I'm going to go inside now and get to work."

"You do want her job, don't you?"

Suddenly I'm tired. Just overwhelmingly exhausted by all this. This same battle—us against them—that's been waged and has raged for far too long.

I want to be free of this.

"I don't know," I tell him truthfully and shrug one shoulder. "Most days I think I really don't care anymore."

I've annoyed him. I can tell. Good.

"You spent a good part of your twenties just flitting from place to place, burning through money, having zero responsibilities," Pascal remarks, sounding almost bitter. "Then one day you came back to Paris and wanted a job at the company, and we gave you that job. Any power you have isn't because you're a Dumont—it's because we let you in and we gave you that power. Now you want to throw it away."

I'm not sure how it's possible for my brother to be both delusional and right at the same time, but there you go.

"Maybe I think I've outgrown the company," I tell him.

"Maybe your loyalties lie with the wrong side."

I take a step toward him, sick of him beating around the bush.

"Is there something I should know?" I ask. "Because you keep harping on about Seraphine. If you don't want her to work for the company, then have Father fire her. And find someone else to take over her position, because I won't do it. And if you don't want her to look into the death of her father, then say something to her. Deal with it. But stop dragging me into this mess. Whatever problems you have with her are with her, not me."

He studies me for a moment before puffing back on his cigar. His hair at this point is black with wet snow and stuck to his head, but he doesn't seem to notice the weather at all. He never does. Sometimes I wonder just where my brother came from, because he doesn't seem of this world.

"You're very good at pretending you don't care, brother," he says as he stubs out the cigar on a nearby chestnut tree. "You've done that well your whole life, but you've never been able to fool me. You care deeply about some things, and I've always found it curious just which things—or people—capture your attention. Certainly it's never been anything worthy. Remember when you were in Thailand for years, training in martial arts? Where did that get you? Is that training still in your blood, or did you cast it aside, looking for something else to tide you over?" He pauses and his eyes take on a weakened gleam that makes my hackles rise. "Remember when we were in Mallorca and you decided to seduce your cousin? That also didn't get you anywhere, did it?"

I still, my breath catching in my throat. So he knows. I figured he did, but even so, it's a shock to hear it now, after all this time.

I don't say anything. There's no point.

"Oh, don't act so surprised," he says reproachfully. "I know you saw me. I would have thought you'd at least be a little grateful that I managed to keep it a secret all this time."

This has got to be a trap, but still . . . "You didn't tell anyone?"

He flicks the cigar into the snow and shoves his hands in his coat pockets. "No. Why would I?"

"I don't know. Because you're fond of blackmail?"

He shrugs. "With my own brother? No. Now if it were someone else and Seraphine, perhaps a pool boy, then you can bet I'd drag her and her fake French name through the mud. Just for fun. But you? I should feel insulted that you'd even assume that."

I'm not convinced. "You didn't tell Father?"

"What do you think?" he says dryly. "If I told Father, you would have heard about it right away and in more ways than one. No, really it was none of my business, and so I treated it as such. Unfortunately, with what I know and what I see now, well, you're making it my business."

"Is that why you asked me to watch her?" I ask.

He shrugs. "Yes. I was curious to see if you'd do it and you did. You did fine. You impressed me. That first night, anyway. The second night, well . . . then you decided to get involved."

I have a hard time swallowing. "You were watching me?"

"I had to know if I could trust you with all of this," he says mildly. "Now I know that I can't."

My fists clench and unclench. "You do know she was being attacked, don't you?" Then the realization of what Pascal would have witnessed comes over me. "Did you even know I'd step in? You would have seen what happened with Jones, what he did to her."

He doesn't look the least bit concerned. I'm two seconds away from punching his fucking head inside out. "I figured it taught her a lesson. He scared her, that's all—and she deserved it, with her high and mighty attitude. But your reaction right now, well, now I know that when it comes to this predicament, we can't quite trust you to do the right thing."

"And what is the right thing?"

His lips twist into a sour smile, like he ate something out of spite. "Leave her to us. That's all."

We're locked in a staring contest, and the more I search my brother's eyes for signs of how genuine he is and how big a threat to Seraphine he is, the more I can't make out anything except that he's serious.

Dead serious.

"Fine," I tell him. "Can I go now?"

"I was never keeping you," he says, suddenly blasé, the intensity in his eyes fading to nothing.

Bullshit.

I hurry along my way, and by the time I get to the office, I look like a drowned rat.

"Interesting," my father remarks as he passes me in the reception area, heading outside. "I know the cold-and-shivering look was a hit with our runway models during the spring show, should have figured you'd be the first to emulate it."

I give my father the fakest grin I can manage. "Can't help that you're so damn influential, can I?"

I turn around and head to my office just in time to see his smile falter.

I can't remember the last time I talked back to him.

Back when I was young.

Back when I was in love.

Back when I thought I knew what I wanted, and what I wanted was a million miles away from this.

When the fuck did I lose that version of myself?

When did I get so fucking *scared*?

I walk right into my office, relieved that my father left, and take out my Post-it notes from my drawer. I lean over my desk and quickly scribble something down, making a conscious effort to hunch over my writing, as if cameras from above are recording my every move.

Then I head over to Seraphine's office on the other side—fucking hell, how my father drilled in how much of an other side it was—and I knock.

"Come in," she says, sounding as tired as I feel.

I open the door to see her at her desk, talking to one of the interns, who is sitting across from her. This particular intern is exceptionally bright and has a million worthy marketing ideas that she keeps bringing to the table. She's the type of person who should be working alongside Seraphine, not me.

Seraphine's initial reaction is to look shocked to see me, but she hides it well under her professionalism. This is the first time we've seen each other since last night, and even though she has dark shadows under her eyes, she looks as beautiful as ever.

Every cell in my body pulls toward her, like my veins have been filled with iron and she's the magnet. I literally have to hold myself back and keep it together. I have to look away from those big beguiling eyes of hers—the ones I know mistrust me, the ones that sometimes hate me—and focus on the desk, on the floor, on anything else.

"What is it?" Seraphine asks tersely.

I give the intern a warm smile, and she blushes in response. At least my charms work on someone, as rusty as they are. I place the note on the desk, folded in half.

"Message for you," I say, and then I quickly leave the room before I lose my mind.

It was Pascal's idea that I start working in Seraphine's department.

I'm starting to think that it was a test all along.

To find out where my alliances were.

To see if I still cared for her.

To see if I would protest should anything bad happen . . .

Something tells me it's coming.

CHAPTER FIFTEEN

SERAPHINE

I stare down at the note in my hands.

Watch yourself. They know.

A chill runs down my spine as I say the words out loud, as I've been saying them to myself over the last few hours. After Blaise slipped me the note, I waited until I was done with work and sitting in my car before I read it. Call me paranoid, but I've always assumed there are cameras and hidden microphones all over the office.

And judging by not only the fact that Blaise had to pass me a note like we're in fucking high school but that it said I had to watch myself, I'm probably right.

They know.

I don't have to ask who *they* are.

I already know that.

He already told me.

This note is telling me something else.

What, I'm not sure.

What I do know is I spent a good hour in my apartment with the hair standing up on the back of my neck, jumping at every single sound I heard, before I decided I should go to my favorite café and be around people and civilization. I thought about contacting Blaise, but I wasn't sure how since we've resorted to paper forms of communication, and to be honest, I'm still torn over my feelings for him.

The other night, he said everything that I've always wanted to hear.

He answered a question that had been burning through me for nine years.

He became the person I always wanted and needed him to be. Not in the dreamy teenage-crush kind of way, but a man. A man who wants to protect, a man who wants to be with me, would choose me over his family.

And even though he is my cousin, that's no longer the outstanding issue between us. We're both adults, and from the world looking in, I suppose it would be strange if we ever got together. As teenagers it felt hopeless, but now, if I look deep enough, I can see there's a way out, and it has a lot to do with not giving a shit what people think.

But we still need to care what his father would think—he's only gotten more dangerous. He's become a murderer, after all. And beyond the threat of, well, death, there's the fact that Blaise might just be lying about everything.

He sounded sincere, he looked sincere, but his brother is the master of acting and deceit, and I have no reason to believe that Blaise hasn't learned a thing from him. After all, Blaise used to be the boy that hated his family. Then he ended up working for them. Now he's back to saying he hates them. I have no idea what to believe with him, but I would be a complete fool to think that he's actually placed his loyalty with me instead of them.

Who am I really to him, anyway?

Is it actually true that he was pining for me all these years, eschewing sex and relationships, carrying a torch for me while I was married?

I don't want to think about that. I know that my heart will latch itself to the idea; it will want to believe that I've had that effect on him, it will tell me that it's all I've ever wanted.

I also don't want to think about the fact that he kissed me.

That when he did, everything came flooding back, like time was held behind floodgates and finally released in a raging torrent that flowed through every hollow and forgotten bend inside me.

I was a teenager again, giving myself away with a kiss.

I was feeling all those years of pent-up sexual tension and frustration and yearning around him being let loose for the first time, and had I kept kissing him, had I not stopped him out of fear, I would have drowned.

No man has ever made me feel like that.

It's just so fucking fitting that it happens to be the man I can't have.

No—the man I shouldn't have.

Not if I expect to survive with my heart and pride and perhaps even life intact.

I'm just about out the door when my phone beeps, and I get the text I've been both waiting for and dreading.

It's from Jones.

My time to pay him has been ticking to a close, and even though I texted him throughout the day, telling him I had a cheque ready to go or the means to do a wire transfer, he never replied until now.

I thought maybe he'd forgotten.

Silly me.

Meet me by the community garden in Jardins d'Eole at eleven p.m. Bring cash.

I stare at the text, blinking.

It's not just that he wants to meet me in a park that's considerably unsafe at night, but that I have to bring cash.

169

I don't fucking have €50,000 in cash!

Fuck me. What the hell am I going to do?

Panic starts to claw up me like a wild animal.

Think, Seraphine, think.

I can only take out so much from the *distributeur*, and the banks aren't open. I do have about ten thousand in cash in my safe, but that's not going to be enough.

I start wildly looking around my apartment, searching everything I have and quickly assessing their apparent value. I have valuable art, rare printed books, handbags, but none of those things will do.

I'm going to have to give him everything in the safe.

Which includes a lot of jewelry I inherited from my mother—jewelry I don't ever want to part with.

It also includes a gun.

Not valuable cash-wise but perhaps valuable in saving my own life.

I head over to the safe, enter the code, and open it.

The handgun gleams. It's completely illegal. But my father always taught me to protect myself. He said that being part of a famously wealthy family like ours only opens ourselves up to kidnappings and the like.

If only he knew that the real threats were coming from inside the family.

I take out the gun, the jewels, the cash, though I leave behind Ernest, the teddy bear I've had since I was adopted, and I know I'm going to need help in this. Help I don't want to ask for, help that might backfire.

But if he does help me, maybe there is more to what he's been saying.

I text Blaise: Want to grab a drink? Meet me at the café at eight?

I don't know how things work, if his texts are monitored by his father or if that's even possible, but I want to be as vague as can be, and I assume he knows what café I'm talking about.

He responds immediately: see you soon.

Damn. The tiny little thrill that rushes through me at seeing that response is completely inappropriate, considering I'm not sure I can trust him and I'm about to ask for a whole load of cash to pay off a thug who threatened to kill me if I didn't.

Blaise lives in the Right Bank, almost right across the Seine from me, so it doesn't take him long to show up at the café. It's too cold and miserable outside to sit on the terrace, so I'm inside the shop, tucked away in the back corner. I'm alternating between a cappuccino and a glass of red wine, wanting a clear head but also trying to temper my nerves and my heart, which are all over the place and making me feel nuts.

I hate to admit it, but he's a sight for sore eyes as he walks toward me; his black wool coat with the popped-up collar matches his dark hair and even darker eyes.

He takes the seat across from me and studies my face for a moment before he says, "I need to apologize to you."

I should wave away what he's about to say, because I'm about to ask him for €40,000, but I want to hear it.

"For what?"

He gives me a look like, *You know what I'm talking about.* "For being inappropriate with you. Right now, that's the last thing you need, the last thing I should be doing. We have bigger problems, and acting on my impulses isn't going to get us anywhere."

He's completely right, and I'm impressed he admitted it.

Still, when he talks about impulses . . .

Stop it. Don't be a fool. You're not a teenager anymore. You're a woman with her own life in her hands and a gun in her purse.

"Luckily I know how you can make it up to me," I tell him.

He nods, his expression open and interested. "I'll do whatever it is, as long as you know that you can trust me. That's all I ask."

"How did you know I still don't?"

He shrugs, licking his lips. Beautiful lips. "Since I don't think you've ever trusted me before, I guess I'll know it when I see it."

I manage a wry smile and lower my voice. "I need forty thousand euros tonight. In cash."

He doesn't flinch. Instead he calmly opens up his coat to me and sticks his hand in an inner pocket, pulling out a very thick wad of bills. "I have fifty."

I stare at him and the cash open mouthed. "How did you know?"

"I knew how much you owed him, and I knew when you owed him. You were at work all day. I'm not sure when you would have gone to the bank, and I'm pretty sure you didn't have money lying around your apartment."

I swallow hard. "I have some cash. And I took my mother's jewelry." I gesture to the bag hanging off the end of the chair. I'm not about to tell him about the gun.

"You're not selling your mother's jewelry," he says sternly. "I promise you that. I'll take care of it."

"But how did you know he wanted cash?" I pause, trying to not let the ever-present suspicions get the best of me. "Did you talk to your father about it?"

He lets out a caustic laugh. "My father? Honestly, you're going to have to push that fucking nonsense out of your head right now. My loyalty is with you. This money is for you. I know someone like Jones would only accept cash because that's how these things work. You're essentially paying off a hit man who never got to take a shot. And that's good. Keep it that way."

I look around the café to see if anyone is listening, but everyone is chatting loudly, not paying us any attention.

"I'll give it to you on one condition," he says, sliding the bills back inside his coat.

I raise my brows. "Please don't tell me I have to sleep with you."

"It wasn't part of the plan, but I can always make an adjustment," he says smoothly, heat flashing behind his eyes.

I try to ignore that, but the tightness building in my core won't let me. "You're being inappropriate again."

"Guess I can't help it around you."

I fight the urge to roll my eyes. "So what's the problem? What's the condition?"

"That I go with you. I don't want you doing this alone."

My stomach flutters with relief before I have a chance to rein it in. I have to think about this. Yes, I want him there, and I am beyond terrified that I have to do this alone, and the gun in my purse doesn't help either. But . . . what if he . . .

No. Either you trust him or you don't.

I have to make this decision right now and stick to it.

And judging by the look on Blaise's face, that's exactly what he's thinking too.

"Okay," I tell him, and even though I'm sure I only hesitated for a second, it feels like a million years have passed. "But you have to stay in the background. Like, hidden."

"I know. He can't see me. He won't see me. I'll just be there in case something goes wrong."

I take in a deep, shaking breath. "Do you think something is going to go wrong?" I'd pick up my wine and have a drink, only I know my hands are trembling so much the wine would go spilling everywhere.

"I've never been an optimist, Seraphine," he says gravely.

"Except when it comes to me, that is," I add, testing him.

"In that case, one might confuse an optimist for a fool." He pauses, his eyes resting on my lips. "Don't you?"

If I didn't know any better, I'd swear I was blushing. It's definitely a lot hotter inside the café than I expected. I clear my throat and give him a leveling look. "Back to business. What did your note mean this morning?"

If there was any lightness in Blaise's features, it fades into something grim. "I ran into Pascal this morning. Before work. He wanted to speak to me alone."

That's never good. I quickly slam back the rest of my red wine before my hands start to shake again.

He goes on, leaning in and lowering his voice to raspy levels. "He wanted me to stop following you." That should be a relief, but I know it's not. "More than that, he was following me this whole time."

"You? Why?" What a psycho Pascal is.

"He doesn't trust me for the same reasons you don't trust me. You think my loyalty lies with him. He thinks my loyalty lies with you."

"But why?"

"Because of what I told you the other night. In Mallorca. He told me he did see us."

I blink hard. "He's known all this time?" Oh, bloody hell. That must mean the rest of the world knows.

My heart sinks to new lows.

"He knew. But he said he never told anyone."

"How can you be so sure?" I say, scrunching my face.

"I can't be but . . . think about it. He definitely didn't tell my father or your father or anyone else. We would have known by now. He just kept it to himself because he didn't think it was his business."

"That's awfully mature of him," I say slowly, and I don't care what Blaise says, but I'll never trust Pascal.

"I'm not taking his word on it, I'm just taking in the evidence that supports what he's saying is true. I don't think anyone knows. But he does. And that's why he wanted me to follow you to begin with. To see if . . ."

"What?"

"If I'd interfere with whatever they have planned."

If I was a pile of nerves earlier, then this is something else entirely. Every single part of me is at attention and frozen with fear.

It's like I can barely breathe. "What do you mean?"

He stares at me for a moment, trying to think. "I don't know," he eventually says. "I really don't. All I do know is that it's in your best interest to pay Jones and forget everything, and before you start getting worked up as you usually do and say you owe your father, why don't you ask yourself what your father would tell you right now? He would tell you to value your life over the truth. He'd agree with me in wanting you to drop this."

"It's so easy for you to say that," I say softly. God, I'm trying so hard not to lose it right now on him, especially with all that he's agreed to help me with, all he's said, but it's so damn hard. "Do you know what it's like, to know that my uncle is a murderer? That he murdered his own brother?"

"I can imagine." A line forms between his brows as he studies me. "I can imagine because . . . you're talking about my father. And do you know what it's like to know that the man who raised you is a murderer? The man you're supposed to idolize and love, the man for whom you tried to do both things and he never gave anything back? Do you know what that's like? Spending your whole fucking *life* asking for someone like that to love you?"

I exhale slowly, realizing that, perhaps for the first time, Blaise doesn't have it much easier than I do. I'm convinced his father murdered my father. He's becoming convinced of the same.

"So now what?" I ask, wanting to get the subject away from what's making Blaise go to a dark place. I can see it in his eyes, the change. I don't want him to go there. I saw him go there the other night when he beat the shit out of that guy. Tonight I need him by my side and focused and levelheaded in ways that I can't be, just in case something goes wrong.

"So now we go pay Jones and be done with this."

"But what if I can't do that? What if I can't be done with it? Then what are you going to do? Leave me? Turn on me?"

"I'm going to be by your side for all of it."

"I'll believe it when I see it."

"That's fine with me. I'm used to my patience being tested, especially with you."

I don't have anything clever to say to that. I'm starting to think I might not ever.

I finish my wine and then, to Blaise's amusement, I finish my coffee, and then we're out of the café and out to the blustery streets of Saint-Germain-des-Prés. The snow and cold rain have stopped, but the wind is blowing something fierce and the sidewalks are slippery. Before I can stop myself, I'm leaning into Blaise, and he's putting his arm around me as we walk down the street to the Uber pick-up point.

Is this wrong? I think, and for once it's not so much about whether I can trust Blaise or not, because I know now that I have to. But it's about the fact that he is my cousin, even if not in an icky way, and being this close to each other in public is something new.

But I don't let those thoughts stay in my head for very long. In a way it's refreshing to worry about that, because it feels like such a simple and mundane problem to have: the world might not approve of our relationship. The reality is, I might fucking die tonight, and I'm not sure having Blaise there is enough to save me.

Also, you don't have a relationship for people to approve of, I remind myself. *So stay fucking focused like your life depends on it, because it does.*

CHAPTER SIXTEEN

BLAISE

The car ride seems to last forever.

Seraphine sits beside me, her purse clutched to her chest like a child. She stares out the window at the passing lights of the city and the occasional hit of wet snow on the windowpanes that turns Paris into a distorted mess, mirroring how I feel inside.

I wasn't sure she'd contact me tonight. Her pride is a mountain that can't be summited, and I feared she would go to Jones trying to strike a bargain. I thought that she would rather appear meek and unprepared and naive to a bona fide thug than to ask me for help. Not to say I couldn't blame her, but it gnawed at me all the same.

Still, I was ready. I lied when I said optimism wasn't my forte. When it comes to Seraphine, it's all I've got. I figure the consequences of being wrong aren't enough to cancel out the chance that I'm right.

And now we're beside each other in this car, in the darkness of the back seat, and I am so fucking torn that it's rendering me useless.

There's fear on one hand. I don't know Jones; I just know that if my father, who has connections with every Mafia group across the globe, trusts him to do shit, then this asshole is the real deal, and he is to be feared. I have no shame in admitting that I'm afraid of what will happen when we get out of this car. Will Seraphine's life be in jeopardy? Will mine, when I step in to try to protect her? Pascal brought up all that training I did in Thailand, and though I can take most normal people on and leave relatively unscathed, I have never fought one of my father's henchmen before. Probably because *no one* fights his henchmen. You either kill or be killed. There is no fighting.

There's lust on the other hand. But it's not just the lust that I've learned to deal with over the years. The physical lust that turns you inside out, that reduces you to nothing more than an animal. It's not that, which is so much easier to compartmentalize. It's the lust of the heart. It's the yearning, the pining, wanting someone to feel the same way about you that you do about them.

Maybe it just comes down to hunting. I am forever the predator when it comes to Seraphine, not just in body but in spirit. I want to possess her heart and her thoughts and her soul the same way that she's taken ownership of mine. I want to seek out what I want and need for survival and call it my own. That's the kind of lust I'm talking about on a larger scale. The lust of craving someone's very being, of needing every single molecule that created them at some point.

Maybe I beat around the bush for too long when I was younger, maybe because I didn't know what I wanted.

But now I do know.

I know very well.

She's right beside me.

And I'm going to do everything I can to make sure she stays there.

This part of the 18th arrondissement isn't the best neighborhood, so it's no wonder that the Uber is pulling over outside a park as per Seraphine's instructions.

At this point, I'm lying low in the back seat, and she's given me but one glance as she gets out of the vehicle.

The glance said *Stay out of trouble.*

Wish I could say the same to her.

It's too late for both of us.

Somehow the Uber driver is used to weird nonsense and doesn't so much as blink when I tell him to circle around and then drop me off on the street on the other side, nearest the train tracks that lead into the Gare de l'Est.

A park beside train tracks—great location for late-night dealings.

I keep low and run quickly through the darkness until I can see Seraphine, standing around the entrance to the community garden. There is only one light above her, illuminating her and the gravel beneath her feet a faint orange color.

Smart, Seraphine. Stay where you are. Don't step out of the light.

I'm about fifteen meters away, far enough to stay hidden behind the tree line but close enough to get involved in case something goes wrong. She's looking around, up at the apartment buildings across the street, which should be a comfort, but they also look dilapidated and abandoned. If anyone lives in them, I bet they're the type to turn a blind eye to anything happening in the park across the street.

She's nervous, tapping her boots against the ground, clutching her purse, which holds the money I gave her. I wish I could trade places with her and do the deal that way, but I know that if I show my face, there will be hell to pay.

I'd venture to guess that a lot of the thugs, hit men, criminals, and dealers in this town all have connections to my father. Growing up, there always seemed to be an "acquaintance" of my father's, as he would always explain it, and they'd disappear into his study. Sometimes they would be there for a few minutes, others a few hours. Even when I was young I knew there was something off about these meetings. The men were rarely charming; they all had hard, scarred-up faces that didn't know how to smile. They looked at me like I was a cockroach and they were the shoe; all they needed was a signal from my father and it would all be over.

As I got older, as I became more privy to the goings-on in my father's life, I realized that he was involved in something far reaching. He had power beyond just being Gautier Dumont. His whole life, he'd been in his brother's shadow—the brother who had it all, was beloved by all, had the brains and the drive for the business. My father had some brains, but more than that, he had the drive for dominance and a distinct lack of morals. He couldn't compete with his brother on the business scale, but he could grow his own power through every legal and illegal channel known to him. He was born with money, and he used that money to amass more money, blood money, and then created an underground empire to rival anyone else's.

I keep out of my family's business. I always have. I know that a variety of terrible things have probably been done by my father, and perhaps Pascal too, but I've turned a blind eye. Even when I joined the company, looking and hoping for a chance to feel like I belong, I still kept out of the darkness, and they willingly kept me out.

They see me as an outsider, just as they see Seraphine as one. They don't trust me, and I don't trust them. But that willful ignorance can only go on for so long.

I know now, as I stay crouched behind these bushes, the bare branches of a maple tree above me, that I've drawn a line in the sand. I won't stand by and let my father frighten Seraphine to death, or whatever it is he planned to do through Jones. I won't pretend anymore that he's a man not capable of murder, because I know he is. Life is pretty good at throwing things you instinctually want to ignore, just to preserve yourself, preserve the life you've carved out for yourself, your way of seeing the world. Change is scary, and when it's time to confront something big, most of us pretend it doesn't exist.

I can't do that anymore.

And if I can't help Seraphine prove that my own father murdered his own brother, then I want nothing to do with this family anymore.

I don't want to be a Dumont. I don't want to add to the legacy. I want to throw my name away, quit my job, start again.

I want to do that with her.

Somewhere far, far from here.

In fact, the longer that I'm watching her waiting in this darkened park, the more I know what our next steps are. She has to pay Jones, there is no question about that. If she doesn't, there will be consequences that I can't help her with. But after this, my life in Paris is over. And with any luck, I'll convince her of the same.

Jones approaches her from the left. His footsteps on the gravel are so silent that Seraphine doesn't hear him coming.

She spins around at the last moment, and I can tell it takes all of her not to scream.

"Do you have the money?" he asks, holding out one hand.

Seraphine nods anxiously and reaches into her purse, pulling out the wad of bills and quickly placing it in his hand. "It's all there."

He glances at it. "If these turn out to be counterfeit . . ."

"Surely you can tell right now from glancing at them whether they are or not."

She's getting attitude in her voice.

Not a smart move, Seraphine. Keep it meek.

"Hmmphf," Jones says, tucking the bills into his jacket pocket.

Then he continues to stare at her, legs in a wide stance, hands clasped at his stomach.

"What?" she asks. "Do we have some other business?"

"I want to know what you have planned next."

"What do you mean?"

Just then a cry rings through the air, enough to give me a heart attack. But it's just some drunken bum on the sidewalk between them and the road, pushing a cart down the street and yelling at no one.

Jones jerks his head toward the trees, in the direction I came from. "Let's step away for a moment."

She stiffens, doesn't move. "We're done."

"We aren't," he says calmly, but the intensity in his eyes says something else. "We aren't done until I say we are, you understand? Now come here, away from the road. You want people to know that you just paid me fifty thousand euros to try to off your uncle?"

Her eyes bug out. "That's not what it was for," she cries out softly. "You know it wasn't."

"I'm just saying, it's easy to twist things around. I'm very, very good at it, among other things. And believe me, you don't want me to prove any of it."

Don't do it. Don't follow him, I think frantically. Other than me, that light is her only hope.

"I'm going to run away," she threatens. "I'll scream."

He looks mildly amused, raising his brow. "That will save you only in the meantime. I guarantee you'll be dead before you get back to your apartment."

She's hesitating. I know she wants to look for me, but that would be a giveaway.

"I'm not moving," she finally says, but she doesn't sound as determined as before. "I gave you the money. We have nothing more to discuss."

I'm holding my breath, ready to spring into action if needed. I don't stand a chance against this guy normally, but he doesn't know I'm here, and if I can catch him off guard . . .

"Fair enough," Jones says. He gives her a nod and then turns around, walking away toward the street, in the opposite direction he came. "Hopefully our paths won't cross again."

Seraphine watches him go, tense and unmoving, until it looks like Jones has disappeared behind the wall that runs along the garden.

Then she carefully looks around for me.

Just in case Jones isn't out of earshot, I don't want to call to her and draw attention to myself, so as she walks away from the light and farther into the trees, I stand up and hurry through the bushes to her. My plan is to grab her hand, and we'll run to where I was dropped off, head a good distance away before we call for a ride.

But just as I'm about to break through the bushes into the clearing where she is, two men emerge from the trees, one from the side of her, the other from the front.

She lets out a cry of shock, and then she realizes as quickly as I do that these aren't random men. Both are tall, dressed head to toe in black, with close-cropped hair, blank faces you couldn't pick out of a lineup.

Much like Jones.

Disciples of his.

The first man reaches for Seraphine, and she opens her mouth to scream, but then the other clamps his hand around her mouth. They both pull her back into the trees as she's kicking and trying to free herself.

I don't think.

I just move.

In seconds, I'm at them.

I get to the first guy at her side, winding up for a lead hook that I know will only get his attention. I punch the side of his face, getting his cheekbone. Because I surprised him by coming out of nowhere, he drops Seraphine and is slow to face me, so I get him at the back of his knee with a fake low kick that brings his attention down to the ground, then I pivot around in a circle with my other leg out, striking him with a high kick to his chest.

He doubles over, but I'm already moving past him and bringing my forearms up to block the fists of the other attacker, parrying against him and protecting my head as he swings. He's bigger, so one hit nearly sends me flying, the world growing darker for just a second, but I come back at him with an uppercut, striking his jaw before I slip out to the side.

I'm rusty, and I know that the element of surprise has already worn off. I haven't practiced in a while, though when I was living in Thailand, Muay Thai had become like my religion.

But back then I was lost and looking for something to sustain me. Now I'm fueled by anger.

The purest, most devastating power there is.

I don't even feel much pain as the other guy comes at me from behind, clocking me on the back of the head.

I fall to the ground but land in a plank position, and I'm able to spring to my feet just out of the way of one of their kicks.

"Run for help!" I manage to say to Seraphine, who is scrambling to get up, free of their grasp. But focusing on her has taken my focus off them.

The other guy gets me right across the face with an elbow strike, and that's when I know he knows Muay Thai too. Of course he does— every guy now wants to be the next MMA fighter.

Blood is running into my eyes, pouring from my head where I know he's split the skin, and though my world is wavering from the hit, my instincts are still right on the money.

I duck another hit, then jump backward, getting enough power through my shuffle to strike a knee right under his rib cage.

He gasps, doubling over, but doesn't fall.

So close.

Before the other guy can come at me, I slip left and then deliver a palm strike to the same spot where my knee hit him, clinch my knee up into the same area, almost a bull's-eye; then, while he's winding up to hit, I quickly place my hands against his chest, pushing back to give myself enough room, and go in for a head kick, striking him full force against the side of his face.

He whirls around from the kick, almost a one-eighty, blood spraying from his mouth, and he goes down to the ground on his knees.

If I'm going to get out of this at all, I have to take one of them out, unconscious, because I can't keep fighting two guys at once. I am good, but together they're better.

I leap into the air and bring my body weight down with my elbow to strike right where his neck meets his shoulder, knowing that will put him out, but just as I make contact and feel the tendons on his shoulders snap, I'm tackled from the side.

This is the bigger guy, the guy who can take a beating, and he's straddling me, striking his elbow against my solar plexus repeatedly until I can't breathe. When my instincts seem to dry up, I try to remember my training on how to get out of a maneuver, knowing I have to twist my body, and when his hands go for my neck, squeezing tight enough to break my windpipe, I think I might be able to twist free and do an elbow strike to his face, but then my thoughts slow.

There's no more air left in me.

It was a race to see if he could weaken me before I could fight back, and I think I'm . . . I think I'm . . .

Hold on, hold on, don't close your eyes.

The blackness is coming for me, right from the trees, like a phantom.

"Stop it!" Seraphine's voice comes through the darkness, and I know I have to fight back for her. I know that if I die, she'll be left with them. She probably won't survive. They'll probably rape her, torture her, and I'll have to die knowing that my own father had this ordered.

And this guy doesn't care that she's yelling. He doesn't hear what she's saying.

She's saying . . .

"I'm going to blow your fucking brains out!"

He doesn't hear that.

But I do.

With what little strength I have left, I tilt my head to the side to see Seraphine holding a gun with both hands, aimed at my attacker.

She glances at me quickly, and there is so much fear in her eyes that I'm not sure she'll be able to do it.

But she does.

She pulls the trigger and there's a blast of light, and she's thrown back a step and the guy screams, right above me, blood splashing on my face.

He lets go of my throat and falls over, screaming, holding on to the side of his neck.

She didn't blow his brains out, but she did a lot of damage.

I don't even have the strength to wonder where the gun came from; all I can do is focus on getting enough air back into my lungs to get out of this situation.

"What have I done?" Seraphine says, clearly in shock.

I manage to get to my knees, eyes closed, breathing in and out as much as I can, ignoring the pain in my throat, and then her hands are under my arms, trying to haul me to my feet.

I stare at the gun in her hands and can tell she's about to throw it into the bushes. "Take that with you, don't ditch it."

I glance back at the guy who is holding on to his neck and writhing on the ground, and I see the other guy starting to stir. I have no idea if he will die or not, if his friend will save him, or how close Jones is to all this. I'm guessing he's in a car around the corner, waiting for them, waiting for their collected prize.

"We need to get out of here," I tell her, taking her gun and slipping it into my coat pocket. Then I grab her hand, and we start running as fast as my beaten body will allow.

We stagger through the trees to where I had been hiding and then follow the tree line that borders the railway tracks along the back of the park, not looking back.

We're about to cross the road when the screech of wheels fills the air, and a black SUV rounds the corner, followed by another. This isn't the police coming to the rescue—this is something else. They aren't here to save us.

I wait, trying to figure out the best option. If we run through the streets, the chances of Jones and whoever else my father has on speed dial finding us are pretty high, and I'm not sure how long it will take to find a cab or wait for an Uber.

So I wait until there's a break in the action, and I pull Seraphine across the street the other way, heading to the apartment building that looks abandoned from the outside.

"Where are we going?" she whispers as we run up the slick stone stairs to the main door. All the apartment names next to the buzzer have worn off, and when the door opens, I'm not surprised.

We step inside. There's a broken chandelier above the foyer with only one broken light. The place is damp and dirty. I lead Seraphine over to one of the two doors on this floor and try it. It's locked. Same with the other.

"What are you doing?" she hisses at me. "Blaise, we need to call the cops. We need to . . . oh God, I don't know. What if I killed him?"

I give her hand a tight squeeze. "We need to get somewhere safe before we can think about anything else, okay?"

I lead her up the stairs to the second level, to the empty apartment I spied from down in the park earlier.

It's also locked, but I knock and wait. The sound of our breath fills the space in the hall.

I put my ear to the door and listen.

Silence.

I take a chance.

I run my shoulder up against the door in a jab and it flies open, the lock weak.

Just as I thought, it's empty except for a threadbare love seat and a coffee table with a broken leg. A thick layer of dust coats everything and has scattered into the air like snow. I reach for the lights, and only one comes on, in the kitchen. It's weak and won't stop flickering.

Seraphine stands in the middle of the room and stares blankly at the studio apartment. I close the door behind us and then get the love seat, pushing it up against the door since I broke the lock coming in.

Then I head over to the window, keeping a low profile and staying close to the wall. I sidle up along the side of the shutters and peer out.

There is one SUV farther up the street, and I can just make out dark shadows passing underneath the light in the park. Then some of the shadows disperse, heading out along the streets in different directions. They run right past this building, which makes me relax just enough to be able to think about our next move.

I leave the window and head to Seraphine, who is still standing in shock, shaking from head to toe.

"Hey," I say softly, placing both my hands on her shoulders. She flinches, eyes wide as she looks at me, like she forgot I was here at all. "You're safe now. You're going to be okay."

She shakes her head violently. "I . . . I shot that man. I killed that man."

"You don't know that," I tell her, trying to get her to meet my eye. "And even if you did, you had to do it. He would have killed me, and then he would have killed you, and you know that's what would have happened."

But she's not looking at me. She's staring at nothing, eyes wide, chin trembling.

"You're okay now," I tell her again, squeezing her shoulders. "I've got you. Okay? Nothing bad will happen to you, we just have to stick together and figure it out. For now, we're hiding in here. His men are searching the streets right now to see where we would have run. After a while they'll give up and we can leave, but for now, we have to hide."

"No ambulance came," she says. "Why didn't they call an ambulance for him?"

"Because these guys don't operate on that side of the law. You do know that they were meaning to kidnap you. Fuck knows what would have happened if I hadn't been there. And if you hadn't brought that gun. I'm not even going to ask where you got it, I'm just glad you had it and had the guts to pull the trigger."

"I was aiming for his head," she says softly. "I missed."

"It doesn't matter. You stopped him. You saved us both."

Finally she meets my eyes, reaches for my forehead with a shaking hand. "You're bleeding." Her fingers gently press near the wound, as if she's trying to see that I'm really alive. "Oh God, Blaise." The way her gaze stops at my brow and my nose and my eye tells me that I'm not looking too handsome at the moment.

"I'm fine," I tell her, and truly the pain isn't sinking in yet. I'll deal with it when it comes. "Just a few scratches. I've been in worse."

"You actually fought them off."

I wince. "Not really. If I had, there would have been no need for your gun. I'm sorry you had to use it."

She blinks at me, taking it all in. Then her eyes widen in shock, overwhelmed and lost. "What happens now? He, Jones, he's still out there. They're going to come looking for me, for us."

I nod. It hurts to swallow. I'm sure I have bruises up and down my throat. "I know. We have to plan our next moves really carefully."

"I can't go back to work. I can't go to my apartment. He's going to kill me. Your father is going to kill me."

"I'm not going to let him do anything to you. I promise." My words come out sharp and harsh, but I desperately need her to believe me. I won't ever let anything happen to her from now on, and if it comes down to my father, then I'll kill him myself if I have to, if that's the only way we can be free.

"I'm alone," she says before she gasps, her hand dropping from my face and going to her chest, starting to breathe erratically. "I'm alone, I'm alone. Oh God, I can't breathe, I can't fucking breathe!"

She drops her purse, starts pulling off her coat, shaking it from her like it's covered in snakes. The apartment has no heat, it's freezing cold, and I try to put the coat back on her, but she pushes me away. She pushes so hard against me that she goes flying backward onto the ground.

"Fuck!" she yelps as I get to my knees beside her. "Fuck!" she screams again, her eyes pinched closed as she starts to wail, crying and convulsing with sobs.

"Hey, hey," I say to her softly, trying to bring her up, cradling the back of her head with my hand. "It's okay."

"It's not!" she cries, tears streaming down her face, lit only by that flickering kitchen light. "I'm alone! I'm alone, I'm alone, I'm alone." She keeps shaking with each ragged sob, trying to catch her breath. "I'm alone, I'm alone."

"You aren't alone. I'm here."

"I'm alone!" she yells louder. "Oh God." She makes fists in my coat, holding on to me for dear life. Through her tears she looks at me, and I see so much pain in her eyes that all resolve and strength I have breaks.

I'm shattering for her inside.

"I have no one," she says, wild eyed and gasping. "No one. My mother and father are dead. My birth parents are gone. My brothers are on the other side of the world. I've been abandoned over and over again. I have no one at all, no one to love me, no one to want me, no one to take care of me. I have nothing."

I try to swallow, trying to keep it together for her even though my own forgotten emotions are threatening to engulf me once and for all. "You have me," I say emphatically, holding her head in place, searching deep in her eyes, looking for a sign that she understands. "Even if you don't want me, you have me."

This seems to make her still. She blinks at me through her tears. "How can I know? How can I know, Blaise? How can . . . how can I believe you?"

"You just have to take that leap and believe me, Seraphine. That's all. It's all a leap anyway, everything in life. I'm not just on your side, I'm not just here for you . . ." I place my hands on her face and hold her. "I love you."

Words I never thought I'd say out loud to anyone hang in the air. They are words I have never tested before on my lips, words I'd always swept away if the emotions came calling.

Now she's in shock. At least she's stopped crying.

I take in a deep, shaking breath and go on. "I love you, and I've never loved anyone before. Never said it to anyone. Never even thought it. Because ever since you came into my life, those words have belonged to you, and they've been waiting and waiting and waiting for the chance to be heard. So do with them what you like. But I'm in love with you, and I will do everything in my power to make sure you never feel alone and unloved again."

She's still staring up at me in awe, and I'm still holding on to her face, but I won't kiss her; I won't subtract from the moment, I won't dampen what I said. I want her to feel those words and wear them and decide how it makes her feel.

I'm giving her all the power, all the power she's always deserved.

I stare at her, waiting, and her eyes flash with something that might be anger, might be a slap in the face again.

But then it isn't.

She's kissing me.

CHAPTER SEVENTEEN

Seraphine

I don't know what's come over me, but I'm not about to dissect it, question it, or rip it apart.

There is no space in my brain.

There is no room for those feelings.

I'm on the floor in this cold, dirty place, and I feel like I could sink into the dusty floorboards, let it engulf me or spit me out.

I only have one anchor here.

My hands are wrapped around his neck.

My lips press against his, open and hungry and dying for something to take me away from this night, take me away from who I am.

He told me he loved me.

I need to sink into those words.

I need to believe them.

I've heard them before.

From Cyril.

From the men before.

Maybe a man after.

But not like this.

Not with the conviction of a man on death row, a man who knows he only has the truth and nothing left to lose.

And so I kiss him like I have nothing left to lose too.

Because I don't.

I kiss him and kiss him until he's really, truly kissing me back, and I feel all the power of him take over, the way he grabs my wrists and pins them back against the floor, the way he takes my lower lip between his teeth and tugs hungrily, grunting and moaning and filling me with so much fuel that I'm afraid I may just combust.

"Blaise," I say breathlessly.

But there isn't much more to say. Nothing I can convey with words. I almost died tonight.

I need him to make me feel more alive than ever.

My hands go to the bloody collar of his shirt, the wound on his head bleeding less now, and I try to undress him as he tries to undress me. We're both a wild mess of torn, bloody clothing and feral appetites.

He rips my blouse down the middle, the buttons popping until they expose the lacy trim of my bra.

I gasp and his lips start nibbling up the tender soft skin of my swells, then pulling the flimsy lace aside until my nipple is exposed.

He licks and teases and flicks and sucks until I'm groaning and gasping and holding the back of his head against me so he can't escape, so he can do this to me forever.

My eyes are closed, and I'm drowning in the feeling, and then he's tearing the rest of my clothes off me until I'm like a dog on the floor, rolling around in heat. I feel his fingers grip me beneath my elbows, and I'm brought to my feet. I can barely walk as I'm led over to the decrepit love seat, barely in charge of my limbs, barely in charge of anything.

At this point, I just want to be taken.

And Blaise takes me, he takes me and possesses me like that's the only thing he was meant to do.

I'm naked before him, legs spread and panting. Totally vulnerable.

But this kind of vulnerable is different from what I felt earlier.

This vulnerable is something I want him to see.

He told me he loved me.

I'm telling him I'm his to take.

I run my hands down my thighs and spread them wider, watching the hunger in his face turn into something uncontrollable; I'm pushing him to lose control.

Take me, I think. *Make me yours.*

Undo this mess.

And he does.

He does by removing his bloody shirt and then his pants and socks and shoes until he's completely naked, standing before me.

I've never been with him like this before.

Had I known he was sculpted the way he is, I wouldn't have pushed him away to begin with. I certainly wouldn't have second-guessed any of his martial arts training in Thailand, because the man is fucking ripped, every single hard and rippled part of him.

And of course there is his cock, long and hard and thick, which made me blush when I was younger and now fills me with a wild sense of need.

This is so fucked up.

I'm his cousin.

He's mine.

Family, if there ever was such a thing from one side to the other.

We're both naked and succumbing to our desires.

But if it felt wrong at one point in our lives, all I know is that now it feels right.

All we might have needed is each other.

Blaise places his strong hands over my hips and helps to lift me up over on his lap as he sits back on the love seat. I straddle him, feeling his cock jut out between us, hungry for him.

He grabs my breasts hard, kneading them before taking my nipple into his mouth and going at me like a wild beast.

I groan, head thrown to the ceiling, back arched, giving him access to every part of me. I've never felt so exposed and explicit, but I'm vibrating on a whole new frequency now.

Taking control, I put my hand against the back of the love seat, taking on the weight, and then I lift myself up so I'm just brushing against the tip of his cock. It feels lush and wild and taboo, and I'm still so aware that I should be curled up in the corner and crying, yet everything is making sense. This desire is just the desire to live and the need to be with the one person that makes me feel like I'm alive.

Blaise grabs the base of his cock, the whole length jutting out in front of us, and I meet his eyes.

They aren't full of the same chaos that surrounds me.

They're full of something obsessive and singular.

Me.

Because he's only wanted me.

I hold the couch as I slowly and carefully lower myself onto his cock, knowing he only wants what I'm giving him.

I've never felt so free.

His eyes go back in his head as I slide down, pushing on the ridge of his cock.

His lips part.

He moans.

He looks like he's been transported to another planet.

And then he opens his eyes and fixes them on me, and I know I'm not his version of a drug den.

He sees me.

Every part of me.

He sees me and he wants me. His hands slide down my waist to the curve of my hips, and he holds on tight, moving my body up and down and up and down until there's a rhythm.

And where there's rhythm, there's magic.

And where there's magic, there's belief.

Belief that I can escape this night and everything I've been feeling, everything that has been torn apart can be put back together again.

With him.

Only with him.

I rock on top of Blaise's stiff and commanding cock until his fingers find my clit, and his mouth comes up to taste my skin. Then I'm just a swirling mess of emotions, close calls, sins, and renewals, and I know that Blaise isn't just someone who will make me forget everything that happened now and before now and forever.

He will remind me that it happened.

And he will remind me of who we are in the midst of chaos.

This is my chaos.

This is my Blaise.

This is me, coming so hard that I can't speak, that I'm bucking and I'm feeling, and no matter what has happened, I know I'm alive.

I'm alive.

CHAPTER EIGHTEEN

BLAISE

I wake up on the love seat, naked, with one leg on the floor. Seraphine is lying on top of me, her head on my chest, her black hair spilled around her like silk. My coat lies on top of both of us.

The air is cold, and I can see my breath when I stir, yet the heat between the two of us is palpable. I lean my head back toward the window and see the sun just starting to rise above the buildings of the 18th arrondissement, filling the cold, empty, stark room with a warm glow.

Seraphine begins to stir, and I run my palms down the naked planes of her back, feeling the dip and rise of her curves. My dick is already hard as a rock and pushed up against her. I fight the urge to just start fucking her again, because now that we're in the clear light of day—in an abandoned apartment, no less—all the dangers and worries and fucking craziness of the night before come flooding back. The sex was something I'd dreamed about, and it was better than my dreams, but while we gave in last night, those wants and needs have to be shoved aside for now.

This is a matter of life and death.

And I need to keep my promise.

To never let her feel alone. To protect her and keep her safe.

To keep loving her.

I close my eyes and drift off a little, warmed by my thoughts, until she stirs again and lifts her head.

I open my eyes and stare right into hers.

"Good morning," I say softly, pushing her bangs behind her ears.

"Good morning." She gives me a small smile. "I honestly didn't think we'd make it through the night."

"But we did," I tell her. "And naked too."

Another quick smile, this one fading as she looks at the window and the rising sun that makes her brown skin gleam like gold.

There's nothing in this world more beautiful than her, not even a million rising and setting suns.

"We should probably get out of here." She gets off my body as I try to sit up, and she's quick to pull my coat around her shoulders, shivering. She stares down at me, naked. "Though with you, you wouldn't know it's cold out at all."

I glance at my cock, still hard and throbbing, the hard, thick ridge of it spanning up to my stomach. The more she stares at it, the more I want to grab her and make her ride me, maybe throw her up against the wall and fuck her until she's crying my name.

God, this is fucking impossible. How can I be around her after this and not want to keep feeling her inch by inch from the inside?

"Blaise," she says, clearing her throat, looking me in the eye. "We can't . . ."

"Can't what?" I challenge, ignoring everything I had decided before she woke up. My willpower has been thrown out the window. "Don't pretend that you didn't like what happened last night, that you didn't want it." I pause as fear washes over me, the fear that last night was it and won't ever happen again. At the moment it's just as powerful as the fear for our lives.

I know that look in her eyes. She's trying to find a way to argue because arguing with me is what she loves to do best, perhaps even more than fucking me.

"Speechless?" I ask, getting to my feet.

I walk over to her, my cock bobbing in front of me, not minding the cold, and I grab her gently by the back of the head. "Just because you're not talking doesn't mean I don't know what you're saying," I say gruffly, pulling her lips to mine.

The coat slips off her shoulders to the floor, and I press my body against hers, her soft skin against my hard torso, my erection against her hip. I kiss her softly at first, but that quickly turns to hunger, a ravenous, wild sort of hunger not unlike last night.

That feeling that each moment we have with each other might be the last moment we ever have.

I know she feels it too.

I can tell by the way she kisses me back, matching me with wild abandon.

Her hands disappear into my hair, making a fist, and I bring my mouth to her neck, biting and licking and kissing down to her shoulders until her head is back and she's moaning breathlessly.

We don't have a lot of time.

All we have is now.

I reach down and shrug her plump ass into my hands and then pick her up, spinning her around until she's pressed up against the wall. Her legs wrap around my waist, and I grab my cock, guiding it into her.

She's slick as sleet, and I slide into her with one hard push, the breath leaving my lungs as I fill her to the hilt.

"Fuck," I swear hoarsely, pushing her up against the wall as I slowly pull out. I glance at her face, our noses rubbing against each other as we succumb to every note of pleasure.

She stares at me through her long lashes, mouth wet and open. Even though danger lurks outside these walls and our lives have been forever changed, what we have right now between us is more powerful, more raw, more primal than anything. It's overriding the fear and replacing it with connection, that deep-seated need we have for each other, that tells us we belong.

I belong with her.

And she with me.

Just as it always should have been.

With each hard, strong thrust as I pump inside her, with each squeezing pulse as she wraps herself around me, together we rock each other until we're heating this cold place with just our bodies. Sweat rolls off my nose and drips onto her chest, and her fingernails dig into my back, and I spread my legs, steadying us as I rut faster and faster.

I'm close to coming, and I slide my fingers down over her puffy wet clit and press, swirl, and tease, and then she's gasping, breathless, greedy.

"Blaise," she cries out hoarsely, and I close my eyes because she's never cried out like this before, never said my name with such need and reverence, and it's something I never knew I needed to hear.

"I'm coming," I say through a groan, kissing the side of her mouth, her jaw, her ear, and then she's coming.

Her cry is choked off, and she starts quivering, her limbs jerking as she pulses around me, hot and wet and tight and . . . heaven.

"Fuck me," I cry out, the words escaping me as the orgasm sneaks up on me and nearly takes me out. I do what I can to stay upright, to keep rubbing her clit, to keep thrusting my dick deep inside of her, harder and harder and harder until I'm sure we're going to go right through the wall.

When we're finally done and she's milked everything out of me, I gently lower her to the ground, and she nearly falls over on shaking legs.

I hold on to her arm, keeping her steady. "Easy," I tell her.

She glances up at me, her cheeks flushed, lips red and wet, eyes shining, and I don't think I've ever seen her look so beautiful.

"You made me forget how to walk," she jokes softly.

"Glad I have that ability," I tell her. "And I'll be happy to make you forget over and over again."

She grins at that, showing her perfect white teeth, and then it fades as she picks up her clothes, clothes that are dirty and torn from last night's fight. My own are splashed with blood. Thank God our dark coats will cover up everything.

Reality has come knocking.

It's just outside this door.

It's waiting for us, and we have no idea what to expect.

We dress quickly and soundlessly. She goes to use the washroom but looks disgusted when she's done, which suggests things in this apartment have been untouched for a long time.

Even though our rocking moved the love seat, it's still blocking part of the door, so I move it out of the way.

We step outside into the hall. There is some sound in the building, the soft murmur of a TV from the apartment across, and I guess we're just lucky that the sound of us fucking didn't make anyone think twice, although I wouldn't be surprised if most places in here are used for exactly that.

We make our way downstairs and out the front door, looking up and down the street. I expected to see police cars, maybe investigating the sound of a gunshot or the spilled blood in the park, but there's nothing. It's cold and calm as the city slowly wakes up, and birds are calling from the trees.

"It's like it never happened," Seraphine muses quietly.

"We both know it did," I tell her, opening my Uber app on my phone. "Now, do you have a friend you can go stay with for today?"

She looks at me in shock. "A friend?"

"Yeah. Someone to harbor you and keep you hidden."

She stares at me for a few seconds, and it's like everything is becoming real to her. "I can't go home."

I shake my head and grab her hand, holding it tight. "I know. That's why you need to go to a friend's house. Or call Olivier and see if he can arrange something for you at one of his hotels, but you can't go home right now."

"What about your place? Where are you going?"

I look off into the distance and frown, not liking what I'm about to do. I exhale loudly. "I have to talk to Pascal." I pat the side of my coat where the gun is. "And I won't leave until he listens to me."

Seraphine clutches my arm. "Don't be stupid."

"I'm his brother. He has to listen to me."

"Don't be so naive, Blaise! He'll throw you to the wolves. Fuck, he *is* the wolf!"

"Even wolves can be tamed," I tell her. "So give me an address."

"I won't let you do this alone."

"You have to let me. This is the only shot we've got."

She stares at me pleadingly, the pale morning sun bouncing off her face. Her breath hangs in the air as she speaks. "You said you'd never let me feel alone again."

Fuck. She's got me there.

I lean in and kiss her hard, my features contorting as I feel everything, just everything. I pull away, holding her. "This is the only way we can be together. If I don't do this, we don't stand a chance."

"You mean I don't. You're not the one who had one of my father's henchmen try to abduct you."

"No, but whatever happens to you happens to me. Besides . . . don't you think by now that the men talked? That they gave my description to Jones, and then Jones gave my description to my father? I'm surprised he's not calling me right now. Maybe he thinks I'll walk into work like nothing's happened, my face busted up like this, and sit right down at the conference room table."

"And that's exactly why you need to—"

"What? I need to do something, Seraphine. If you think we can just go on the lam like Bonnie and Clyde, the family version, then you're not thinking clearly. I have to set things right, and I can't do that until I know you're safe. So please, I need an address." I wave my phone at her.

She closes her eyes, her lips moving though no sound is coming out. Finally she says, "Marie. My friend Marie. She'll still be home, she doesn't go to work until ten. She lives in the thirteenth arrondissement." She opens her eyes and takes the phone, scrolling through the map until she enters the Nationale métro stop into the address bar.

It turns out there's an Uber just around the corner from us.

We get in the car, and it takes forever to reach Marie's place; it's on the other side of the city, and the morning rush hour is thick.

"Are you going to your apartment first?" she asks me.

I shake my head. "I can't risk it. People could be waiting for me."

She studies me, frowning deeply. She glances at the driver and then leans in, whispering, "Do you really think your father won't hurt you?"

I shrug and give her a sour smile. "He's done it before, remember? I'm sure he'll have no problems now, when I actually deserve it."

She eyes my coat, where the gun is resting against my side. "Are you sure we're not better off with the police?" she says, keeping her voice barely audible.

"Did you learn nothing from last year? From the car chase with Olivier? We reported it to the police, and they did nothing. They did nothing because it's like it never happened. That's what my father can do. One word and it's like everything . . . and everyone . . . disappears. He has everyone in his pocket."

"Except you."

"Not anymore."

The Uber driver must have caught some of what we're saying, because he's eyeing us in the rearview mirror with interest.

I take it as a sign to shut up.

Eventually we get to Marie's neighborhood, and I make sure that Marie comes to the door to greet Seraphine and let her in the building just in case.

Seraphine looks back at me in the car and nods stoically, trying to be strong in front of her friend. Marie peers over at me, concerned, then maybe almost happy to see me, and then the two of them disappear inside.

I lean back in my seat and breathe out a long, rough sigh.

"Bad night?" the Uber driver asks.

"You can say that again."

"Are you not getting out?"

"No, I'm afraid not. Not yet. Can you give me a minute?"

I know the drivers hate having to go to a new destination on the fly like this, but I need to make sure I'm going to the right place.

I make a call to the office and get the receptionist, Nadia.

"Nadia, it's Blaise," I say. "Is my father or Pascal there? By the way, don't tell anyone I'm calling."

"Okay," she says brightly. I guess she's used to the eccentricities of the Dumonts. Probably why she's still working for us. "Your father is in his office. I don't know where Pascal is. He hasn't come in yet, but he's usually here by now. Where are you and Seraphine?"

"Uh, I've got a dentist appointment. I don't know where Seraphine is. I'm sure she'll be in."

"Okay. Will I see you later?"

"Of course. And if anyone asks for me, tell them I'll be in then."

I hang up and decide to take a shot. I lean forward and tap the driver on the shoulder. "If I pay you extra, are you up for taking a drive into the country?"

"Where in the country?" he asks me suspiciously.

"Just outside Versailles. Take the A-13 to Saint-Nom-la-Bretèche."

His face says it all: *No fucking way.*

I sigh and reach into my wallet, pulling out €500. My wallet has been a revolving door of cash lately.

I wave it at him, and his eyes follow it like it'll disappear if he doesn't. "This is five hundred. This is for taking me there, dropping me off around the corner, and waiting for maybe an hour. Is that okay?"

He nods, eyes widening. "Yes. That's fine."

I give him three hundred and put the rest in my coat pocket. "That's for now. You'll get the rest later. And if you can get us there quick, well, that would be great."

"No problem," he says, straightening up and pulling away from the curb. "Though I do have to say, if you're willing to spend that much on Ubers, you might as well buy yourself a car."

"I hate to drive," I tell him. The truth is, I'm not about to chance going back to my place and getting my car. I'm not trusting anything at the moment. Do I really believe my own father would put a car bomb under my car? Probably not. But Jones could be operating on his own now.

Hell hath no fury like a hit man scorned.

CHAPTER NINETEEN

BLAISE

By the time the Uber pulls up alongside the country lane, a few meters from the entrance to the driveway to my family's estate, I'm a mess.

It's not just that I don't know what's going to happen next.

And that I don't know what I'm going to do.

It's that Seraphine hasn't answered any of my texts over the last thirty minutes.

She had been sporadically, saying she was sitting with Marie in her kitchen and having coffee and that Marie would be going off to work soon, but now it's like radio silence. I've tried calling a few times, too, but it goes straight to voice mail. I can only hope that she's just busy, as she should be.

Planning a new life for herself.

A life that hopefully includes me in it.

Everything has changed so much and so fast, I'm not sure when we'll ever be able to come up for air and make sense of what happened.

And if I don't play my cards right as Blaise Dumont, we may not come up for air at all.

I stick my hands in my coat pockets and hurry down the lane. Out here, the fields are full of frost, and though the birds are singing, the sound is muffled. It's overcast and gloomy, and the chestnut trees look deader than ever before. It's like spring doesn't exist for a family like us.

I head up the long and winding driveway, passing underneath the skeleton trees, then head straight for the front door.

I ring the bell and wait. Pascal's Audi is in the driveway, so I know he's definitely home. I wasn't about to phone him to make sure, so the gamble to come out here has paid off.

For now.

I ring the bell again, and when the door finally opens, I expect to see one of the housekeepers who live in the servants' quarters at the edge of the property, but to my relief, it's Pascal. I want to be completely alone with him.

He doesn't seem surprised to see me, but he fakes it.

"Blaise," he says, brows raised. "Why are you here? What the fuck happened to your face?"

"Got in another bar fight. I was hoping to have a word with Mother."

"She's not back yet," he says warily, taking in my busted features.

I knew that, of course. Our mother has been at a fitness and wellness resort in Portugal for the last two weeks, which I know is code for plastic surgery and liposuction. She'll come back thinner, with a face tighter than an elastic band, and she'll blame it all on yoga. "Shouldn't you be at work?"

"Shouldn't *you* be at work? I just came from there."

He frowns, trying to figure out if that's true or not. "I wasn't feeling well," he says. He looks over my shoulder at the driveway. "Where's your car?"

"I took an Uber," I tell him.

"Why?"

"Can I come in?"

I put my arm against the door and hold it so that he can't shut it on me. I make sure my body is wedged in there and that I'm looming over him, hoping to intimidate him.

He doesn't intimidate easily. "Something wrong?" he asks, holding his ground until he eventually relents and lets me walk in.

He closes the door behind him and turns to face me. "Well?"

I don't say anything. I don't know what to say. The gun is burning a hole in my pocket.

My expression must be saying something, because he seems to be a bit on edge now, his posture straighter, stiffer.

"Blaise?" he prompts.

"I need to talk to you," I tell him. "Brother to brother."

"Okay . . . isn't that how we always talk?"

This isn't going to be easy. I really hope to use the gun as a last resort. I have no plans to shoot him, I just need it to threaten him if things don't go the way I want.

I have a feeling they won't go the way I want.

Not with Pascal already on the defensive. I don't know if he has a gun; I'm going to assume he does, but he's already very slowly making his way back into the study.

The cane is still leaning against my father's desk.

The sword inside.

Interesting. He obviously knows that this isn't a friendly visit between two brothers.

"Come in here and talk, then," he says, gesturing to the study and heading for the desk.

He leans back against it, legs crossed at the ankles, seeming ever so casual as he reaches for the cane, as if he fiddles with it out of habit. Perhaps he does.

I stop in front of him, just far enough so that the sword couldn't reach me, not about to let my guard down and sit down.

"So what do you want to discuss?" he asks carefully, slowly twisting the horse's head around and around.

"Pretty much what I told you before," I say. "I want to quit."

His brows knit together. "So then quit. I'm not stopping you."

"And I need for you to get Seraphine a job at the new office in Dubai."

Now I have his attention. His eyes widen. "What the hell are you talking about? Dubai?"

"We just opened an office there. I think it would be a great environment for her."

He flips the cane around in his hands, still frowning. "And why are you speaking for her?"

"I think you know why," I tell him calmly, even though I'm anything but calm inside.

"Are you saying I should reward my cousin by giving her an even better job than the one she has right now? And what would I be rewarding her for? The fact that she thinks our father is a murderer? The fact that she will do anything to prove that he is, even if it means throwing one of us under the bus?"

"She's not throwing me under the bus," I tell him. "And depending on what you did and your involvement, she won't throw you either."

"What I did?"

"Where were you last night?"

"Here," he says.

"And let me guess: Father can back you up?"

"And the help."

"Also under your payroll."

He studies me for a moment, his grip tightening on the cane. "What are you getting at, Blaise? You want to try to set me up for something I had nothing to do with?"

"It's just that you said you had been following Seraphine when I was following her. So I have reason to believe that you were following us last night when Seraphine made her payment to Jones."

He shrugs. "I wasn't there."

"Do you know what I plan on doing to you if I find out you were there?"

It's like he perks up at that threat, like a fucking dog. Seraphine was right about him being a wolf. "Do tell me what you plan to do. I would love to know."

My gaze hardens. "Were you there or not? So help me God, tell me you didn't witness everything that happened to us. Tell me you didn't see what they did, that you didn't watch it all unfold and didn't say or do anything."

"I don't know what you're talking about."

"That's bullshit."

"I don't."

"You know what happened!" I scream at him, spit flying from my mouth. "You knew she was meeting Jones, you knew what was going to happen to her!"

He swallows, shakes his head. "You need to calm down."

"Calm down?" I yell. "I don't think I'll ever fucking calm down again!"

I reach into my pocket just as he slides the sword out of the cane.

But before he can bring it around to point at me, I've got the gun aimed at his face.

And my hands aren't shaking.

"What the fuck," Pascal cries out. "What the fuck is wrong with you, a gun? Get that fucking thing out of my face."

"Drop the sword. What the fuck do you think you are, a musketeer?"

But he doesn't drop the sword, and even though I don't need to cock the hammer, I do so anyway, for emphasis, my finger firm on the trigger. "I said drop it," I repeat.

I've never seen him so taken aback before.

Good.

He shakes his head in disbelief and then drops the sword and cane so both clatter at his feet.

"If you try and reach for that, reach for anything, I'll fucking shoot you. I might not blow your pretty-boy head off, but I'll make sure it fucking hurts."

"Blaise, you have lost your damn mind," he says roughly.

"I haven't. I'm thinking more clearly than ever. So I need answers. I need them now. Tell me what you knew about last night, and I'll tell if you're lying. You pride yourself on being such a good actor, but let's just say this gun is like a truth seeker."

"I was here last night."

"But you knew Seraphine was meeting with Jones."

"Yes," he says hesitantly. "I knew she was going to pay him and then hopefully drop this whole thing."

"And how did you know that?"

"How do you think? Father told me."

I take in a deep breath, trying to put out the fire I have rising inside me, the anger that wants to lash out at the mention of my father. I have to keep a cool head, especially when I've got the barrel of a gun aimed at my brother's face.

"What did he tell you, exactly?"

Pascal doesn't say anything, his mouth pressed into a thin white line.

I aim the gun at a point just off his shoulder and pull the trigger.

The blast reverberates throughout the room, the bullet going straight into a book, hopefully a rare edition of some bullshit.

"Fuck! Blaise!" Pascal screams, and I have to delight a little in scaring him. That's not easy to do. "Calm down, okay, just calm down."

I cock the hammer again for show and grin at him with no love left. "My patience is being tried, brother. What did he tell you?" I grind out the words.

"Okay, okay," he says, raising up his hands. He licks his lips. "He said that he wanted to scare her. To rough her up a little."

My heart is beating so loud in my head it's like I've got a drum inside me.

"He said what?" I eke out, my hand starting to shake just a little from the pure fiery anger. "He wanted her roughed up?"

Pascal nods slowly. "I don't know what happened. I just assumed that meant maybe, uh . . . maybe . . . he—"

"You knew that Jones was going to fuck her up, and you were okay with that? Ignore the fact that she's your fucking cousin, a girl you grew up with, she's a fucking woman! What the fuck is wrong with you?"

"I don't know!" he yells. "I didn't think it would be bad; maybe just a slap, maybe just to scare her. He just wanted to scare her, okay? I know that much, and I was okay with that because she needed to be scared, okay? She needed to know she had to knock it off before it was too late."

"And what the fuck is considered 'too late' to you? Huh? Because if I hadn't been there to stop them, then it would have been too late. Do you understand what you're dealing with here? Do you understand just what you let happen?"

"Whoa, hey. No," he says, shaking his head. "I didn't let anything happen."

"You did. They fucking attacked her. Two other guys, trying to drag her off to a waiting car. What do you think they were going to do with her, huh? Give her a slap?"

"Maybe they were random thugs."

"They weren't random thugs, they were with Jones—Jones, who threatened Seraphine right after she gave him the money. Don't try to justify this. You knew they wanted to scare her, you should have known that scaring meant rape and possibly murder."

"Father would never—"

"He would!" I yell. "He would and he has before."

"Oh God." He sneers with a roll of his eyes. "Not you too."

"Yes. Because I'm not a fucking sheep. I'm not blind, not anymore. We both grew up in this house knowing what he was capable of. Somewhere along the way you decided you wanted to be just like him."

"Wait. No. I am not just like him," he protests, shaking his head and coming toward me.

"Get the fuck back!" I put my other hand on the gun and aim it right at his forehead. "Don't you fucking make me shoot you, because I will. Just to *scare* you."

Pascal freezes and then immediately backs up against the desk. "You're going to be in a lot of trouble."

"No, I'm not. And frankly, I don't fucking care about your threats. Or Father's threats. When I'm done with you, I'm walking away, and I'm walking away with her."

"What are you, in love with her?"

"You know I am," I say, and there's nothing but truth and conviction in my voice.

"It will never work."

"That's none of your business. As you said, it never was. And it never will be. I'm in love with Seraphine, and when I leave this place, both of us are leaving Paris for good, and you're going to set it up so that we're never bothered, never followed, never threatened again."

"I can't do that," he says in disbelief.

I fire the gun again; this time the bullet goes over his other shoulder, slicing through another rare book. I think that one might have been Dickens.

"Fucking stop it! Just stop it!" Pascal yells, covering his ears. As he moves, though, he goes for the desk, sliding open the drawer and reaching for something.

I don't take the time to guess what it is.

I leap over the desk, using it as leverage, and drop-kick him right in the chest so he goes flying back against the books.

He scrambles for the drawer again, and I strike up with my knee until he's doubling over, falling to his knees. I bring my elbow down on his shoulder until he's fully collapsed on the floor and then pistol-whip the back of his head. Serves him right for making fun of me and my Muay Thai training in Thailand.

I reach down and pull him up by the collar, pressing the tip of my gun into his temple. "Now you listen to me, brother," I growl in his ear. "You're going to do everything I've said, and I'm going to let you live. I probably won't even shoot you. Roughing you up a little, just as you wanted Seraphine roughed up, actually feels pretty good."

Pascal doesn't say anything, he just moans.

I push the gun into his head harder. "I mean it. I want Seraphine and me to walk out of here, and I don't want to see you, or Father, or Mother ever again. I want nothing to do with the Dumont name; as far as I'm concerned, I'm no longer part of the family. Maybe I never was." My heart is racing so fast but so hopeful with the possibilities of starting over. "I want Seraphine to have the head job in Dubai, and if she deems it not acceptable, then she's free to do whatever she wants. But the point is, both of us are free."

"Then you tell her to stop blaming Father for Ludovic's murder," he mumbles.

I laugh bitterly. How naive can he be?

"She'll stop," I tell him. "She'll stop because she'll have no choice. You and Father will be free to do whatever the fuck you do here, but we won't have any part of it, won't have any ties to it."

He doesn't say anything for a moment. Then he says, "Fine."

"Is that a promise?" I ask, and when he doesn't answer, I haul him up to his feet, pressing him against the books with my forearm against his windpipe, the gun at his head. "Tell me it's a promise. Or else."

"You'll shoot me," he says, wincing. "As if I were never your brother."

"No," I tell him. "Seraphine will share the files I've been recording since I got here. From my phone in my pocket. The microphone picking up everything, it's going straight to the cloud that she has access to. She's in a safe place. Maybe you've bought the Parisian police, but she can take this to the tabloids, and you can bet they're just dying to run something against the great team of Gautier and Pascal Dumont. A murderer and an accessory."

"You wouldn't dare," Pascal whispers, but there's fear in his eyes. He believes me, even though I actually lied through my teeth. My phone isn't recording, and I can only hope that Seraphine is safe.

"I'm starting to think you don't know me very well," I tell him. "But I'm always willing to prove myself. Now promise me that you'll sort something out for us, because if you don't . . . I will ruin your whole life, and that's going to hurt a lot more than a bullet to the head."

He closes his eyes and sighs. "Okay."

Just then the sound of crunching gravel comes from outside.

I continue to hold the gun at Pascal's head, and I drag him over to the windows and peek outside.

My father is home.

And it's not just my father.

It's him and Jones and three large men. More disciples.

Two of them are from last night.

One of them with several layers of gauze wrapped around his neck, hunched over and in pain.

So Seraphine didn't kill him after all.

Shit.

Now I wish she had.

Pascal and I exchange a glance.

You know them? his look says.

215

I bring him back over to the desk and sit him down, then I crouch down under the desk so I'm hidden. I keep the gun trained on him and whisper harshly, "Handle it."

Pascal stares down at me, maybe calculating how fast he can turn me in and if I'll shoot him before that. Then he glances up at the door as the front door opens, and I hear the men step inside the house.

"Pascal?" my father's voice says, echoing in the hall. "What are you doing in the study?"

I have my head craned up at Pascal, watching his face carefully, waiting for him to give a nonverbal signal to our father that his crazy son is under the desk with a gun.

But so far Pascal just shrugs, easily playing back into his lackadaisi-cal attitude. "Wanted to pretend to be you for a while." He then frowns as his gaze goes from my father to someone else who walked into the house. "Is everything all right?"

"No, everything isn't all right," my father says, sounding tired and on edge. "Have you heard from Blaise?"

I hold my breath. This is it. My brother could rightfully turn me in and take a chance with a bullet.

He shakes his head. "No, why? He wasn't at work?"

"No," my father says. "Listen, we have a major problem on our hands, and I'm going to need your help with it. In case you haven't met before—I can't remember these days—this is the infamous Jones. These other guys, it doesn't really matter—the only thing you need to know about them is that two of them were involved in a fight last night in Paris."

"I can see that," Pascal says evenly. Even though his face and upper body are cool as a cucumber, he's tapping one foot right beside me. It's a light, quick movement, and it's enough to tell me that he's actually nervous as hell.

That makes two of us. I'm starting to think I won't come out of this alive.

Maybe Seraphine was right.

"What happened?" Pascal goes on.

"He was shot."

"Shot?"

"By Seraphine."

Pascal's eyes widen, and his shoe-tapping stops. I didn't tell him that part.

"Sorry . . . you said *Seraphine* shot him? How? Why?"

"You know why," my father says gruffly.

"Then tell me again because I don't remember that part," Pascal says, frowning slightly.

I hear my father sigh, and I can picture him dragging his hand down his face. "Let's just say the roughing-up part didn't work out as planned. She fought back. And more than that . . . I think Blaise was involved."

"What makes you say that?" Pascal asks as he tilts his head, surveying the men.

A throat is cleared. I hear Jones speak: "When I met with Seraphine, she was alone. She was on her guard. She wouldn't come with me. So I had my men here try to take her. They say a man came out of the bushes and started fighting them."

"Could be any good Samaritan."

"What a lovely world it would be if that were true," Jones says. "Except most random strangers aren't trained in martial arts, and this guy was good enough to handle these guys. Or at least one at a time. When Seraphine pulled a gun on them and shot Rufus here through the neck, I knew the two obviously knew each other."

"Do you know where Blaise was last night?" Father asks.

At least now I know that Pascal was telling the truth about staying home. He hadn't been watching it all unfold. I probably would have killed him had I known he'd stood by and let it happen.

"No," Pascal says. "Are you sure it was Blaise? Why would he be involved with Seraphine?"

Hmmm. The way he says this makes it sound like he truly never discussed the relationship between Seraphine and me. Part of me would feel relieved, if only I could feel relief right now, crammed under this desk, the gun slick under my sweaty grip.

"I have suspicions I won't dare let myself think about," my father says. I notice he doesn't outright say that he thinks I'm in love with her or we're having an affair. He might only suspect those, but it's an embarrassing thing—for him—to admit in front of other powerful men. "But Blaise is soft around the edges, and Seraphine has no one. It's possible that she went to him for help."

"But she suspects you of murdering your own brother," Pascal points out. My father snorts at that, like it's amusing, like it's true. "How could she know that he'd believe you did that?"

"Oh, come on, Pascal. We both know that Blaise is a waste of space in this world."

Pascal stiffens. My fingers tighten around the gun.

My father goes on with his insults. "The only reason he came back to work for us was because he wanted the status symbol. I understand that. Living in Thailand and whatever else the fuck he was doing, that gives him nothing. No name. Nothing to show to the world. Try as you might, after a while, being a Dumont is all that becomes important. It's the legacy and the bloodline that pulls you back in. You can try to escape it, but it turns out you can't. And that boy has been trying to escape who he is for his entire life."

"Doesn't mean that he'd throw it all away for his cousin."

"Perhaps he's more like her than us. Maybe he should have been Ludovic's son, pathetic and weak. I don't know what it means. But I know what we have to do now."

I swallow and wait. Whatever he says, I'm not going to like. I just have to hope that Pascal doesn't like it either.

"What?"

"We need to take Seraphine out of the picture."

My father's words have extra weight in them as they hang in this cold room. As angry and hot as I was earlier, now I feel the pit of my stomach turn to ice. Not that this was unexpected, but to hear him say it like this in front of Pascal . . .

I watch my brother carefully. One of his hands is by his knee, and he's clenching and unclenching his fingers around the material of his pants.

Pascal blinks at him for a few moments. "What do you mean, 'out of the picture'?"

"You know what I mean," my father says, voice lowered as if he is being recorded in his own house. "And you don't need to worry about it. I just need your help."

"What do you want?"

"I need you to contact her and bring her to me."

Pascal gives a twisted smile. "She won't go anywhere with me. She hates me."

"But she's soft and you're family."

"I don't think you know her like I do, Father, but she is not soft. She can be a vicious little bitch."

I can't help but smile. *Thatta girl. You've been scaring Pascal all this time.*

"Then you deal with it. You're the charming one. You bring her to me, use force if you have to."

Pascal swallows uneasily. I wait with bated breath, not knowing what he's going to do or say. Is he going to go along with this as he always does, or is he actually going to do the right thing for once? I don't think Pascal has ever done the right thing in his whole entire life.

"This isn't really part of my skill set," he goes on carefully, trying to be funny and deflect. "That's what you hire those guys for, isn't it? I'm more of the subtly-terrorize-and-stalk-people variety."

"We don't have a choice. She's going to turn us in."

"Us? What the fuck do I have to do with any of this?"

"You let it happen," my father says smoothly. "Don't you dare think for a second that I don't have all the evidence in the world to pin Ludovic's death on you. Because I do. We're Dumonts, after all. Double-crossing is in our nature. A good father prepares for the fact that one day his son may not want to do as he's told."

"But what evidence?" Now Pascal is sweating. "I had nothing to do with it."

"We know that. Other people don't, and I can easily make it so that it looks like you did. So fucking easily, Pascal. Now, are you going to get Seraphine for me or what?"

Pascal stares at him, and he's breathing hard, his hand clenching until it turns white.

Our father is actually blackmailing him.

The tables have turned.

At one point I would have found it amusing that Pascal, for all his shifty dealings and power plays and actually blackmailing our cousin Olivier, is now being blackmailed by my father.

But it's not amusing.

It's sad.

And absolutely frightening to know just how far my father will go to keep going; he'll throw his most beloved son, his wolf, to a pride of lions.

"I have a better idea," Pascal says evenly, as if my father's words had no effect on him at all. "Less messy, more legal."

"What?" my father asks after a beat.

"Transfer Seraphine to the new office in Dubai," he says.

My eyes widen in surprise.

"What? Why the fuck would I do that?" my father practically spits out.

"It's easier. It won't raise any questions. It will keep her out of our hair. She'll gladly go, I know she will."

"This doesn't solve our problem of what she's trying to do."

"It will. Look, she's just one woman."

"Not when Blaise is involved."

"I'll talk to Blaise about it. I'll get him to reason with her. Seraphine is scared, okay, I guarantee that. She shot a man. That's what someone who thinks they're going to die will do. You did your job and you scared her. She's not going to continue to poke around; she's learned her lesson."

"And how do you know this?"

"I've worked with her long enough to know that she's human. She will preserve her own life. Let her think what she wants about us, but if she goes to Dubai, she'll drop it."

"Her love for her father is extreme."

Pascal presses his lips together in thought. "I don't think it's extreme. I think it's normal. For a normal family. Not for us."

"Not for them either. They aren't normal. They have everyone fucking *fooled*," Father says. "You know what my brother did to me, don't you? Your saintly uncle? You know why he deserved to die?"

I still, not knowing what he's going to say.

Pascal shakes his head. "Not really."

"You were there on Mallorca," he says. "And you didn't pick up on it."

"There's always something going on—"

"Right. Well, anyway. Don't go ahead thinking that their side is the good side. It's not. They share the Dumont name too. The same wicked blood pumps through all of our veins, only we're the ones who aren't scared of being who we are. We embrace it. They do it in secret and pretend to be good. It's all a mask, son, all a mask."

"Seraphine isn't even related."

"And that's why she has to go."

"She will go. I'll make sure of it."

There's a pause, and I hear my father's footsteps on the parquet floors, coming closer to the desk. "I'm not talking about Dubai."

"You should be. I know your emotions are all mixed up right now," Pascal says, his posture stiffening as my father gets closer and closer to him, to me. "But it's the smart thing to do. Forget about it being the right thing—it's the smart thing."

My father stops in front of the desk, and I hear it creak as he leans on it. I see his shadow fall as he leans toward Pascal, staring him right in the eye.

I freeze. If I move, there's a chance that my father will pick up on the movement out of the corner of his eye, and I have zero doubt that I'll be killed. If he's willing to blackmail his favorite son, he's willing to kill the one he hates.

But I'm also willing to kill him.

"What a world we live in," my father says in a low voice. I can see the bottom of his throat move as he talks. "You telling me what decisions to make. Smart ones, no less."

Pascal doesn't shrink. He holds his ground, stares right back into our father's eyes. "There's a first time for everything," he says.

"Right," he says, and the staring contest ensues.

I can't even breathe, I don't fucking dare.

If he looks down at all, he'll see me.

He'll see me and I'll have to shoot him and maybe even kill my own brother, and then I'll have to fight the rest of them, and then I'll be dead too.

And then Seraphine will be dead.

And our legacy will come to an end.

Maybe that's the way it's supposed to be.

But then my father reaches forward and patronizingly taps the side of Pascal's cheek. "Okay."

He stands up straight, and I don't dare exhale because he would hear me, but at least I'm hidden by the desk again. "If the men come back empty handed, then we'll send her to the Middle East."

What men?

"What men?" Pascal asks.

"We sent some men to find her."

"I thought . . . I thought you wanted me to kidnap her? Bring her to you?"

My father laughs. "Oh, son. You really thought that I'd have to rely on you? I know you're soft too. I just wanted to see where you stand on the whole thing. And it's fine, really, I don't expect you to be exactly like me. Roughing your cousin up, you didn't seem to have a problem with that. Kidnapping, maybe. Kidnapping that leads to death? Perhaps that's where you draw the line."

"Where is she?" Pascal asks, saying what I wish I could ask, what my heart is lurching around in my chest over. "She wouldn't be dumb enough to go to her apartment. Or Blaise's."

"Jones?" my father asks.

"We had some men check out their apartments," Jones says coolly. "They weren't there. So we started going through Seraphine's contacts. The men are checking them out as we speak. If not a friend, then perhaps her brother's hotels."

Marie.

They're going to know about Marie!

"So we'll see," my father says. "If they find her, well, I guess you don't have to get involved with that, Pascal. You can cover your innocent eyes. But if they don't, okay. She's off to Dubai. But you would have to make sure she doesn't have any contact with us and, more than that, that she doesn't keep sticking her neck out. She has to drop this. You say she's scared and she's learned her lesson—well, I'm taking your word on it. But if you're wrong . . . well, you know what the consequences will be. And it won't be just for her. It'll be for you too."

"And Blaise? What do we do about him?"

He sighs. "I don't care. If she's gone, then it doesn't really matter. Maybe he'll go with her. Maybe he'll stay here. As far as I'm concerned now, he's not my son and he's not your brother. You understand that? If he's going to take Seraphine's side over ours, then we have no choice but to cut him loose. This is his decision, you see. He can't matter to us if we don't matter to him. We'll take him one day at a time."

If I get out of here, I'll spend the rest of my life making sure that I'll never see these two again.

I have no family, except for Seraphine.

And that suits me just fine.

Only there's a chance now I won't have her either.

I wish I could check my phone, that I could call her, text her of the danger, but I can't risk any movement. Not now.

"Now," my father goes on, "if you'll excuse us, we're going to need to use this room for our meeting."

Oh fuck.

Pascal seems to freeze. "Oh yeah?" he asks, slowly getting to his feet. "You want him bleeding all over here?"

There's a shuffle and a gasp.

"Jones, he's making a mess on my floors," my father snaps, and I can only assume that the guy Seraphine shot is losing a lot of blood. My father is incredibly anal about his office. Thank God he hasn't noticed the bullet holes in the books yet.

"I think we should maybe take him to the hospital," Jones says.

"You mean the vet?" my father says. "Because I know that you're probably on every hospital's most-wanted list."

"He's about to pass out."

My father grumbles. "Fine, fine. Take him. I'm going upstairs to take a shower now. Pascal, don't go anywhere, I'm not done talking to you. And go to the servants' quarters and get Charlotte or one of those other lazy fucking maids to clean this shit up. I want it gone before I come back down."

"Fine," Pascal says, and I watch his expression as the men leave the room. I hear shuffling and footsteps and then the front door closing.

His eyes then go to the left, probably watching my father head upstairs. Then they go to the right, out the window. I hear car doors slam and then engines start and then wheels crunching gravel until I hear nothing at all but the sound of the pipes groaning as the shower upstairs is turned on.

Then Pascal looks down at me. "You better get the fuck out of here," he whispers.

For the first time, I lower the gun. My arms and hands are screaming from stiffness.

There's a moment of vulnerability when he steps aside and I try to scramble out from under the desk, and then he's grabbing my arm and helping me up.

We stand, facing each other.

Brother to brother.

Maybe for the last time.

"Did you mean what you said?" I whisper. "About Seraphine in Dubai?"

He nods. "Get out of here. Go to her. Now."

I hold his gaze for a second longer, trying to see the humanity inside my brother's cold eyes.

When I find it, I know.

As quietly as I can, I run across the study, nearly slipping on the spilled blood, then go out the front door, carefully closing it behind me. I check up and down the driveway, and then I slip my gun back into my coat pocket and take out my phone, running down the long winding driveway as fast as I possibly can, trying to call Seraphine.

CHAPTER TWENTY

SERAPHINE

"Do you have a phone charger I can use?" I ask Marie. "My battery is almost dead."

"Of course," she says, coming over to me and taking my phone and bringing it into her bedroom. When she comes back out, she's shaking her head.

"What?"

"I just can't believe this, Seraphine," she says. The teapot starts to whistle, as if emphasizing her disbelief. She heads into her tiny kitchen and takes it off the burner. "What you say is fantastical. It only happens in movies."

"If my life is a movie, it's horror at the moment," I tell her as she pours us tea.

I wasn't sure what I was going to tell her when I got to her apartment. Do I tell her that I shot and possibly killed a man, even if it was in self-defense? Do I tell her that I spent a night in an abandoned apartment and slept with Blaise? Do I tell her I was part of an attempted kidnapping?

I decided to go with the last one. I told her that I was in a lot of trouble, that I was on the right trail and getting in over my head. I told her about Cyril and Jones and paying €50,000 last night, then I said that men had attempted to kidnap me.

Then I told her I needed a place to hide out for a few hours.

Suffice to say, it's a lot for her to believe.

I don't care at this point if she does or not.

I just need to stay alive.

"But you have to go to the police," she says, bringing the cups of tea and putting them on her coffee table. The sight of the steam rising and the sound of the mugs clinking against the glass are so banal, so soothing, so normal, that for a moment it tricks me into thinking everything is all right.

But it's not.

"I can't," I tell her again. "I told you, he has them under his thumb. Did you know what happened to Olivier, Blaise, and me last year? Just when I started to suspect my uncle? He hired someone to run us off the road. That's how my car got totaled, it had nothing to do with a guy running a stop sign. This guy was trying to kill us. I reported it to the police, but they waved it off. The only reason we weren't all killed is because my uncle discovered Blaise was in the car with us. Though I doubt that would stop him now," I add under my breath.

"But your uncle, he's so powerful. He has so much to lose," she says, blowing on her tea. "Why would he risk this?"

"Because he's also a fucking psychopath. A narcissistic monster. He thinks he's above everyone, including the law, and especially his brother and his family."

She sighs, shaking her head. "I don't know what to say. I think you need to go to the police. You have to try. When I get back from work, that's what we'll do. Together. Until then, you can hide out here."

"You do believe me, don't you?"

"I absolutely believe you. But I don't think you have anything to hide from. They did let you go, didn't they?"

"I escaped," I say carefully. As much as Marie is my friend, if I tell her I shot someone, I think she might kick me out. Harboring a fugitive and all that.

"Escaped," she repeats. "Again, this is like a movie."

And now she's looking at me like I might be the delusional psychopath.

"And what about Blaise?" she says. "He was with you? Where did he go?"

"He went to talk to his brother. I think."

"Why was he with you again?"

"He's on my side."

She raises a brow. "I thought you were bitter enemies."

"We were . . ." I trail off and pick up the tea, taking a tepid sip.

"'Were'? What happened?"

I shrug delicately. "I guess we got to know each other. He's not like them."

"And you can trust him?"

I give her a brave smile. "I trust him with my life."

For a moment I'm hit with the images, him fucking me up against the wall in that cold, dirty place, bringing light and warmth to my heart in a time when it feels like I have nothing left.

I trust Blaise with my *life*.

I trust him with everything I have.

He saved me yesterday in more ways than one.

He loves me.

And I know, in my heart of hearts, that I love him.

That I always have.

God, I hope he's okay.

I don't know what I'll do if he's taken away from me.

"Hey, I need to go to work," Marie says, glancing at the clock on the microwave and putting down her tea. "Remember, you can feel safe here. I'll text you from work, to check up on you. Okay?"

228

I nod, feeling a wave of nausea run through me, my nerves twisting inside my stomach. I don't want to be alone, but I don't have a choice. It would be pathetic to ask if I could go with her to her job. Blaise was right. This is probably the safest place for me.

"Okay," I tell her. "Don't worry about me."

The look on her face says it all: too late for that.

She gets up and grabs her purse, and then she's gone, locking the door behind her.

I try to take a sip of my tea, but my hands are shaking so bad I'm spilling. It's a wonder that I hit that guy at all last night. And yet the moment I saw that Blaise was about to die under his hands, I knew what to do. All fear went away. I pointed the gun, and I pulled the trigger, and even though my soul is warring with me over potentially taking someone's life, I also know that I had no choice. Blaise did what he could to save me, and I did all I could to save him.

For now, it's worked.

I get up, shaking my arms out, trying to calm my racing heart, and go over to the window, looking out.

I spot Marie leaving the apartment.

Just as two large men dressed in matching black suits push past her, catching the door before it has a chance to close.

I know beyond a doubt that those two men are coming for me.

Marie knows it too. She looks up at the window and sees me staring down at her. Even though I'm on the fourth floor, I can see the fear in her eyes, the realization that I was telling the truth. Then the determination to help me.

She goes into the building after them.

Oh God.

I run away from the window and over to the door. They're going to reach me before she does, unless she passes them on the stairs. Do they know who she is, what she looks like? Do they know she's my friend?

I don't know what to do. Barricade the door? Wait for her? How do I know who is out there?

Shit, shit, shit.

Panicking, I look around the apartment. It's small and tidy, with Marie's minimalist style. The only thing I can see to help would be the bookcase full of books that her TV sits on top of.

I quickly pick the TV off and start pulling the bookcase away from the wall. It's heavy, but that's what I need. I push it across the floor, wincing, as I know the bookcase is making deep scratches in her beloved hardwood.

I push it up against the door, using all my strength, and then hold it there, waiting.

I hear footsteps coming down the hall outside. Heavy and echoing.

Oh fuck.

They're getting here before Marie.

The footsteps stop outside the door.

I suck in my breath.

Someone knocks on the door.

Loud.

I don't say a word.

Now someone bangs on the door.

"Hello?" a deep voice asks.

"Shoot the lock off," another voice says.

Shit.

Shit!

I glance at the lock and slowly move out of the way in case a bullet comes flying at me.

The floorboards creak loudly under my feet.

I freeze.

"Did you hear that?" the deep voice asks. "Someone's in there."

There's a pause, and I know they're getting ready to either smash down the door or shoot their way through it, and either way, I'm dead. I'm dead.

Then . . .

"FIRE!"

Marie's muffled voice screams through the apartment building, and before I can figure out where she is or what she's doing, the fire alarm goes off.

It's so loud that it makes me jump. It vibrates through the whole apartment.

"Fuck!" one of the men outside yells, and then everything explodes into chaos as people start screaming and doors start opening, and I can tell from the shouts and the stampede of feet that people are rushing out of their apartments, trying to figure out what's going on.

"Come on, there's a fire!" someone yells, and I know they're talking to the men. "Get moving!"

"There's someone in this apartment," one man says.

"No, there isn't; Marie would be at work," the neighbor says, sounding suspicious. "Who are you again? Do you live here? I've never seen you around, and I remember every face."

God bless that neighbor for questioning them, because I hear their footsteps fall away, and when I take a chance and lean up over the bookcase to look out the peephole, I can see the two men going down the hall, the neighbor—an older woman—following them like an escort.

Now I know there's no fire, that this was a clever diversion by Marie.

I run to my phone and see a million texts from Blaise and a few missed calls since it's been charging. My heart leaps into my throat, thinking something has happened to him, until I see the last text.

Get out of there! There are men coming for you.

Are you okay? Please answer me.

I'm heading to Marie's.

I breathe out a sigh of relief and lean back against the wall.

He's alive. He's okay.

He's coming to get me.

I can only hope that the men have dispersed, especially as the police and fire trucks show up. I can hear their sirens beyond the shrill noise of the fire alarm.

I can also hear someone knocking at Marie's door.

My heart skips a beat.

"Seraphine!" Marie yells from the other side.

Thank God.

I look through the peephole to make sure she's alone.

With what strength I have left, I push the bookcase to the side and open the door.

She rushes inside, locking it behind her, and immediately pulls me into a hug.

"Are you okay?" she cries out.

I nod. "Did you pull the alarm? That was genius."

"I didn't know what else to do. God, Seraphine. Those men. They were after you, I know it."

"I know it, too, they wouldn't leave either. One of your neighbors practically scolded them."

"Madame Langlois. About time her nosiness became a blessing." She heads over to the window and peers out. "I don't see them out there, but the fire trucks have arrived. They're going to come through the building."

"Then I think we're going to have to get an escort out. Blaise is on his way."

I bring out my phone and quickly text Blaise back. I'm okay. Marie pulled the fire alarm. We have to leave the building and I'm not sure if the men are still there or not.

He responds immediately. Okay. I'll come by with an Uber and you guys get in right away. Is there a back entrance to the building?

I look at Marie. "Is there another way out of here?"

"There's an emergency entrance, but the fire alarm sounds when you open it."

I give her a wry look, since the alarm is already going off. "Then they probably went out that way. I don't think they're going to risk being seen by going out the front, not with the cops and firefighters showing up."

"You're right," she says. "I think I hear the firemen now."

She goes to look through the peephole, and I text Blaise back.

We're going out the front. It's safer in a crowd. We'll get a fireman escort. See you soon.

Marie opens the door to two firefighters in their gear, staring at us. "Are you okay?" one asks.

"We panicked," Marie says. "We didn't know where the fire was."

"So far we can't find any sign of one," he says.

"We're still scared. Can one of you escort us through the building?"

"I will," the other firefighter volunteers. He's younger and has an appreciative look on his face as he looks Marie over.

Whatever. We just need to get moving.

We follow the young firefighter as the other roams the hall, knocking on doors, and others are running up and down the stairwell. I feel bad that they're here for no reason, but it did save our lives. And as I look at Marie as she talks with the fireman, flirting with him, I know she thinks it was worth it too.

Once we're outside, there's chaos, but I manage to scan the crowd of apartment dwellers, firefighters, policemen, and lookie-loos, and I don't spot the men in suits anywhere.

I don't know how long we stand outside, the firemen and police checking the building from top to bottom, being extra thorough, though the more I stand outside, the more I feel like a sitting duck with a target on my back.

After what seems like forever, a white Toyota pulls up beside us, screeching to a halt, and the back door opens. Blaise is inside, waving me in.

I look at Marie. "Are you going to be okay?"

"Are you?" she asks.

"I think so." I look back at Blaise and then to her. She's gazing up at the firefighter, and I know that no matter what happens, she's no dummy. If she sticks around him, she'll be fine.

"Text me," she says. "We'll get through this. Whatever you need, I'll do for you. I love you."

"I love you too," I tell her, ashamed for a moment that I even thought she would ever turn her back on me. Then I quickly get in the back of the car.

I've barely closed the door before the car is pulling away down the street and Blaise is pulling me into his arms. "Seraphine, Seraphine," he whispers. "I thought I lost you." He cradles my face in his hands and kisses me over and over again.

I wrap my fingers around his coat collar and bury my head in the crook of his neck, breathing in deep. His smell, his warmth, the fact that he's alive and I'm alive, and in this moment in time, we're safe.

We're together.

"What happened?" he asks, and I lift my head to stare into his eyes. God, how could I have ever thought that his eyes held anything but love for me? I see it now, clear as day. "Did you see the men? Are you okay?"

I nod, trying to keep from crying, the fear of everything slamming into me like a fist to my chest. "They came as soon as Marie was leaving. She saw them, she knew they were coming for me. I locked the door, but they knew I was in there. Then Marie pulled the fire alarm. It was the only way out."

"Your Marie sounds like a good friend."

I nod. "Yes. But . . . how did you know they were coming?"

He closes his eyes and pinches the bridge of his nose. "I had quite the morning." He looks up at the driver in the rearview mirror. "We're not being followed?"

The driver grins at him. "No, sir."

It's only then that I realize it's the same driver from earlier this morning. "How long have you been in this Uber for?" I ask Blaise.

"He's starting to feel like a long-lost friend."

"Most exciting morning of my life," the driver says.

"And where are we going?" I ask Blaise. "What do we do?"

"We're going to a hotel outside Paris. We'll take a few days to figure it out."

"What can we possibly figure out?" I ask.

But Blaise just gives me a tight smile, and I realize that as much as this driver has been a big help to us, he's not ready to hear everything.

I close my eyes, rest my head in the crook of Blaise's neck, and fall asleep.

CHAPTER TWENTY-ONE

SERAPHINE

The Uber ends up taking us to Disneyland Paris, which is far outside the city. When we pull up outside of one of the Disneyland hotels, I look at Blaise, and he just gives me a small smile, his eyes shining brightly for the first time in what feels like forever.

"I figured when it feels like our world is ending, we might as well spend it at the happiest place on Earth. Besides, I don't think anyone would look for us here."

I don't dare argue. As soon as we get out of the Uber—it looks like Blaise has handed the driver the entire contents of his wallet, plus a business card—and we're enveloped in the sprawl of the resort, surrounded by happy families and laughing children running around in costumes, it really does feel safe. It feels normal.

We don't have any luggage, but the front-desk person doesn't seem to notice, though she takes a second glance at Blaise's black eye and bruises, and soon we're heading up to one of the suites at the top floor.

The moment the door closes behind us, I nearly collapse to the floor. Blaise locks the door, and then he's at my side, pulling me into an embrace and kissing me wildly.

There are so many questions going through my head, so many unknowns, but they all dissolve into dust the moment I feel his lips on mine. The adrenaline that was surging through my body is now funneling into the desire for him and only him.

Always only him.

All we've been through in the last twenty-four hours is coming out in surges and waves, and just like last night, I'm craving the release, needing the escape, wanting that connection to him.

His hands pull my coat off, and I'm pulling off his, and it's then that we both look at each other and realize what a fucking mess we both are. My blouse is torn, my pants ripped and dirty. His shirt is splattered with blood, so much blood.

"We need to get ourselves clean before we get ourselves dirty again." He takes my hand and leads me to the large marble bathroom, and we quickly undress as he turns on the showerhead. He leads me into the shower, the water powerful and hot, and he brings my naked body right up against him.

He lays kisses down my neck as he brushes the hair off my shoulder, then his head dips to my breasts, where he gently cups and cradles as his tongue swirls around my nipple.

I moan, my eyes closed, head back in the falling water, feeling it wash everything away. I'm becoming new, my sins are being cleansed, and yet nothing feels so lush and decadent as Blaise as his wide palms roam around my slick body, running down between my breasts, over my stomach, and between my legs.

I immediately let him in, the slow tease and push of his fingers, while he pulls my nipple into his hot mouth, pinching the hardened tip between his teeth.

Another noise escapes my mouth, this one harsh and sharp and full of mindless need. That's what I want right now—to feel just this and only this, only him, as he makes my body run wild with desire.

"I need to be inside you. I need to feel you, to know that I have you," he says hoarsely, the lust dripping in his voice. But it's not just lust. It's not just this primal drive that I know is awakening within each of us. It's a need for each other on a deeper level, a place so deep that only our bodies together can seem to reach it.

But before I give myself to him in that way, I want to give myself to him in another way.

I grab his cock, making a fist, and kiss him madly as I pump my hand up and down his shaft.

He groans, biting his lip, eyes pinched shut from the pleasure. I step back an inch, just to see the water pour down the sculpted planes of his body, the battered features of his face, the way his eyelashes glisten when wet.

Then I sink down to a crouch and take his cock into my mouth, slowly, carefully, wanting to take my time in teasing him, in letting him know that I want to do this for him, want to bring him pleasure.

His hands go to either side of my head and hold me in place as I grip the base of his dick and start pumping him into my mouth faster, harder, my teeth occasionally scraping along the stiff, veiny ridge, which prompts a breathless gasp from him.

"Seraphine," he says, voice gruff, and his words are like a prayer said in the middle of the night. The kind of prayer you make even if you don't know anyone is listening.

I want to answer his prayers. This man who was once my cousin and yet ended up being even closer than that. A man who saw in me what ailed him, someone who didn't have a place in the world. Someone on the outside.

Now we have each other.

I'll do my best to hang on to that.

"Stop," he hisses. "Stop. I need to come inside you."

I pull my lips away from his hot shaft and smile as I get to my feet.

Before I can say anything, he's kissing me fiercely, violently, and then he's spinning me around until my arms are up high, palms pressed flat against the glass of the shower, my sensitive nipples barely grazing it.

He parts my legs by sliding his hand between my ass and the back of my thighs and grips my waist as he pushes himself inside me.

I gasp from the feel of him, a shock to my system, then I relax as he slowly eases in and out, and my body starts writhing with greed.

Yes. Yes, this is what I wanted.

This is what I needed.

For him to reach me deep inside here and turn my world upside down.

Make up for all this fucking lost time.

And make up for it, he does.

He fucks me thoroughly, pumping himself up into me from behind, more and more, faster and faster, until he's slipping around on the tiles and I'm pressed up against the glass, and I wouldn't have it any other way than this.

He pulls my hair and tells me he loves me.

I cry out his name, begging for more.

He gives me more.

More and more.

And then we're both coming, lost to each other and swept away by the falling water. Every care and worry and wish I had gets swept down in a circle toward the drain.

At least for the moment, but a moment will do.

Then, when we both regain our breath and give each other a flushed and slightly shy smile, we soap each other up from head to toe, making sure that when we step out of the shower, we're different people than when we stepped in.

When we're clean and dried off, I walk right over to the bed and throw back the covers, getting in. I don't care that I'm naked, I don't care that it's the afternoon. I just want to rest.

Blaise follows, coming in to be beside me and pulling me close, tucking the covers around on top of us. This is the first time I've been in a bed with him, and I have to say that it feels as natural as breathing.

I rest my head on top of his chest, relishing the sound of his heartbeat, the warmth of his strong body, a body that would die to protect me.

I love him. With every fiber of my being, I love him.

I want to live in this feeling, hold it close, now and forever.

But I know that finding love doesn't mean that life stops.

It means that you want more than ever to keep on living.

"What happens now?" I ask softly, wanting both to talk about it and to pretend that everything is fine, that all we need for the rest of our lives is in this hotel room. And maybe it is.

"Well," he says, inhaling slowly as his fingers play with my wet hair. "I struck a deal with Pascal."

"You did what?"

"I know. But believe me when I say he'll honor it, because he will. A lot went down this morning, a lot of stuff I don't want to get into right now. But we have a way out of it. Both of us."

I'm almost afraid to hear what it is. I lift my head and rest my chin on his chest, staring at him. "What?"

"You're getting transferred to Dubai."

"Dubai?" Now I'm sitting up straight. "Why?"

"Because, as you know, that's where the new Dumont office is. And they're looking for someone to head the company there. That someone will be you. Or you can take any of the other roles if you want. Or you don't have to take any. But for now, that's the solution."

"What if I don't want to go to Dubai?"

He gives me an apologetic smile. "You can't stay in Paris. You know that."

"Tell me what happened."

He exhales noisily. "Everything happened. I got Pascal to cover for us. To get my father to call off his fucking hounds."

"How did you do that?"

"Your gun came in handy."

My brows raise to the ceiling. "You pulled a gun on your *brother*?"

He nods. "Was I not supposed to?"

"Blaise . . ."

"It was the only way he'd listen, and you know that. I was hiding there when Father showed up with Jones and his cronies. By the way, the guy you shot is alive . . . not well, but alive."

"You saw him?" I'm almost embarrassed at the relief I feel at his not being dead.

"As I said, I was hiding. But I heard it all. Pascal stayed true to his word. We're both cleared to leave. He doesn't care where I go and neither does my father. It hurt to hear that part, not going to lie, but at least I know it was honest. As for you, well, you can go to Dubai. It would be what's best for the company, but I already quit, so I don't give a flying fuck about the Dumont brand. Don't think I ever did. Just wanted to belong, that's all. But if you want it, you can have control at the Dubai office, the power. You're good at what you do, and you've earned it. But if that doesn't appeal to you, we can go anywhere you want. And when I say we, I mean it. It's you and me. I can't leave your side, even if I wanted to."

It's too much to handle all at once. I don't even know if I want to work for Dumont anymore, but perhaps a new city in a new country, as a boss . . . maybe that's what I need. Or maybe I need to cut ties altogether.

"Can I figure it out when I get there? What if I don't want it?"

"Then we'll do what you want. You can get a job anywhere, and you know it. We just can't be here. Not in Paris. That's where it all ends."

"That's the only part of the deal?"

"That and dropping the investigation into your father." He pauses. "I know that's hard. I know it's so hard, especially when we both know, well . . . the truth."

"Which is?" I demand. I need to hear him say it.

"That my father killed your father," he says.

And it's like my whole world changes into something new.

I am no longer alone in my conviction.

I am no longer alone.

I swallow, feeling tears well up inside me. "You believe it," I whisper, my nails pressing into his chest. "You believe it."

"I do. And I am so sorry," he says, his eyes growing wet as he stares at me, brows drawn together in determination. "I am so, so sorry. So sorry that he's dead. So sorry that I didn't believe you. And I am so, so sorry that it was my own father who took his life. That it was someone whose blood runs through my veins. I am so sorry that I am his son."

I'm already breaking, and Blaise looks close to it.

"It's okay," I say through a choked sob, reaching for his beautiful face and running my fingers down his cheek, which is still bruised from last night. "You don't have to say anything. I was there, Blaise. I only had eyes for you growing up. I watched you and your family, and I knew how it was, even if you didn't tell me. You aren't like them; you never were and never will be. In my eyes, you're not a Dumont. You're just Blaise. And you deserve peace and family and forgiveness as much as anyone."

"I love you," he whispers again, his voice ravaged with the emotion that seems to roll through him. "I've always only loved you, even if I didn't know how to feel it, how to say it, it's still true. You're mine. You were always mine."

"And you're mine." I lean up and kiss him on the lips, feeling the tears run down my cheeks and onto our lips, tasting the salt, tasting each other. "I love you. I think I always did. When I was young, you broke my heart, Blaise, because I'd given you my heart, and I swear I never got it back until now. It's yours and I'm yours."

He kisses me back, and we're immediately wrapped in each other's limbs, both of us spilling tears for the things we've let go of and the things we've gained. For the love we've been denied, the love we've lost.

The love we've found.

The next morning I wake up in a haze. Despite the copious amounts of coffee I consume from the hotel room's coffee maker, I can't seem to get my head on straight.

There's a lot to process: What just happened to us. What's coming up next. The longer I'm in the hotel room—almost like Blaise and I are biding our time, because I guess we are—the more I feel like I'm trapped.

"I want to go for a walk," I tell Blaise as I slip on a Minnie Mouse dress, eyeing myself in the mirror. It reminds me of the shirt I had when I was in the orphanage. We don't have any clothes other than the bloody and dirty ones we showed up in, so Blaise had the concierge bring up a whole assortment of clothes from the gift shop. Of course, most of them are Disney themed, but I don't really care. It's all pretty surreal right now as it is.

"I'll go with you," Blaise says, getting up off the chair. He's been on his phone all morning, looking at flights to Dubai and places to stay, and everything is just moving oh so fast.

"No," I tell him. "I want to be alone. I just need some fresh air and some space to think." His face falls, so I walk over to him and wrap my arms around his waist, momentarily giddy that I can do this with him. That he's mine. "Don't worry. It's nothing bad. This is just how I process things, and there's a lot to process. Besides, I need to call Olivier. I need to tell him everything that's happened."

"I worry about you," he says.

"Well, you shouldn't," I tell him. "I'm going to go for a walk in the actual park. Happiest place on Earth is also the safest, most secure, and most-monitored place on Earth. You have to be screened to get in, and security cameras are absolutely everywhere. Nothing is going to happen to me."

He frowns and then kisses me on the forehead. "Okay. But if you're not back here in an hour, I'm going after you, and I'm bringing the police in tow."

"If it's not the *Goof Troop*, I'm going to be very upset," I tell him. I can tell by his bemused expression that he doesn't know what the *Goof Troop* is, so I leave it at that.

I slip on some Daisy Duck–print leggings, plus my boots, and grab my coat and purse, and then I'm out the door. I feel ridiculous, like I'm an adult in kid's clothing, but the feeling only lasts as far as the park entrance, where I go to buy the day pass. It seems almost everyone, of all ages, is dressed similarly to me. It actually makes me smile—the first bit of lightness I've felt in my chest since yesterday.

Even though being with Blaise now has opened up my world to love, something I'd only dreamed of sharing with him, at the moment everything is tainted by the fear of the unknown, the fear that at any moment, someone might appear and ruin everything. All we have is Pascal's word. We don't have any closure whatsoever.

Which is why I have to phone Olivier. It's going to be late at night, but I don't think it can wait. I need to hear my brother's voice, especially since he's gone through almost the same thing I have.

Once I'm in through the park gates, I relax a little. Even though it's a weekday and it's winter, it's still crowded and loud, so I set out across the park looking for the quietest place possible. I finally find a little duck pond by Cottonwood Creek Ranch in the frontier section of the park. I sit down on a bench and call.

He picks up on the fifth ring. "Hello?" he asks, voice thick with sleep.

"Olivier?" I ask, letting out a breath of relief at the sound of his voice.

"Seraphine?" He sounds more awake now. "Are you okay?"

"Yes. No. I'm sorry to wake you," I tell him. "I know it's early."

"It's okay," he says, and I'm surprised he's still speaking English. He sounds really good. "I get up early anyway."

"Who is it?" I can hear Sadie mumble nearby, and I feel bad for waking her too.

"It's Seraphine," he says. "Go back to sleep, baby, I'll take this in the other room."

"Baby?" I ask with a chuckle as I hear some shuffling and the shutting of a door. "You guys are pretty cute in the morning."

"She's the cute one," he says with that same softness he always has when he's talking about Sadie. He clears his throat. "So what's going on with you? Last we talked you seemed a bit . . . distant."

I bite my lip. "Yeah. Well, I had my reasons. And before I explain, I just want you to know that I'm okay. I'm alive. I think I have a future ahead of me, much like you had your future ahead of you when you stepped on that plane and went after Sadie."

"Oh shit. What happened? Is it Gautier?"

I swallow and try to keep the tears back. I should be all cried out after these last few days, and I don't want to lose it in the middle of Disneyland Paris. "I did something stupid, Olivier. Or maybe it wasn't stupid, because it led me to the truth. But it's changed everything. Everything."

"What truth?" he asks cautiously.

"That our uncle murdered his own brother in cold blood."

· There is silence over the line. I hear him exhale a shaky breath. "And you know this how?"

"Because I got too close to the truth, and he found out. Because I trusted the wrong person."

"Blaise."

"No," I cry out softly. "No, not Blaise. Blaise is the only one I can trust. I . . ." Shit. Never figured out how to break this part of the story to him. I leave it for now. "It was Cyril. I told Cyril what I suspected, and he went straight to our uncle."

Olivier grunts. "Those two don't even like each other."

"Birds of a feather," I tell him. "Cyril wants revenge for not getting a single penny from me. And I guess Gautier trusted him because Cyril has always been weak and spineless. He knows how to manipulate the desperate."

"So then what happened?"

I take in a long breath, and I start from the beginning, from when I went to the castle in the middle of the night, all the way to having Jones's men come after me yesterday morning at Marie's.

"And you're where?" he asks, and I know he is having a hard time wrapping his head around everything. So am I.

"Disneyland Paris."

"With Blaise?"

"He's in the room, but yeah."

"And you're going to go to Dubai . . . with Blaise?"

I nod. "I am."

"Seraphine," he says cautiously, "I don't . . . I'm not one to judge much, and I don't want to ask but . . ."

I don't want him to ask either. "I'm in love with him, Olivier."

More silence. Even though it's practically vibrating through the phone, I swear it puts a hush over the whole park.

"I don't expect you to understand at all," I go on. "And I know it's weird because he's my cousin, but we have a background, a history, that no one knows about and—"

"It's not that," Olivier says. "I know you're not blood related, and believe me, I have noticed very weird fucking vibes between you two for pretty much our whole lives. I can't say I'm that shocked, to be honest. But what I have a hard time with is . . . it's him. It's Blaise. He's one of them. How can you trust him?"

"Because I do. I can't explain why, other than he risked his life for me, other than he's protected me, other than he's chosen me over his own family. But I trust him with my heart, Olivier. And you don't need to trust him at all—"

"Good, because I don't."

"But just trust that I trust him. He loves me. It's crazy to say, but he loves me. And I really don't know what the future holds for us. But I do know we'll be in it together, and that's honestly good enough for me."

Another long silence. Then I hear him exhale. "I get it, Seraphine. I really do. Sometimes you find that someone, and that's all you need. Nothing else matters but them—not the life you built for yourself, not the land you once called home. Not the truth and not the injustice and not the need for revenge. They become more important than all of that, more than yourself, even." He pauses. "But I'm going to worry about you. You can't stop me from doing that. I think you should come here."

"I'm not leaving Blaise."

"Then bring Blaise," he says, even though it sounds like it's killing him.

"I'm going to be okay, Olivier," I tell him, and the more I say it, the more I believe it. "And if things get tough and I get scared, then I will come to California. With Blaise."

"Shit," he says.

"What?"

"My battery is dying. Here, let me call you back from Sadie's phone."

"Okay," I tell him, and he hangs up.

I stare at the phone in my hands. I knew Olivier couldn't really help my predicament other than to ask me to come to California, but even so, I feel better for having talked to him. Just to have someone else know besides me and Blaise that—

Before I know what's happening, a shadow looms over me and swipes the phone out of my hand.

I jerk back on the bench and look up to see Gautier staring down at me, slipping my phone into his coat pocket.

"Seraphine," he says. "I thought you'd be too cynical for a place like this."

The disgust I feel toward my uncle overtakes all the panic and fear. I can't even speak, the anger choking me, though I do start looking around for help. I have no idea what he's here to do, how he even found me.

"Oh, don't worry," he says, putting both hands in his pockets. "I'm not here to make a scene. I just wanted a word with you and my son."

"Blaise isn't here," I tell him.

He gives me a tight smile that makes him look monstrous. "I would have thought you'd know my son better than that." He steps to the side, and I see Blaise standing behind him, face red, fists curled at his side. "You think he'd really let you come here all alone?"

I look at Blaise in shock, wishing he hadn't followed me, but also so damn relieved that he did. I don't want him to go through whatever we're about to go through, and at the same time, I'm selfish enough to not want to go through it alone.

"What the hell do you want with us now?" Blaise asks, his voice practically a growl as he approaches his father.

I have to admit, as angry and scared as I am, this is fascinating to watch. I haven't seen father and son interact since this all started.

"Watch your language, son," Gautier says, turning to face him and giving him an easy smile. "This is a park for children."

"I am not your son," Blaise says through gritted teeth.

Gautier purses his lips like he just ate a lemon. "No. I suppose you're not now, are you? A real son of mine wouldn't turn his back on his family. He wouldn't believe the false accusations of someone else, someone who has always proven to be flighty and insignificant and untrustworthy. He wouldn't choose them over his own flesh and blood. But you did all that, didn't you, Blaise?"

"You're the liar," Blaise says, coming closer. "Cold-blooded killer. You were so envious of your own brother because he was better than you in every way possible, you let that envy turn into hate. You let that hate turn into murder."

"*Murder*. Such a strong word," he says with a laugh. A couple with children walking past us gives him a funny look. He smiles at them merrily, and then when he looks back at me, his eyes turn dark and hard, practically soulless.

"But to say that he was better than me," he says, raising his chin. "We all know he wasn't a saint. Or perhaps you believed he was this perfect and pure man until the very end, Seraphine. Such a doting daughter. Such a stupid woman."

"What do you want?" I ask him. "You just came here to steal my phone?"

"You'll get it back," he says. He looks at Blaise. "Actually, I want a word with my son, though I suppose you're not about to give us a minute alone, are you, Seraphine?"

"I wouldn't count on it." No fucking way would I let Blaise walk off with his father. That man murdered his own brother; I have no reason to believe he wouldn't do the same to someone he's practically disowning.

"Say what you have to say and then go," Blaise says, his eyes burning holes into his father.

Of course, Gautier takes no notice. He's as cold and apathetic as ever. I'm starting to think he likes the idea of his son hating him. I suppose he thinks it gives him power, some kind of upper hand.

"I just wanted to see you face to face and wish you good luck on your journeys," he says.

"Bullshit," Blaise says, and I watch his hands ball up into fists again. I hope for his sake he doesn't lose it here in the park, because even though Blaise has every right to beat the ever-living shit out of his father, he'd get in a world of trouble for doing it here. It would be caught on tape, and the news of Blaise Dumont attacking his own father in Disneyland would spread like wildfire. No way that anyone would understand the truth of it all.

Maybe that's why his father is here after all. To provoke him one last time. Get his son put away so he can never leave. So that I am left alone. I don't think I could get to California fast enough.

"Such bitterness," Gautier remarks. "I guess I haven't taught you very well in the end, have I? Bitterness is not fuel, Blaise. Only anger is fuel. Bitterness will rot you from the inside out."

"Is that how you're so rotten?" I ask.

He raises his brow at me. "You really think you're that clever, don't you? Even after everything that happened. You fucking pretending to be Columbo and nosing around, stirring up trouble and who the fuck knows what. Contacting your ex. Your ex! You stupid woman, he was just waiting for the opportunity to sell you out, and you know I could never pass that up. Not a chance to take you down a few pegs, wipe that self-assured, righteous smile off your face. And I did. And yet you still didn't listen, you still didn't learn."

He looks at Blaise. "You think that I'm a bad father, but if it weren't for the fact that you obviously care for her, I would have blown her fucking brains out right away. Or perhaps that would have come at the end, when she was begging those men to end her life."

A rush of rage roars out of Blaise's throat, and before he can lunge at his father, I leap to my feet and get between them, pushing Blaise back.

"Listen to me," I tell him quickly, trying to get him to look me in the eye. His face is red, the veins at his temple are throbbing, his eyes are pinpricks. "This is what he wants. He wants to provoke you. He wants you to hurt him so that he can then hurt you. Don't you see? Don't fall for it."

"You'd better listen to your dirty-skinned whore, here," Gautier says.

This time my eyes go as wide as Blaise's.

I don't even think.

I just whirl around and spit right in Gautier's face.

"Fuck you," I say with a sneer. "Even my spit is too good for your face. I know what you did. One day everyone else will know too."

Gautier glares at me, breathing in deeply, trying to control his rage as Blaise tries to control his own. Like father, like son. Calm as snakes until they fucking snap.

He slowly wipes my spit off his cheek under his eye. "We had an agreement," he says tersely, and I can feel the raw anger rolling off him. He came here to provoke us, but I don't think he was expecting that.

"And that agreement is what? We drop it and you let us live free?" Blaise says. "This doesn't look like you're letting us live free."

"Live free," he repeats with a dry chuckle. "How fucking dramatic." He turns his back to us and walks a few steps away before turning around, his gaze sharp. "I just needed closure, that's all. I could listen to Pascal yammer on about Dubai and what you both wanted, but the truth is, I can't trust my son for anything. I needed to see it for myself. And I needed the two of you to understand just how serious I am."

He licks his lips and gives us a quick smile. "I'm only letting you go, Blaise, because my blood is in your veins, and there's little you can do to erase that. Believe me, I now wish I could erase you from my life as much as you feel the same. But we can't. We're still family in some shape or form, maybe just by technicalities and maybe that's too much. Besides," he says with a sigh, "I made a promise to your mother that I would let you go to Dubai. If you have anyone to thank after this, it's her."

He reaches into his pocket and pulls out my phone, holding it out for me. I quickly go to snatch it from his grasp, but he hangs on to it. He stares right into my eyes with venomous intensity. "But if you ever dare try anything again, if you ever try to raise hell over the dead, I promise you, *I promise you*, that you will be next. And perhaps before that, it will be your brothers and their loved ones. They aren't safe. No one is. Especially not you. Unless you stay in line."

He lets go of the phone, and I clutch it to my chest. "So stay in line," he says. "Keep your head down. And remember everything you have to lose—most of all, each other."

Gautier then turns around, shoves his hands back into his coat pockets, and starts walking away.

I stare, watching him go, needing to do something. But what?

I look at Blaise, knowing how hard this must be for him.

He's trying to keep it together. His jaw is clenched, his eyes are as hard and dark as coal, his breath ragged with rage that's slowly coming down.

"What do we do?" I ask him, quickly glancing at my phone and seeing a missed call from Olivier. "We can't just let that be it."

He shakes his head, pressing his lips together until they turn white. He watches his father disappear into the crowd of happy park goers, then he looks at me, his features softening. "But that was it. And it was enough."

"He can't get away with it . . ."

"He won't," he says, grabbing my hand and holding it tight. "But it won't be because of us. The truth always comes out. Somehow, at some point, the truth about my father will come out. You can't operate the way he does, careless and driven by ego, without the whole deck of cards coming down. They will come down, Seraphine. And we will watch from someplace far away, someplace happy, someplace where we are together and nothing can touch us. We will watch justice be served, and we will live free."

"Are you okay?" I ask him, putting my hand on his cheek. "I know that must have been so hard to see him again, to have him say those things . . ."

He nods and kisses the inside of my palm. "I will be okay. And so will you. I promise you that. I promise you everything, Seraphine."

Even though it doesn't seem possible, how any of this could ever be okay, how losing my father in that way and losing my life in Paris could ever be rectified, I believe Blaise.

It's not going to be easy.

But I have him by my side.

And we're going to live free.

EPILOGUE

SERAPHINE

Dubai
Six months later

I stare down at the stick in my hands, second-guessing what the symbols are supposed to mean. I pick up the box and look at the instructions again.

Two pink lines means you're pregnant.

One pink line means you're not.

And I'm staring at two pink lines.

Two pink lines that I know, deep in the heart of me, are about to change my very world.

And to think I once hated the color pink.

"Blaise!" I call out from the bathroom. He can't hear me anyway, so I grab the stick covered in my pee and charge out into the hall, looking for him.

He's out on the balcony, a glass of iced mint tea in his hand. He's leaning against the railing, watching the blue waters of the Persian Gulf beyond the busy sands of Jumeirah Beach. I stop in the doorway and absorb this scene, absorb him, taking in the dark aviator glasses on his face, the way his dark hair has lightened up a bit in the relentless sun. It's longer now, and a few strands wave in the ocean breeze.

He's wearing what he wears every day he's at the apartment and not at the office: dark board shorts, a gray polo shirt or dress shirt. He has a necklace that says *love* in Arabic around his neck. I picked it up at a market. He's not wearing shoes.

He looks absolutely and utterly relaxed. He looks at peace.

And I'm not sure if I'm about to ruin that peace or not.

"Blaise," I say again, and I'm unable to stop grinning.

He turns and lifts up his shades to get a better look at me, and that's all it takes.

He knew I was taking the test, knew I had missed my period.

Knew we had been pretty reckless with unprotected sex from the start.

But even so, I didn't know how he'd react.

Hell, I didn't know how I'd react.

I didn't even think about having children when I was with Cyril. It didn't seem right. I was so scared and so worried that we would have a child and it would end up just like me. That something would happen to us, that he would leave and I would die, and then our beloved would end up in an orphanage, going through the same things I did.

But of course, I came to realize it was because I wasn't in love. I didn't love Cyril, and even though his cheating was a shock, I saw it coming. My subconscious knew this wasn't a man to have children with.

And then came Blaise. Blaise, for all intents and purposes, should have never looked at me like he first did, and I him. He was my cousin. We were family from opposite sides of a perceived moral compass. We never should have had feelings for each other at all.

There's a reason I'm using past tense.

Because he's no longer my cousin.

He's just my man.

And I'm just his woman.

And even though I still am proud to call myself Seraphine Dumont, even though I once was Jamillah Bains, he doesn't consider himself his father's son.

So we are family to each other more than our family, more than the bloodlines and backstabbing could have ever controlled.

"You're kidding me," he says, mouth agape, eyes wide and shining.

To see Blaise happy is the most beautiful, humbling sight in the world.

I had never seen him happy for the sixteen years I'd known him until we moved to Dubai.

Once here, once in the heat and the sunshine and the desert air, I could see the grime and stress of Paris melt off his body. There was a reason he'd always gravitated to places like Thailand and Bali. The sun brings out his soul.

"I'm not kidding," I tell him, holding out the test. "Two lines. It means I'm pregnant!"

He whoops and hollers joyfully and pulls me into a tight embrace, crying now, grinning, kissing me. "I can't believe it. I'm going to be a father."

"You're going to be a great father," I say against his mouth, feeling every single emotion known to mankind flood through my body.

I can't believe it.

It's like, until this moment, I never knew what I really wanted from life. I worked hard, and I did what I could to make sure I deserved the life I was given, but even so, I didn't know what I wanted. It wasn't the money or the fame or the power that came with the name I was gifted.

It was this.

It was a future.

It was love.

It was creating a life and sharing a life of love.

And I found it with this man.

I grab his face in my hands and kiss his forehead, his soft eyelids, his pretty lashes, his high cheekbones. I kiss him all over, and I laugh and laugh and laugh because I've never been so happy.

He holds me tight and brings me off the ground, swinging me around like we're two teenagers in love. Maybe that's what we still are, but I wouldn't trade it for the world.

This is my world.

And it just became a world of three.

"What do we do now?" he asks as he lowers me to the ground. "Do you have to tell your boss? Or will she let it slide?"

I grin at him and smack him across the chest.

I am my own boss.

Oh, I'm not working for the Dumont label. I took advantage of the transfer that Pascal orchestrated—anything to let us live a new and free life without their involvement.

I worked for two weeks at the new office in Dubai as the head boss. I liked it. I liked the people.

I didn't even have to deal with Pascal or my fucking murderous uncle. Sorry, but I can't quite forget that.

No, the company is big enough now that there are those who manage the different branches in different countries.

But even though I am Ludovic's daughter and I got all the respect in the company, in the business, in the fashion world, the designs and the style and the attitude just didn't jibe with mine anymore.

I wanted to merge the classical style I'd grown up with and been trained on with something a little more me.

So I started my own label.

The name?

Seraphine.

The ladies in Dubai are loving it so far. Turns out, this fashion-forward, rich, vibrant city was the best place to start something new, something catered to the well-to-do woman who wants class with some edge.

And believe me, it's very new.

We're still looking for an office after operating out of this apartment for a while. But everything is coming together. We have designers and social media experts, and once we cut that red ribbon, the world won't know what hit it.

Of course, Blaise is my CFO. Even though his family was never known for managing their finances, Blaise was always very aware of the money he had and what to do with it. He's been instrumental in getting Seraphine off the ground. I couldn't do it without him.

The tabloids love to report on us, by the way.

They talk about how we're the outcasts of the Dumont brand, how I had a nervous breakdown after my father's death (which isn't untrue) and wanted to follow in my brothers' footsteps by distancing myself from the Dumont name as much as I could.

As for Blaise, well, the media is a little kinder. Figures—he's a man with money, after all. They like to say he rescued me, that he brought purpose to my life.

Maybe that's true. He's saved me on more than one occasion.

But I like to think that I brought out the best in him as he's brought out the best in me.

And now, well, the two of us will do what we can to bring out the best in her.

Did I say *her*?

I grin at Blaise. "I think it's a girl."

He grins at me right back. "I wouldn't be surprised. Perhaps she can design for the label."

"Maybe," I say, pressing my head into his chest as he hugs me. "Or maybe we'll start a new tradition and let our children do whatever the fuck they want to do."

"Sounds good to me."

Sounds damn good to me too.

ACKNOWLEDGMENTS

If you've read the first book in the Dumont series, *Discretion,* and happened upon the acknowledgments there, you'll be happy to know that the writing experience for *Disarm* was a lot different (better!) than the writing experience for *Discretion.* I've gotten a lot of feedback from readers thanking me for my honesty and transparency when it comes to my (albeit short) battle with depression and how difficult it was to write while in the throes of it, so if those acknowledgments helped you in some way, I'd be happy to hear about it.

But as I said, writing *Disarm* was an easier process. Thank god. That's not to say it was all a breeze. It was definitely a book written on the go. I started the book at the end of my time in Kauai and was writing it while in LA. The Lamill coffee place in Silverlake was a godsend, and I loved going there with my husband every morning and putting in the words, surrounded by creative people furiously typing on their laptops. I was *also* writing it during our road trip up the West Coast heading back home, drinking wine and spending many nights typing my ass off in La Quintas in Paso Robles, Healdsburg, Port Orford, and finally typing THE END in Portland. Whew.

Of course, all of this was made easier thanks to many people who helped me along the way. Thank you to Kathleen, Nina, and Sandra for being shoulders to cry on when I was totally losing it. (Have I mentioned writing on a deadline while traveling is stressful?). Thank you to my ever so patient agent, Taylor Haggerty, for all your support and understanding. Thanks to Maria and everyone else at Montlake for again putting up with me and my wacky writing process. I know I keep putting you guys through the ringer, but your passion for the book and your patience and help have not gone unappreciated! Holly, your editing skills are amazing and you definitely deserve all the credit in shaping this book and making it the best it can be. Special mentions to Hang Le for knocking another awesome cover out of the park and everyone at the Social Butterfly team.

I also have to give a shout-out to my readers! I had to push back a book release because I needed to work on this book and you guys are so damn understanding! Thank you for supporting me through everything I do, and I hope you enjoyed Seraphine and Blaise's journey in *Disarm*. Stay tuned for book number three because Pascal is going to win you over, I promise.

Finally, last but never least, my husband, Scott. I can't do any of this without you. You truly make me a better person and a better writer. Every crazy thing I'm going through, you go through it too, and you never complain, and your love and support never wavers. You deserve all the medals in the world.

Honorable mention to my sweet pit bull, Bruce: if you weren't such an awesome dog and the best traveling buddy, I don't think I could get my books done as fast. It's almost as if you know these books pay for your abundance of Milk-Bones!

ABOUT THE AUTHOR

Karina Halle is the *New York Times, Wall Street Journal,* and *USA Today* bestselling author of *The Pact, A Nordic King, Sins & Needles,* and fifty other wild and romantic reads. A former travel writer and music journalist, she currently lives in a rain forest on an island off the coast of British Columbia with her husband and their adopted pit bull. There they operate a bed-and-breakfast that's perfect for writers' retreats. In the winter, you can often find them in California or on their beloved island of Kauai, soaking up as much sun—and inspiration—as possible. Visit Karina online at www.authorkarinahalle.com.